Praise for the w

"From beginning to end, *Blacque/Bleu* offers something different in the usually overfilled field of supernatural stories."

– *Whipped Cream Erotic Reviews*

"Blacque/Bleu is passion and acceptance combined with sizzle and heat. The power of this story is that even as you find satisfaction you want more and that is a true gift."

– Kimberley Spinney, *Sensual Reads*

"*Blacque/Bleu* has a little bit of everything for paranormal fans: emotion, hot sex, plenty of action and conflict, and a satisfying ending. Read it!"

– Cassie, *Joyfully Reviewed*

Belle Starr

"Belinda McBride's *Belle Starr* was a right off the bat an action packed novel. Space fights, hot steamy sex with a sinful were, intrigue and mystery and throw in a ménage, and man...you have one great story."

– Lila, *Two Lips Reviews*

An Uncommon Whore

"An absorbing story with thrilling intergalactic adventure, steamy man-on-man sex, romance galore, friendship and an extremely satisfying end."

– Kathy K, *Reviews at Ebook Addict*

LooseId®

ISBN 13: 978-1-61118-362-7
BLACQUE/BLEU
Copyright © August 2011 by Belinda McBride
Originally released in e-book format in October 2010

Cover Art by Anne Cain
Cover Layout and Design by April Martinez

DISCLAIMER: Many of the acts described in our BDSM/fetish titles can be dangerous. Please do not try any new sexual practice, whether it be fire, rope, or whip play, without the guidance of an experienced practitioner. Neither Loose Id nor its authors will be responsible for any loss, harm, injury or death resulting from use of the information contained in any of its titles.

This book is an original publication of Loose Id. Each individual story herein was previously published in e-book format only by Loose Id and is a work of fiction. Any similarity to actual persons, events or existing locations is entirely coincidental.

Printed in the U.S.A. by
Lightning Source, Inc.
1246 Heil Quaker Blvd
La Vergne TN 37086
www.lightningsource.com

BLACQUE/BLEU

Belinda McBride

Dedication

To my friends, whether you are gay or straight, bent or queer, kinked or vanilla. You taught me to toss out the labels. You are simply my friends.

Most particularly:

To CB: You came to me for advice on how to tell your mother. You honored me.

To JS: You cried before you turned your back on your true self. You made me cry too. (But I still want your clothes... They're in the closet...)

To CH: You not only came out, you managed to capture the prettiest girl in the department!

To HH: You broke my heart during the last days of your life. I didn't know you well, but you changed my life.

To J and L: You two still confuse the hell out of me!

Not only is this story for you, this is your story.

Happy tales!

Chapter One

Oliver Bleu was locked in paralysis. He could only watch and listen as the chaos of war swirled around the muddy grave in which he was trapped. Blisters rose on his skin in spots where the mustard gas had settled. His lungs closed off and filled with foul, viscous fluid... He couldn't breathe... A beautiful, hateful face gazed down at him, fangs distended, cruelty displacing love...

With a choked cry, he woke from the nightmare, still frozen in place, but instead of horrified screams and the roar of artillery fire, he heard the muffled sound of a man's deep voice and the haunting melody of southern rock on the radio. Lynyrd Skynyrd soothed him with "Free Bird" as the burns on his face faded and the blisters were absorbed back into his skin. He took a chance and drew breath, pleased when he didn't choke.

The dream had released him, but Bleu was still trapped, held immobile by the presence of the sun. His limbs were heavy, and the mattress under his back felt rough and lumpy. He labored through another heavy breath and sighed, just for the sake of hearing something other than the fading sound of battle in his ears.

He didn't have the refined sense of time some vampires possessed. He only knew the sun was still up and that he was awake and aware, though weary. He wondered how many more hours it would be until he could rise and return to the night. He wondered how much longer he had until fatigue crippled him and he starved or fell victim to a bigger, stronger predator.

If he could have laughed, he would have. Oliver Bleu was undoubtedly the only vampire on the face of the earth who suffered from chronic insomnia.

Resigning himself to the long day ahead, he closed his eyes, focusing on the sounds of the day outside his resting place.

* * *

For whatever reason, the muddy, greasy undercarriage of the battered Studebaker held a lot more appeal to Lukas Blacque than the flashing light on his answering machine. He'd listened to the voice on the other end of the line and then cranked up the radio before pushing himself under the car on a rickety old creeper. He knew who was calling. He simply didn't want to hear what he had to say.

Since he'd been a kid, cars had been his solace. He'd tagged along with his grandpa to auto shows, and then in high school had escaped from the drama of daily life in the shelter of the auto shop. His reputation as a tough had been hard earned even then. It had bought him distance from the cheerleaders and the jocks who wanted to be his friends. It had kept him safe from the curiosity of the kids in the new high school in the town he had moved to. He played sports because he loved to, but didn't necessarily cherish being dragged into the limelight at every pep rally and homecoming dance.

He'd done his duty and gone on to college to earn his business degree. He'd come home to Arcada and surprised everyone by buying old man Foster's garage, located in a small industrial park. Blacque had followed his dream and now made a modest living bringing old cars and trucks back to the artistic beauty of their prime.

He hummed along to an old Allman Brothers song as he worked before cursing briefly as chunks of mud and rust flaked away, showering his face with grit. In all, he was in his happy place, working on his own terms and on his own time. Could you see a tattooed, pierced guy like him in a nine-to-five office? Not likely. Mated, with kids? Even less so. And what his old man was proposing in the numerous voice mails he'd left lately? No fucking way. He'd heard enough to know he didn't want to hear more.

He groped for a tool, taking pleasure in working on something simple. This old lady was his, the project car of his dreams. His days were spent with sleek new cars that ran on electronics and computer chips. You pushed a button to raise the window, and another button engaged the locks. If something went screwy, it took an advanced degree in technology to figure out the problem. But this old Studebaker was all simple elegance and efficiency.

When he finished her, he'd send her out for new paint and upholstery. He'd seen the work that Bleu next door was capable of; maybe he could talk his neighbor into doing custom leather seats. That is, if he was still around. Every time he saw the vamp, the poor guy looked sicker. He wondered if vampires were inclined to contracting some sort of blood-borne virus or something, 'cause hot as the man might be, he was looking pretty ragged these days. He'd been a sight to behold when he'd first opened his shop a few years ago. He was still sexy in his heroin-chic way. These days he had a drawn, elegant beauty that tugged at Blacque's protective nature. He doubted the aristocratic vamp would welcome a big wolf like himself as a guardian. But he kept an eye on the man when he could, worried about him when he couldn't. He figured one of these days Bleu simply wouldn't wake when the sun went down. It would be a damn pity.

Maybe when he lay down in his coffin at night, his cheeks were flushed with blood. Blacque usually saw him at dusk, just as the sun was setting. Of course, that would be the start of Bleu's day. Blacque was never at his best in the morning either. Maybe once Bleu fed, he returned to the glossy picture of health he'd been a few years back.

The player switched to Stevie Ray Vaughan, and Blacque kept his groove, carefully examining the exhaust system of the car. He heard the shop door swing open but ignored it. He had flipped the sign over to CLOSED. He was on his own time now.

Footsteps echoed through the bay, and he cursed softly, remembering that Davey had gone home at five. There was no line of defense between Blacque and whoever was intruding into his world. And thoughts of Bleu had taken their usual effect on his body—he was hard as a rod inside his old, worn jeans.

He glanced toward his feet and saw slender legs in a pair of bright red fuck-me heels. He imagined long legs that went on for a mile and most likely were revealed by an exquisitely made skirt that seemed to show everything but in reality showed nothing at all.

He sighed.

One red-clad foot nudged his.

"Hey, sexy. Come on out and play." Her voice was smooth as fine whiskey, low pitched, and seductive. Blacque rolled his eyes.

"Hey, Dru. Gimme a sec."

Drusilla. What had their mother been thinking when she filled out the birth certificate? Drusilla Blacque sounded like a damn pretentious TV vampire, not a werewolf.

Digging in with his battered work boots, he then slid the creeper out from under the car and sat up, looking as if he'd been showered with grit. He grinned as his sister hopped back. She wouldn't want to get her pretty suit all dirty.

"So." She stood back, hands on her hips, her head cocked to the side. "This is what you do for fun?"

"After hours. Project car." Blacque scrambled to his feet and headed for a workbench to dip his hand into a tin of degreaser. He smeared the stuff over his fingers and nails, blatantly ignoring Dru as she waited impatiently.

He finally wiped his hands on a red rag and turned to face his sister. He imagined they made an interesting contrast—Dru in her neat black suit and he in his dirty jeans and sleeveless work shirt. Her thick black hair was neatly coiled into some sort of elegant bun, while he kept his hair shaved close to the scalp. He looked her over slowly.

"Can't believe they let you teach school dressed like that."

She raised an arched black brow at him. "What's wrong with the way I'm dressed?"

He snorted. She knew damn well what she looked like. No doubt she had hordes of horny teenage boys tied up in knots on a daily basis.

"And I don't teach anymore. I'm the high school vice principal now."

"I knew that." And he did. He'd even sent her a little bouquet of flowers when she got the job. He had to wonder if she kept a neat black cane hidden under her desk. She probably had volunteers lining up to take their punishment.

Blacque leaned back against the old car, propping his ass on the hood. Outside the vapor lights had come on in the parking lot. He hadn't realized it was so late. Bleu should be up and stirring soon. He didn't see him much these days.

"So, are we supposed to do something tonight?" He frowned, trying to remember if he'd missed an appointment.

"You got Dad's calls? He said he's just getting your voice mail."

"I got the *alpha's* calls." He pushed off the car and headed to his little office. "I'm busy. Business is good. Can't take every personal call that comes in." Blacque dropped into the ancient chair in front of his computer. He winced at the Mail icon on the toolbar. The old man was determined, wasn't he? Blacque glanced up at his sister, and he knew by the look on her face that he didn't want to hear what she had to say. He leaned back in the chair and propped a booted foot on the scarred surface of the desk.

"If you had come to the meeting on Sunday night, you'd have an idea what's so important."

She brushed off the chair across the desk from him and sat. Outside the stereo switched to Willie Nelson. Automatically his mind reached for the music, letting it lull him just the tiniest bit. His sister looked damn relaxed, crossing one long leg over the other.

"Okay, Dru. I'm braced. What's so damn important that the alpha is calling me a dozen times a day?"

"Our *father* has decided to drop restrictions on breeding for the next few seasons. That's what's so damn important, Lukas. He's decided we need fresh swimmers in the gene pool."

Blacque snorted. It was about time. His father had been dropping pups into the community like confetti for a couple of decades now. Their birth certificates might read *father unknown*, but he claimed every one of his offspring. Not a one could complain that Dane Blacque ignored his children.

"Well, we're off the hook. The two of us are hardly fresh blood."

"Don't get your hopes up. Or are you disappointed? All the other males are practically humping air, they're so excited."

He put his hands behind his head and studied the ceiling, where a cobweb waved in the breeze. He'd have to knock it down when she left.

"Never really thought about having kids before."

"Well start thinking, Sparky. Dad wants grandkids. Specifically, he wants *your* grandkids. And mine." She added the latter as though it were an afterthought, prompting Blacque to look at her. She sounded resigned and doleful.

Blacque dropped his feet and leaned forward. He'd been right; her face was a bit downcast. She didn't look happy. He knew why he wasn't interested in the whole circus, but what was up with his sister?

"Again. You and I are his direct offspring. If he wants fresh blood, there are other males out there."

Dru met his gaze. "Our mother was an outsider. That's where the fresh blood comes in."

"Fuck," he whispered, pinching the bridge of his nose.

Dru folded her arms, glaring at Blacque. "I don't know why you're upset. All you've got to do is poke a few women and make babies. You can walk away. I, on the other hand, get to look forward to morning sickness and nine months of bloat, followed by a couple of decades of dependents on my tax form."

"Damn. I think you're a bit upset by this." He did his best to hide his smile. It was rare to see Drusilla this distressed about anything. She was the ultimate crisis manager.

She stood, tried to pace, but the office was too small. She dropped back into her chair and clenched her fists. "Damn straight I'm upset!"

"You gonna do it?" He was curious how far her rebellion would run. Dru had always maintained a warm relationship with their father. She rarely bucked his authority. Blacque, on the other hand, had always tried to keep his distance. The old man saw far too much. He was far too perfect compared to his eldest son. Dane Blacque was everything an alpha werewolf should be and then some. Blacque? Well, he'd never measure up. And it pissed him off that he felt that way. He pulled himself away from his thoughts and focused on his sister.

"I have a good career, Lukas. I've been accepted into a doctoral program in education. My new position pays well. But... I suppose..."

"What'll the school board think when you put in for maternity leave?"

She shot to her feet again. "Shit! Damn! I hadn't thought of that."

"Well, lots of women have babies without fathers these days. I'm sure the board will be perfectly understanding." As he watched his sister fuming over her situation, Blacque had to congratulate himself for turning the conversation around so smoothly. He loved his sister and trusted her to a degree. But even the most tolerant among the pack would have difficulty with the sort of secret Blacque had carried all his life.

Fluid sexuality wasn't uncommon among their kind—males paired up for brief encounters, and females frequently had intense, passionate relationships. But in all his life, Blacque had never encountered another like himself. So, much as he loved her, he could never tell his sister he was gay.

That would just be stupid.

Chapter Two

"Hey."

Oliver Bleu looked up from the bench seat he was measuring. He took few commissions these days, usually just enough to make his monthly bills and keep the rent paid. His work was declining in quantity, but the quality was still top of the line, as long as he didn't push himself. He released the tape and noted the measurements on a pad, hiding the feral interest that rose at the presence of his neighbor. He took a moment, willing his fangs to recede.

"Hey, Blacque. What's happening?"

He did his best to appear casual, but after the last conversation he'd eavesdropped on, Bleu was itching to know more about the big werewolf who was darkening his doorway. He could understand why Blacque's sister might be reluctant to give in to the alpha's demands to make babies. After all, she had a career on the line. She couldn't just drop a pup and walk away.

But Blacque was a different story. He'd never met a shifter who didn't think with his dick. Speaking of which, it was looking nice and snug there inside those faded denims. And it looked happy to see Bleu. He quickly looked away, wondering if maybe his suspicions about the wolf were correct. Blacque had showered and changed out of his work clothes. He smelled like steam and Lava soap.

"Just gettin' ready to head on out for the night. Wanted to check, though. I've got an old Studebaker I'm working on. Wanted to see if you might be available to do the interior."

He looked slightly uncomfortable, but they'd never really talked much before. Their hours didn't exactly mesh, and the mechanic had always avoided Bleu. He watched Blacque's face as the wolf scented the air slightly. He wouldn't catch the smell of illness on Bleu, and hopefully not weakness either. But shifters' senses were even more acute than those of vamps. Maybe he could smell fatigue and hunger. Maybe he could smell lust.

Bleu certainly scented something on the shifter. Hot, rich blood flowing inside his veins. The musk of a male, the sweat of a hardworking man. It was all like perfume to his libido. He was suddenly very glad the wolf had interrupted his work. His fangs ached to drop even as his cock began to rise. He took another breath and let the cool control of the hunter wash over him.

"Studebaker, eh? Let's go look." He followed Blacque from his little workshop to the garage next door, taking time to appreciate the ripped, muscular build of the were. His ass was tight, and his legs were sleek with muscle. Bleu's mouth watered a bit in spite of the mug of lukewarm pig's blood he'd downed earlier. All that shit did was ease the hunger pangs gnawing at his belly. It did nothing to nourish his flesh. A full-blooded werewolf was like nectar to a hungry vamp.

Blacque paused to unlock the shop door, and he entered, flipping on the overheads in the big auto bay once he did. In the cold fluorescent light, tattoos on his bare arms stood out in stark contrast to his lightly tanned skin. They twisted and climbed like vines on a trellis. His scalp gleamed through the thick black stubble that was growing in. He certainly wasn't trying to hide any shortcomings by shaving his head. Bleu's fingers itched to rub the wolf's bristly scalp.

God, he was butch enough to make Bleu want to grapple him to the floor right then and there! Thing was, the big guy might not appreciate it. Deep down, he might crave it, but he didn't *want* to want it.

After dragging his hungry gaze from the wolf, he looked critically at the old car in the bay. She was a dirty gem, all right.

"Nineteen fifty-five Speedster. Nice." He slowly walked around the car, peering into the windows to look at the tattered seats and headliner. "It'll need everything. Panels, seats, headliner. You want it authentic or custom?"

"As close to stock as we can get. I'd like the seats done in leather, though."

"Original colors?" He opened the door and ran a hand over the dark red steering wheel. Man, where'd the quality go in cars these days?

"I'll keep the paint stock, so let's keep the interior the same as well."

He could picture the Speedster with a gleaming black-and-white paintjob, its chrome polished to a high sheen. He straightened up and gazed at Blacque, taking a moment to appreciate the artistry of his rugged face. As he looked, the wolf colored up slightly.

"Call when you're ready for me." Their gazes held for a breathless moment. Bleu finally exhaled. "I'll work up an estimate. Damn nice vehicle. Can't beat the fifties when it comes to cars. Especially Studebakers." He gave the door a push, and it closed with a satisfying *thump*. He might have more fun with pimped-out cars and customized limos, but restoring a classic brought out the best in Bleu. He followed Blacque to the back door and paused, watching him lock up.

Blacque turned to face him. Excitement fluttered in Bleu's belly. "Thanks, Bleu. I appreciate it." Again the big man hovered, looking ill at ease. He reminded Bleu of a kid angling for his first kiss after a date. Well, that could be wishful thinking on his part. Clearly the mechanic had something to say.

"Well, good night."

Or not.

"Good night, Lukas. You have a good evening."

"You too." The wolf started out to the parking lot, where his big pickup truck waited. Blacque paused and then turned back to Bleu.

"See you around."

He waited for a moment, gazing at Bleu, and then started back out to his truck, moving with swift, graceful strides.

Beautiful. From the top of his bristly head to the soles of his steel-toed feet, the wolf was beautiful. Bleu shifted, letting his cock find a more comfortable position in his work pants. Dickies. What a name for a pair of pants. When he threw back his head and laughed, the tips of his fangs glinted in the moonlight.

This was a bad idea all the way around. Such a bad idea. The were community here in Arcada had been tolerant of him so far. Vamps and wolves never got along particularly well, and he valued the uneasy peace that existed in this quaint little town. Blacque had been a temptation he'd long denied himself, and one that Bleu should continue to ignore.

He laughed again. Hell. What was life without a bit of risky self-indulgence now and then?

Fuck. What was he thinking? Blacque started the truck, catching a glimpse of the vampire before he returned to his shop. He was facing enough shit with the alpha, and now he was hungering for a vampire...a *male* vampire, no less.

He scrubbed at his scalp and then brought his fist down, banging it on the steering wheel. He took a deep breath, gathering his control. He reached between his legs and grasped his cock hard, willing it into submission. Had the vampire's gaze lingered there, even for a moment? Had he mistaken something else for the scent of arousal? He squeezed at the base of his swollen shaft, grunting when his arousal began to wane.

It had been bad enough when his wants had been vague and amorphous. He'd craved another male, but it'd been years since a name or face was attached to his need. These past few years, a pale, tall vampire occupied his lust. How old was Oliver Bleu anyway? He seemed pretty modern, but you never knew. In fact, Bleu probably passed for human to most of Arcada's residents. Other than his scent, the only telltale sign was the slight accent in his voice. He'd originated in Europe somewhere but had been in North America long enough for the accent to have faded.

Shit. He was getting as moony as a teenage girl. His heart raced in his chest, and heat prickled along his skin. He wasn't one to talk a lot, but the damn vamp had him flat-out tongue-tied. In fact, he couldn't clearly remember what they'd talked about.

The air grew crisp and cold, and Blacque steered through town with his window down, barely seeing the town square with its fairy lights and the couples strolling arm in arm. He rolled through a stop sign and headed north, away from the orchards and out toward where the real wilderness started.

The official city limits of Arcada extended much farther than the actual town itself, and within its borders, paranormals like him found a measure of safety. That safety came with a price, though. The town didn't like bad behavior. Not the townspeople, but the *town*. It had a way of punishing those who tried to violate its code of sanctuary. There was no hunting within the unmarked limits. No stalking, no pack wars of any kind. He wondered if the vamp had to leave town to hunt. He and Dru had come here as kids when their mother died, but many of Arcada's residents were outsiders who were drawn to the sense of safety here.

Of course, everyone in Arcada had their secrets, and conversely, everyone knew everyone else's secrets. The place was so rife with oddity that someone had jokingly nicknamed the city "Normalville, USA." That's how the sign greeted visitors as they coasted into town on the two-lane approach strip. Hell, even the most mundane humans in town were far from normal. There were witches and psychics and even the occasional oracle, all busily living their day-to-day lives.

He turned off the highway and took a narrow road out to the little house he'd purchased the year before. It was humble, but sound and private. He could shift, go for a run deep into the surrounding forest, and be back without ever encountering his neighbors.

His father, the alpha, lived in a sprawling two-story farmhouse that was buried in acres of orchards. The old house was always filled with his visiting children. Sometimes he took in strays—shifters who were without pack ties elsewhere. If one of Dane's families was down on their luck, the alpha fed them, and when possible, paid their bills. The vast orchards and pack-owned businesses helped with that, as did his day job as the county sheriff. The pack also paid a tithe to help out.

Damn socialist werewolves, always taking care of each other. The thought made him grin.

Blacque pulled up in front of his house and shut down the truck. The silence out here was complete, broken only by the wind in the trees and the occasional flutter of wings as bats and night birds hunted. He took a deep breath, scenting the wind, and deemed it safe to go inside. Arcada might be a safe haven, but the outside world wasn't. Dane continually preached caution to his pack.

Like most residents of Arcada, he didn't bother locking up when he left. Locks on the doors wouldn't stop anyone here. He skipped the stairs, jumping smoothly to the raised porch, and entered, pausing before turning on the lights. Like the outside, the interior of his house was small and neat. It was old, maybe dating to the 1930s or earlier. At night he loved to lie in bed and listen to its old bones settle.

He headed straight for the fridge, grabbed a beer and popped it, then took a long drink. He drained it, opened a second, and then leaned back against the counter. His cock was hard again, aching and swollen. He reached down and cupped himself, indulging in the brief fantasy of Bleu's swollen, dripping cock sliding into his mouth. He licked his lips, imagining the salty taste of his seed as it melted over his tongue. He took the imagery just a bit further...still on his knees, but leaning forward or maybe bent over the kitchen table...Bleu covering him from behind.

Shit! What the hell was his problem?

Blacque rolled the cold can over his sweaty forehead and swallowed hard. It wasn't going to happen. Not if he wanted to keep all his limbs. He might get away with occasionally fucking another guy, but not a male vampire. He took a second to readjust his cock and then headed into the living room.

"Son of a...!" He nearly dropped the can on the polished wooden floor. "Fuck! What the *hell* are you doing here?"

Had he walked right past his father, or had the old man followed him in? He'd scanned both the property and the house. The alpha sat on the big leather sofa, all sprawled out and at his ease. How was the alpha able to sneak up on him like that?

"Wanna get me one of those?" Dane grinned, his strong white teeth gleaming in his deeply tanned face. He was still in uniform; the olive green of the fabric nearly blended into the brown leather of the couch. His thick black hair, waving back from his handsome face, was a bit long for the uniform; it brushed down past the collar.

Blacque returned to the kitchen and grabbed another beer. Without looking at his father, he tossed it in his direction. He gathered his anger and settled into a battered recliner, then kicked back and propped his boots on the footrest. The can tab hissed, and he hoped the old man would spill brew all down the front of his pristine shirt.

No such luck. Sheriff Dane Blacque sipped at the foam, catching it before it spilled. Too damn perfect by far.

"So Dru says you're busy at work. That's good. Real good." His dark eyes glowed, and goose bumps ran down Blacque's arms. The alpha was pushing power at his son. He was making certain Blacque knew who the boss was. "You got a project car going?"

"Fifty-five Studebaker," Blacque replied.

"Nice. Good year for a car." He took another pull at his beer. "She tell you what's up?"

"Yeah. It's about time you stopped populating the world." To his satisfaction, Dane's face darkened a bit. Blacque didn't know if it was embarrassment or anger, but decided it was safest to back off.

"I talked with a couple of elders. Alice Mitchum brought out genealogy charts and such. Showed me how my bloodline's gotten pretty deep."

Deep as the ocean and wide as the Mississippi.

"You've been alpha for a long time now." Maybe too long. Yet Dane was still healthy and vital. There was no reason for him to step down, and thus far, no one had successfully challenged him for the position. In truth, Blacque couldn't think of anyone better suited to be alpha.

Dane sat back and studied his son. The silence drew out until it began to grow uncomfortable, but Blacque felt no need to fill that void. Blacque and Drusilla hadn't grown up with their father. He wondered how different his life would have been if he had. Would he have developed into another person completely if he'd been under the care of a strong male like Dane Blacque? Would he feel this…small?

"You didn't make the meeting Sunday night."

Well, that had been obvious. He waited for the alpha to continue.

"I told the pack the basics, that we need to diversify genetically. I didn't tell them everything." He sipped his beer and then continued. "It's getting pretty bad with other packs outside Arcada. Their birth numbers are falling. I'm going to send some of you out of the area to move in with other packs for a time."

"I've got a business, Dad."

"I know. That's why we're screening a few females from outside the pack who want children. They'll be coming to stay here."

Blacque stifled a grin. He could just imagine a pack of horny females lodging in with his father. He suspected there'd be a few more little Blacques in the world soon after. Good intentions aside, he'd never seen a werewolf who could stay celibate when breeding season rolled around. His father was the worst.

"So there's too much of your bloodline out there. That should leave me and Dru out of the pool." He couldn't hide the hopefulness in his voice. Maybe Dru had been wrong after all.

"No, you two are my oldest. And you're different. I'd like to see grandchildren soon."

"Different." He snorted. That was an understatement. "How are we different?"

"Well, for starters, you were both born years before I became alpha. I fought for the right to your mother."

"Okay." Blacque sat and did what he was best at doing: he kept his mouth shut. The alpha clearly had something on his mind, and if he had to wait to hear it, then he'd stay quiet. Dane emptied his beer and set the can on the floor.

"I had big ambitions back then. I knew that settling down wasn't in my future." He looked steadily at Blacque. "Still, I was at the hospital when you were born. Spent a couple of months with you and your mom, just till she could get back on her feet."

"And a year later, Dru was born. And then you went on your way."

Dane rubbed the bridge of his nose in a gesture Blacque recognized in himself. The alpha was getting frustrated. Or maybe he was feeling guilty about walking away.

When he looked at Blacque, his eyes were slightly reddened. "I loved your mother."

Okay. He hadn't seen that coming.

"Guess I never stopped loving her. When she died..." He cleared his throat. "Well, yeah, when she passed, I was..." He trailed off.

Blacque remembered those harsh days. He remembered the sudden emptiness in his life where his mother had been and the abrupt move to a new town, into a new home and life. He remembered how quiet Dane had been back then. The alpha had grieved privately and deeply. All the while he was helping two shocked teens absorb the sudden changes in their lives.

"Anyhow...uh, something happened a while back."

"When you were knifed on the job?" Blacque clenched his fist and then released it as his fingers shifted into claws. With some effort, he brought his hands back to normal.

Dane nodded. "I never told you much about the attack."

And that little fact had pissed Blacque off to no end. His father had spent days in the hospital, and nobody had known outside of his inner circle. When Blacque had found out and tried to visit, he'd discovered his father's room was off limits to all except his betas and law enforcement.

That had told Blacque what he'd suspected all along—he was firmly on the outside of the elite circle. If Dane had wanted Blacque on the inside, he could have brought him in at any time over the past decade. At least Dane had the grace to look slightly ashamed as he spoke.

"I nearly died." He didn't meet Blacque's gaze. "I was transporting a suspect to the county lockup. The deputy didn't search him well enough, and the bastard had a shank. Opened me here"—he gestured across his throat—"and caught me in the liver. That's what nearly did me in."

Blacque's skin crawled when he saw the fading scar, but he made no comment.

"Got me to thinking. Before I die, I'd like to see Bianca's face in her grandchildren. And I've got to think of the future. Of the pack."

"What's that got to do with me?" He ignored the comment about grandchildren. That was an issue, but it was the lesser issue. His father rarely talked to Blacque about the inner workings of the pack. In fact, he was as near to being a lone wolf as they came. Even as his father answered his question, Blacque braced himself, knowing that his world was about to fall apart.

"Things happen, Lukas. I wasn't ready when your mother died. Somehow, I always thought she'd be there and someday we'd work things out." He swallowed hard, and the expression on his face was bleak. "She was my mate, Blacque. I left her behind, and now there won't be another for me."

That's right. Their kind mated for life. He stifled a sympathetic groan. Nausea hit his stomach like a fist. He hadn't known. No one had known.

"I wasn't ready to find myself in a hospital. The only reason I didn't have an outside challenge then was that Mallory and Michella had kept it on the lowdown. If I'd died, it would have left the pack in chaos and open to invasion. I don't want to be caught unprepared again."

Dane Blacque looked steadily at his son. "It's time for me to look for the next alpha. And I've decided it's you."

Chapter Three

Things fall apart; the centre cannot hold...

Bleu pondered the words by Yeats as he surveyed the grubby little bar. Maybe this wasn't really a sign of the end of times, but for him, things were looking pretty grim. A few years ago, Bleu had no problem finding willing donors. He'd flash a roguish smile, bat his baby blues, and they'd come. But the more tired he became, the more the hunger ate away at him. Now it was nearly impossible to hunt by seduction.

He'd tried hunting the old-fashioned way, by stalking and sneak attack, but he was too slow, too clumsy. He watched more and more victims run away untouched, reporting the madman to the police. Now here he was, sitting in a bar, hoping to find a hooker or someone willing to be hustled by a pale, ghostly man.

It wasn't so bad, really, when he prostituted himself. It was a fuck and a meal, plus a little spending money to boot.

Yeah, keep telling yourself that, Ollie. Someday you might believe it.

But this was survival, and staying alive was everything at this point in his undead existence. After all, his mother country had a reputation for producing the most excellent whores in the world. Some had even worn crowns.

Bleu nursed his drink and eyed the crowd. The Roadhouse was a rough-and-tumble place, filled with bikers and truckers and those who sought their company. On Thursdays, their doors opened to men who loved men. Tuesdays were ladies' night. Too bad this was Friday—he'd have done just fine on either theme night. Most of the tough, blue-collar men who filled the bar on Fridays wouldn't be interested in someone like him. And their ladies? Damn. They were just dangerous. But still, there was plenty of prey to be had.

He sipped his whiskey and scanned the bar, making eye contact with a likely tough. He'd seen the fellow before and knew the man took the occasional stroll to the other side of the block. He'd want Bleu on his knees and wouldn't object to a little love bite to the groin. One of these days, Bleu was going to glamour the hell out of the biker—he'd have that bastard on *his* knees for a change. He lowered his lashes slowly and tried not to look too hungry as he made the connection. The man met his gaze, flushed, and started in his direction. Bleu exerted a tiny bit of compulsion and…lost his focus as he was jostled by a large body on his left.

He stifled a frustrated growl. His fangs dropped, and he saw the room through a red haze.

"Beer. Whatever's on draft."

A deep voice, an angry voice. It grabbed his attention. Bleu's mark drifted away to check out the pool table. He turned, a slight frown on his face. And then he smiled. Deliverance came in the form of a hot, rich-blooded werewolf.

"Lukas Blacque. Fancy seeing you here." His voice purred with sensuality.

A series of expressions flitted over the mechanic's face. Irritation chased pleasure, which was followed by chagrin. A slow, deliberate glance at his crotch told Bleu exactly from where the chagrin originated. His fingers itched to reach out and stroke the outline of that fine, very substantial cock. "It's a bit late for you, isn't it?"

Blacque glanced up at the old illuminated clock on the wall. It was only an hour out from closing time.

"It's Friday."

Loquacious as usual.

"Saturday morning. Barely time to get a good buzz on." Bleu grinned and looked away, following the path of a harried barmaid. He'd had her once, long ago. She hadn't known she was pregnant at the time. He'd taken a taste and then backed off, not wanting to do harm.

Maybe that was his problem—he was soft. If he were more like his maker, Yves, he'd never have come to this state of desperation. He would never have worried about unborn babies and consent. But he'd never been like Yves and was generally grateful for the difference. Thoughts of his maker made his skin pebble with gooseflesh.

Blacque sipped his beer. His face had closed down, back to the stony mask he tended to wear. His shirt was partly unbuttoned, and Bleu caught the golden glint of a piercing in his nipple. Gold? *That's right, silver burned boys like him.*

His hunger spiked. Tattoos and metal. He swallowed hard, imagining what the gold would taste like on his tongue. Bleu took a sip of his whiskey and let it dribble down to vaporize in his throat. He couldn't really stomach much alcohol, but one drink over the course of the evening was manageable. His metabolism didn't do well with spirits, and he got wasted much too easily. But the glass helped him blend in, and a big tip kept the bartender happy.

"Thought vamps didn't eat or drink." Blacque glanced at him from the corner of his eye.

"So you know."

"Yeah. Sleep all day, up all night."

"I wish." Bleu murmured. "So tell me, can werewolves get drunk?"

Blacque jerked in surprise.

"It's the doggie fragrance. Gives it away every time."

"You can scent us?"

Bleu nodded. "We're predators. It helps to know the difference between a human and a creature that might rip us to shreds."

"Hmm. Guess I can see how that might be important." He tipped back his beer. "And yeah, werewolves can get drunk. Takes a little more than humans. Thanks for reminding me. This isn't my first tonight." He set the glass down on the bar and gestured for another.

"I take it you had a bad evening." Bleu lifted his shot glass, barely tasting the alcohol. He gazed at Blacque over the rim of his glass. The second beer seemed to be working to loosen his companion's tongue.

"Family. Pack. Shit like that."

Clearly the Blacque siblings' baby-making drama hadn't been resolved. If his behavior was any indication, it seemed to have got worse.

"Perhaps you should appreciate the fact that you have such shit in your life. It beats being alone."

Blacque gave him a long, considering look. "Speaking of shit, that's what you look like lately. Are you chasing the dragon?"

The mechanic's meaning came slowly to Bleu. The anger came more quickly, rapidly shifting into fury.

"I don't need heroin or crack to make me look this lovely." His smile was hard and glittery. He knew that if he looked up into the fly-spotted mirror, the tips of his fangs would be in full sight. He reached out and stroked a long, slender finger down the length of Blacque's throat. "So how's that little family problem of yours coming along? Did you explain to your alpha that your baby-making equipment is slightly confused?"

The werewolf's face went still and dangerous. Bleu smiled evilly. He didn't know which hunger prompted the comment, but he didn't bother to hide his need. A big hand gripped his wrist painfully and pulled it away from his throat.

"Don't touch me," Blacque growled.

"If you don't want to touch, then take your hand off my wrist." His warning was filled with wicked fury. If the wolf squeezed much harder, the bones in his arm would break.

"Take it outside, guys." The harried barmaid looked at them sternly, but he caught the scent of fear on her. Bleu didn't look away from Blacque, not even for a second. The wolf was ready to explode. Instead of letting him loose, the grip on his wrist tightened. He growled at the wolf.

"Outside, Blacque."

They rose like dancers, and Bleu resisted the urge to jerk his arm away from the wolf. He exerted just the slightest push on the crowd, making them oblivious to the strange scene the two of them made. He glided backward out the door, his steps matching those of Blacque.

He had one shot at this. Bleu gathered every ounce of strength in his ailing body. He summoned every last shred of glamour he possessed. As soon as the door slammed shut behind

Blacque, he pivoted on one foot, swinging the mechanic off balance, and pushed him around to the darkened corner of the building. He threw the other man into the wall, causing the metal siding to buckle under his weight. A twist of the wrist held the bigger man in place, and Bleu pressed himself flush against the long, muscular body of Blacque.

"This is what you want, isn't it, wolf?" He saw panic and confusion on the werewolf's face. Smelled his lust and felt the iron rod of his erection pressing against his own. Blacque gritted his teeth against the pain and pulled his arm, snarling in frustration as Bleu dug powerful fingers into the nerves of his wrist. Hand capture was an old Chinese fighting trick. It hurt like hell, and the big guys were just as vulnerable as the little ones. If he really wanted to, Blacque could break from his grip. It would likely be exquisitely painful, but he could do it.

Bleu rocked his hips into Blacque's groin, watching his eyes glaze over as he submitted to the vampire. He held him there, mentally processing the wolf's behavior. He leaned close to whisper in his ear.

"This is your secret, isn't it? Not just that you prefer to do men, but you prefer men to do you. Isn't it?" He punctuated the question with a thrust of his hips. They were nearly the same height, so he didn't have to reach to take Blacque's mouth in a brutal, hard kiss. He bit, he licked, he ground their teeth together, tasting the slightest hint of blood as he did so. He kept up the pressure until Blacque surrendered and opened his mouth to Bleu, moaning as their tongues explored, still rough, hard, and aggressive. All the while their hips rocked together, pushing them deeper into arousal.

"You want me to do you, don't you, Blacque? Right here and now." He didn't wait for an answer. Instead he tore open the front of the old denim shirt, baring a muscular, tattooed expanse of chest and torso. The wolf's ink work was as black as the night, as savage as his primal, lupine nature. Thorns and vines twisted around his body. The bars spiked through his nipples were golden and heavy. Bleu bent his head and worried at the metal with his teeth.

"Oh Lukas Blacque. You are such an unexpected surprise." He let go of Blacque's other wrist and stroked down the length of his torso, following the trail of the tattoo. His hands ended up resting on lean hips, and the slightest detour led him to the damp spot at the front of Blacque's jeans. From the fight-or-flight reaction, he'd have to say that Blacque had rarely if ever indulged himself sexually. Not with a male, anyhow. His heart raced under Bleu's palm. He panted and twisted his head away. But he didn't try to escape. He was nearly feral in his reaction to Bleu.

"You ever been blown by another man before?" He grinned wickedly as Blacque's cock jerked under his hand. Bleu spread his fingers and trailed down the length of that tempting shaft.

"No." Blacque's whisper was harsh. The wolf tilted his head back against the wall of the building, surrendering to Bleu's attentions.

"Come home with me, Blacque. Come with me, and we'll make each other feel good...so damn, fucking good." He meant it. His own cock was aching and hard, leaking copiously. "I'll blow you, I'll fuck you...anything you want, Blacque. Whatever nasty dream you've had, I'll do it. Just come with me." Was he begging? Surely not...

"What do you want from me?" Blacque was slowly pulling himself together. He was still shaken, still visibly overwhelmed, but suspicion rose in his eyes.

"I like you too much to lie to you, Blacque. I need to feed. I nearly scored a willing donor tonight. I lost him when you came in. It will be my pleasure to take you as his replacement."

"Blood." That seemed to clear the werewolf's mind. "If I say no?"

Disappointment ran through Bleu like lightning. But still, if sex was on the table, that was a good second choice.

"Whatever you want. You fuck me, I fuck you. I've wanted you for a while now, Blacque."

"I can't. I—"

Bleu pressed a hand over his mouth. "No one will know, Blacque. Our secret." It'd have to be. He really didn't cherish the idea of being hunted by the pack alpha for taking advantage of his son. He pulled his hand away from Blacque's mouth and trailed his fingers over those stern lips. On impulse, he hooked a finger over the wolf's lower lip. He nearly came when Blacque nipped the tip of his finger and drew it deeper into his mouth. He pulled his hand free, reached up, and cradled Blacque's head in both his hands. "It'll be good, Blacque."

"Werewolves aren't food."

Bleu's belly twisted in desperation. He came close for another deep kiss, groaning when Blacque clumsily clasped his hips and pulled them tightly to his. The wolf's inexperience was poignantly obvious.

"Do it now."

Bleu pulled back just enough to look into those obsidian dark eyes.

"The blood. Do it now."

The invitation sang through his veins like the "Hallelujah Chorus." His heart raced; sweat broke out all over his cold, weakened body. He wrapped one arm behind Blacque's neck and dropped his other hand to his ass, digging his fingers into the tight muscle there. Bleu nuzzled his bristly jaw, down the muscular length of his throat, searching for the perfect spot. He trailed his tongue down salty skin, taking a slight nip as warning. He poured every ounce of seduction he possessed into the bite.

He struck, and Blacque moaned, his hips surging forward, his cock grinding against Bleu's shaft. Bleu released, pulling sweet, salty blood into his mouth, pulling in time to the increasing tempo of their thrusts. They grunted and wrestled, hands roaming, muscles flexing. As blood hunger was sated, his climax rose, drawing his balls tight to his body and sending spasms up his spine. It was desperate, it was crude, and it was divine. He threw his head back as he came. His muffled cries mingled with Blacque's as they finished together, bodies straining, their weight held only by the galvanized metal of the wall behind the werewolf's back.

Bleu panted, exhaustion fading as the blood hit his system like a drug, intoxicating and invigorating. Blacque lay back, shuddering, his body racked by the aftershocks of his orgasm. His angular, harsh face was oddly beautiful in the moonlight. Bleu leaned in and rested his forehead against the wolf's.

"That's the beginning, Blacque. Come back to the shop with me. We've got hours still."

Blacque closed his eyes. His face was no longer stony and cold. Now it showed traces of passion. Fear. Hope. Years of pent-up need were plainly written there. This liaison was dangerous for them both, yet resolve began to crystallize in the wolf's face.

Bleu pulled his head back slightly. Blacque still had his arms looped around his waist. One big hand idly stroked Bleu's lower back. "I remember the first time I saw you."

"We met the day you opened for business. You were doing the interior work for a fleet of limos." Blacque spoke without opening his eyes.

Bleu shook his head. "No. I saw you long before that. You were working late. I'd come to look over the building, and you were still there. You were so beautiful, I just sat in the trees across the road and watched you." He'd come back at dawn, waiting for the wolf to arrive for work, and was back again at sunset. He'd spent hours spying on his neighbor.

Even in the darkness, he knew the big man was blushing—the heat radiated from his body. He was ready. After so many years, he was finally ready. It was nearly too late for Oliver Bleu.

"Will you come with me, Lukas?" His voice was rough with need and desperation.

Blacque nodded. When he opened his eyes, the expression there made Bleu catch his breath. Loneliness—deep, wrenching loneliness. He reached out and gently cupped the mechanic's face in his hand. He couldn't help wondering if that expression was reflected in his face as well.

If there were a Nobel Prize for stupidity, Lukas Blacque would undoubtedly be this year's recipient. Having sex with the vampire was dangerous on so many levels. And he'd *fed* him. Nevertheless, he stood just inside the doorway of Bleu's upholstery shop, watching the vampire unlock a closet door. He followed Bleu into the closet and couldn't help but smile at the irony of the image.

The storage closet was large, its shelves lined with rolls of leather and vinyl and various tools that he assumed were part of the vampire's trade. Bleu rolled a panel aside, revealing another room—a hidden room.

He didn't know why it surprised him. Bleu had to live somewhere safe from the sun, but Blacque hadn't expected it to be right there in the shop. He cursed inwardly. With his sensitive ears, the vampire probably overheard his conversations. This room was just on the other side of the wall of Blacque's office. But vampires died during the day, didn't they? So how had he managed to know about his alpha's ultimatum?

The room held a bed and a flimsy freestanding closet and not much else. No mementos, no decor. A couple of books lay on the floor by a lamp. A netbook was plugged in to the wall. He had none of the normal detritus that came with life.

The bed was large and long and covered in a navy blue cotton comforter. The scents of glue and leather lingered in the air, probably from Bleu's clothing. He reached back and slid the door shut behind him. He looked up to find Bleu studying him carefully.

"You've never been with a man before."

"Told you that back at the bar." Though the admission cost him some pride, he couldn't go back on it. Honesty suddenly seemed to be very important to his soul.

The vampire smiled, sending a shiver down the length of Blacque's body. He'd come with a blinding, crashing climax not a half hour ago, and he was again hard—painfully hard. Sometimes he got himself off before falling asleep at night, sometimes in the morning when he woke up hard and needy, but he'd never felt anything like his pain-tinged orgasm with

Bleu. He'd spilled inside his pants; even now he felt the cool stickiness of his cum. It was the sort of experience a man would sell his soul for.

"Women?"

He gave a curt shake of his head. There'd been some fumbling in the dark, hasty handjobs in darkened theaters or under the bleachers, but nothing beyond that. He'd tried, but his heart had never been in it.

"A virgin."

To his relief, Bleu didn't look amused or smug. He spoke quietly, allowing Blacque some sort of dignity.

"I know that werewolves are sexually opportunistic. How old are you, Blacque?"

"I'm thirty-four." He released a huge, gusty breath. Blacque felt as if a huge weight was lifted from his chest. He'd had no idea that sharing his secret would bring such relief.

"When I was a young man, it wasn't unusual to remain virginal until marriage. And to admit homosexuality could be dangerous, even in my country, where we were more liberal about such things."

As he spoke, that subtle accent increased just a bit. Blacque looked at him, studied the finely drawn lines of his face. He looked better than he had earlier. Still not robust by any means, but better. His color was up; the gaunt hollows under his eyes and cheeks had filled out a bit. His carelessly tousled hair didn't look quite so lank. Once upon a time, Bleu must have been a stunning man. Now his sensually formed lips were chapped, and the skin next to his mouth appeared rough with old scars. What could have happened to steal the vitality of a vampire?

"I suppose fucking men is forgivable in your pack as long as it's related to dominance and you're doing women as well. And it wouldn't do to actually fall in love with another man."

That was it in a nutshell. Blacque dropped his gaze to the rug that covered the hard concrete floor. Werewolves couldn't be gay. They simply couldn't. It was completely counter to their nature. Yet here he was, totally oblivious to females, even during their heat cycles. If he'd been human or vampire or even fae, there'd be no shame attached to his homosexuality. But Lukas Blacque was a werewolf, and his species existed to reproduce. He was a freak of nature. He didn't belong.

"Take your shirt off, Blacque. I want to see that body of yours again."

Odd that a quietly voiced command would send a thrill through the pit of his stomach. All he had to do was shrug, and the tattered shirt fell to the floor. He watched Bleu look him over speculatively. His eyes were hooded and mysterious. His tongue flicked out, moistening his lips. Blacque folded his arms over his chest and waited.

"It makes it easier for you if I tell you what to do." He said it as a statement, but Blacque nodded anyway. He'd never have been able to put that concept into words before. It wasn't true of the outside world, but here…now…he wanted to be commanded.

Bleu sat on the edge of the bed. "Come over here, Blacque. Get on your knees."

Fuck! It was all he could do not to rush, to skid into place. His darkest, most shameful fantasies were being played out here in this small, hidden room. Blacque's throat was tight and painful.

"Now." Bleu's voice was low and sensual. Stern.

He took a step, and then another, until he found himself kneeling between Bleu's spread legs. He'd unbuckled his belt, and his jeans were unbuttoned down the front. Blacque studied the front of the vampire's pants. His erection was off to the side, thick and alluring, still hidden behind the fabric of his jeans.

He glanced up at Bleu, seeking... reassurance, perhaps? Permission?

The vampire leaned back on the bed, braced on his hands. "Do whatever you want, Blacque. Suck me. Lick me. Touch me." His eyes were closed, and in spite of his gentle tone, a tremor ran down his body. Blacque reached up and pushed the black T-shirt up Bleu's belly.

The vampire was lean as whipcord. His muscles were flat and sleek under his skin. Blacque supposed he normally carried more weight, as he could clearly see ribs and the lines of his hipbones. His skin was pale and unmarked. He kept pushing at the shirt until Bleu sat up and pulled it off over his head. He looked surprisingly young here in the dim light of the tiny lamp.

"How old were you...?" He faltered, uncertain if he should ask the question.

"When I was turned?" Blacque nodded wordlessly. "Not yet twenty-two. I was a young soldier facing death." He didn't open his eyes as he spoke. "I was in a field hospital. My injuries were not fatal, but they became infected. My maker turned me on my last breath."

Blacque trailed roughened hands down the vampire's belly, then slipped his fingers into the waistband of his jeans. Taking a deep breath, he tugged them down. Bleu's cock emerged from the fabric. He sat back and stared breathlessly. It was thick and long with a slight curve to the left. Jet-black hair curled around the ruddy base. He was uncut; the flushed head emerged from the folds of his foreskin.

Blacque swallowed and worked the jeans off Bleu's legs, cursing softly as he came to his boots. Those came off easily, and soon enough the vampire lay naked before him.

He looked oddly romantic. The softness of youth had never fully left his face, and Bleu had the fragile, drawn look of the starving artist or dying poet. Nudity truly was the great equalizer. He no longer looked like a tough man who hunted in bars—he looked beautiful. His mouth was soft. His black hair grew back from a widow's peak. His nose was aristocratic. For the first time, Blacque realized the vampire had only the barest hint of facial hair on his upper lip. He'd been little more than a youth when he'd been turned. He knelt again and ran his hands up the front of Bleu's thighs.

"When…?"

Bleu understood. "Nineteen seventeen. Ypres, Belgium."

He'd been turned during the First World War.

Blacque looked up the length of him, at the slender body, the beautifully swollen shaft and rounded balls. Instead of speaking, he lowered his head and tentatively dragged his tongue along the seam between thigh and testicles. His own body responded as though he'd been the one touched. He reached down and fondled himself through the heavy fabric of his jeans. With his other hand, he steadied Bleu's shaft and softly skimmed his mouth over it.

There'd been times when he'd ordered porn on a hotel television. He'd seen the act, but when he slid Bleu's cock into his mouth, he choked and gagged. He felt a hand on his head, pulling him back slightly.

"It takes practice, Blacque. Hold down at the base...take a little at a time."

He tried again, using his fist to control the depth. To his satisfaction, Bleu grunted and rolled his hips a little. Blacque cupped the vampire's balls and pulled them away from his body. He tasted the salt of precum on his tongue, and his mouth watered in anticipation. The vampire's hips jerked, and fierce pride flooded him. He was on his knees, but he was in control. It was a heady sensation.

When Bleu halted him, he growled in protest. But he obeyed.

"Come up here, pup."

Blacque stared but saw that Bleu wasn't making fun of him, so he decided not to take offense. He crawled full-length up the vampire's body. In one smooth move, he found himself on his back with Bleu covering him from head to foot. The vampire liked to kiss, and he proceeded to devastate Blacque with lips and tongue and teeth. Their torsos flexed, hips grinding against hips. When the kiss broke, the other man began nipping at his chest, leaving hot, fiery trails on his skin. He tugged at the bars in Blacque's nipples while his hand stroked lower, then fumbled at his fly. Blacque lifted his hips, letting the jeans slide down over his ass. He didn't bother with his heavy boots, and Bleu didn't seem to be inclined to finish undressing him.

And then he was loose and free, his dick lying heavy and hot on his belly. He heard the vampire hiss and knew that he was looking...that he saw what Blacque had done to himself.

"Fuck, Blacque! How much metal do you have down here?" A cool hand cupped his balls and sought out the numerous piercings that studded his genitals. "How much gold do you have on your body?" Blacque moaned as Bleu found the Prince

Albert, lacing the tip of his tongue through the hoop. The tug at his glans gave him just the right amount of bite. One hand moved up his belly and pulled at the barbell through his nipple as a warm, wet mouth swallowed his cock.

He gasped at the sensation. A wet finger probed at his ass. He clenched and gritted his teeth at the pressure. He began spouting inane expletives as he thrashed and rolled against the sensations that were overwhelming him.

Bleu quickly caught on to his taste for pain and dragged his teeth down the fine skin of Blacque's cock. His finger tunneled deeper into Blacque's ass, thrusting and retreating.

"You are so tight, so absolutely fucking hot!" Bleu tugged at a loop on his scrotum and returned to the piercing at the tip of his cock.

"I'm close," Blacque managed to gasp. In response, a strong hand grasped him at the base. He was back in Bleu's mouth, and the vampire was moving with intent now, faster, swallowing him down and holding him in his throat for endless, blissful moments. His long finger pumped into Blacque's ass, hitting the hot spot just enough to make him flex his back, desperate for more.

Wildly he looked down at Bleu. Watching him deep throat his cock just sent him over the edge. He clenched his fists in the comforter and thrust up into the vampire's mouth, feeling his seed burst forth in a scalding wave. He came, and then he came some more, making up for years of lonesome celibacy in one blissful, glorious climax. He cried out as Bleu's mouth worked him, sucking and lapping up the semen that had escaped his lips.

Bleu rose to his knees and straddled his hips, pumping his cock frantically. Blacque reached up and covered Bleu's hands with his own just before the warm, sticky fluid burst through their joined fingers. Bleu rode him, thrusting through the tunnel of their hands, looking every bit as overwhelmed as Blacque felt.

Maybe that was always the way it was with sex. Maybe that was why every man he knew was thinking about fucking every other minute of the day.

Surely it had nothing to do with the ailing vampire who was now draped over his body, pressing soft kisses to his skin.

God, I hope he doesn't want to cuddle.

Blacque was just not the cuddling type. Wolves generally needed a great deal of touching, but too much contact made Blacque feel vulnerable. Another trait that separated him from the pack.

To his relief, the vampire sighed and rolled away to collapse onto his back. They didn't speak. The only sound was the laboring of their breath. Oddly the silence wasn't uncomfortable, and Blacque felt his heart slow to normal. His breathing steadied, and the world hadn't come to an end because he'd just had sex with another man. He closed his eyes and felt something like a smile cross his lips.

Bleu's hand brushed his, and when Blacque drifted into a fuzzy state somewhere between wakefulness and sleep, their fingers were loosely laced together.

Chapter Four

Blacque woke to find his nose buried in the surprisingly smooth neck of another person...another man. Alarm shot through his body, and he held perfectly still, not willing to risk waking the vampire. Bleu's chest rose and fell steadily. He was asleep, but it might be only light, normal sleep. Carefully he brought his arm up to check the time. It was still an hour from dawn. The vampire wasn't yet out for the day.

Blacque evaluated his condition. He caught the musky scent of semen on his skin, both his and Bleu's. So that part wasn't a dream. If that really happened, nothing else really mattered, did it? It was one of those moments when a man knows he's crossed a line and there's no turning back.

Carefully he eased back, moving away from the other man, then rolling onto his back to stare at the ceiling in the dim light from the cheap lamp. He'd been with this man twice. It had been voluntary, no seduction involved. Dismay and delight warred in his gut. His dick grew hard as iron and slid up to rest on his belly once again. Obviously his body opted for delight, though he was still dismayed at his weakness.

Bleu had made it easy. He'd quickly found Blacque's buttons and pushed them all. He reached up and laid his hand over his eyes. Saying no had never even crossed his mind.

What a cluster fuck.

He rolled his head to look at the sleeping man next to him and found blue eyes open and gazing at him.

"Buyer's remorse, Blacque?"

He thought about it for a moment.

"No. I'm not sorry. Guess now I know for sure." Hell, he'd always known. Now he simply knew what he'd been missing. He rolled to his side and finally succumbed to the temptation to touch Bleu's skin. It seemed smoother now, especially the spot on his face that had appeared rough and scarred. He watched his hand as it drifted and then settled on the center of the vampire's chest. He felt Bleu's heart beating strong and steady.

"Thought vamps didn't have a heartbeat."

"Myth. We also need to breathe. And we aren't immortal, though like you, we are long-lived."

"Hmm." Blacque had dozens of thoughts whirling around in his head but didn't really know where to start. As a rule, if in doubt, keep your mouth shut. That had always worked for him. But still, he was curious.

"What happens? When the sun comes up?"

"Well, I don't die, though it might appear so." Bleu rested his head on his arm. "I suppose it's like hibernation. The body goes completely dormant. If we are attached to monitors, they would show no heartbeat and very low brainwave activity. The sun is to me what silver is to you. It won't turn me to ash, but it is painful." Bleu closed his eyes. "You are welcome to stay after I sleep, though you might find it disturbing." Even though he'd been sleeping, he looked weary. He had surprisingly long eyelashes, like a woman's should be. They lay in a dark crescent over the shadows under his eyes.

"Blacque, can I come to you when the sun sets?" For just a moment, the vampire looked uncertain and oddly vulnerable. His eyes remained closed, but one arched brow rose just a bit.

He took a moment to consider Bleu's request. "First I wanted to say no. This is too dangerous. Not just to me." He looked away from the vampire. "You need blood."

The other man swallowed hard. He opened his eyes. "Yes. But that isn't the only reason I want you."

The whispered confession brought blood flooding back to his cock, and looking down, he saw that Bleu was reacting the same way.

"This is so bad. So bad for us both." Blacque rolled over and pinned the vampire onto his back. He looked down for a moment, studying those blue, blue eyes. Carefully he leaned down and pressed his lips to Bleu's.

He'd never kissed someone before, not like this, and not on his own initiative. He held very still, uncertain of what to do next. The rough tip of Bleu's tongue slid over his lips, and he automatically responded, opening his mouth and letting Bleu in. He angled his head slightly, feeling the press of lips and the click of teeth. He swept his tongue into the vampire's mouth, touching, tasting, and finally retreating, stopping to catch Bleu's lower lip. He nipped and then sucked it between his own lips.

To his delight, Bleu gasped and reached up to cradle his head. The vampire's response gave him courage, so he continued, tasting Bleu's jaw, his throat. His ran his lips over rough patches and then smooth. He wondered what had been harsh enough to have scarred the vampire. He didn't remember those marks being there even six months ago.

Finally Bleu clasped his shoulders and held him away from his body. "It's nearly time. I don't want to drop off in the middle of anything." He grinned. "Can you hold that thought till tonight?"

Blacque rose to kneel next to Bleu's naked form. As he watched, the vampire's erection faded, the flush that had suffused his skin beginning to pale.

"Can I come to you tonight, Blacque?"

He struggled to think with his brain rather than his dick. Closing his eyes, Blacque scented the air, remembering the fantastic events of the hours just past. He wanted more—desperately. For the first time in years, he felt he'd connected with another being.

But it was dangerous. Foolish. Once the alpha announced his intention to call Lukas Blacque his heir, he'd be under constant scrutiny. Challenges would soon begin at unexpected times and locations.

"This is such a bad time to start this."

Bleu didn't answer. He didn't try to mesmerize or charm or seduce. He simply watched Blacque's face.

"I can give you...us a weekend. Tonight. Tomorrow night. Then it's got to end." He wondered if it was his imagination, but he thought he briefly saw a devastated look in Bleu's eyes. It was too soon for emotion, wasn't it? Things didn't really move this fast.

"I'll take what I can, Blacque. And I thank you for it." He swallowed, and Blacque watched the movement of his Adam's apple. "I..."

Blacque leaned forward to hear what he was saying, but the vampire had gone still. He watched for a moment and then pulled the bedding out from under Bleu's supine body. He threw the comforter over the vampire and then slid into bed beside him.

He didn't know if vampires felt the cold, but he did, and if he could, he'd keep Oliver Bleu warm as he dreamed. Just for a little while, anyway.

Vampires don't dream when they sleep...or they shouldn't. There was too much violence and savagery in Bleu's life to wish to recall. It had been such a long time since he'd contemplated a future beyond his next meal and finding a spot safe from the sun when he collapsed for the day. With the warmth of Blacque's body there by his side, he'd slept as a human for an hour or two. He'd dreamed of the young days—childhood days when he'd run out in the grass and shade his eyes against the sun, watching soldiers parade through the town in their brilliant uniforms of red and blue.

He recalled meals at the family table, the laughter of his mother, and his father's stern presence. He remembered the slight softening of his father's expression as he looked at his beloved wife. Bleu remembered the feel of the sun on his skin and good food in his belly.

The sleep of the vampire is dark and still. It isn't death as many believe. When a human or vampire truly dies, the spirit flees; the cells of the body break down and disintegrate.

Things fall apart; the centre cannot hold...

Without that temporary respite, the body of the vampire begins to slowly die. The powers that set it apart as a predator begin to weaken, and with agonizing slowness, life begins to fade as starvation sets in.

Bleu was locked in the paralysis of daysleep, and when the dreams came, he was helpless before them. In his mind, he struggled, trying to flee the noxious, oily cloud of gas creeping through the knee-deep mud of the trenches. He tried to run, but the gas was in the very mud that held him fast. It dissolved on his skin, settled on his inner thighs and scrotum. Blisters rose, and he choked, unable to breathe past the fluid gathering in his lungs...

You're safe. I'm here with you.

The voice came from so very far away. A deep, gruff voice. A hand clasped his and pulled him up from the mud and out of the trench. The blast of mortar shells faded, as did the screams of the dying.

Warmth that was foreign wrapped around him, and with a sigh, Bleu slipped away into blackness and oblivion. His belly was full, his body was sated, and he was warm. The trenches of Ypres were thousands of miles and nearly a century away.

Blacque was awakened by the most subtle of warnings. Next to him, Bleu was still and cold, yet the stench of fear radiated from him. Under his closed eyelids, his eyes rolled rapidly. As he watched, blisters rose on Bleu's skin, vile and poisonous in appearance. They trailed from the left side of his beautiful mouth down to his neck. His eyes were red and oily looking. Blacque sat up and threw back the bedding, and he cursed at the painful-looking burns that peppered the vampire's body.

Blisters the size of Ping-Pong balls rose on the tender skin of his groin. His legs were covered with ooze. Blacque scoured his memory for World War One. Bleu said he'd died in Ypres.

Mustard gas.

As he watched, some of the blisters faded back into his body, while others rose like a ghastly stop-action film. The vampire was having the flashback to end them all. Unable to find a spot on his body that seemed safe to touch, Blacque clasped his hand and whispered to Bleu, telling him of safety and warmth. He stroked the dusky hair back from his forehead and moved close, sharing his body heat.

The vampire took a shallow breath that gurgled in his chest. Had he inhaled the stuff too? His throat tightened at the thought of the agony that Bleu must have suffered along with countless other young men. Mustard gas was heavy. It eventually settled to the ground like an oily, caustic trap that the soldiers had been unable to avoid.

The nightmare eventually released Bleu from its grip, and as Blacque watched, the blisters smoothed away; the rough patches around his mouth faded. When he was no longer afraid of hurting the other man, Blacque smoothed his hands over his skin soothingly. If the vampire could dream, perhaps he could sense his presence.

"Don't dream anymore, Bleu. Just sleep."

To his relief, that was exactly what the vampire did.

* * *

Blacque pocketed the keys and closed the door to the upholstery shop behind him. He wasn't completely comfortable leaving Bleu behind, but he wanted to shower the scent of the other man from his body. He needed to dress and eat and move on with his day.

He'd found a pair of work pants and a shirt among Bleu's neatly stored clothing and carried them to his shop, where he cranked up the shower. He had coveralls on hand but didn't want to put on grease after cleaning himself.

Hot water pelted over his head and shoulders, and as he soaped himself, Blacque fingered the piercings that Bleu had been so fascinated with. He couldn't resist a bitter smile. He'd gotten the tats and piercings out of fierce sexual longing, and now they would forever serve as a reminder of the brief hours he'd allowed himself with Bleu. They were only hours into their tryst, and he was already regretting…already missing what hadn't yet ended.

Touch. Werewolves thrived on touch. In fact, in the world outside of pack life, they had to remember that this wasn't a touching culture. Physical contact didn't always lead to sex, but it was as necessary to their comfort as food or rest. Blacque had held others away for so long, he was now uncomfortable with what he craved. That deep, aching need had fled under the attentions of Bleu. Even as he'd rejected the physical closeness while they slept, Blacque had awakened to find himself pressed against the vampire, arms and legs tangled with his.

Perhaps this explosion of lust was little more than the hunger for touch. Perhaps a woman could serve that same need. Holding that thought close, he turned off the water and stepped out into the crudely cemented stall. The shower had originally been an emergency station for cleaning off toxic chemicals. He'd converted it to an actual shower back when he first bought the shop.

Blacque grabbed the last clean towel and dried off, then stepped into the twill work pants that Bleu favored. He wasn't surprised that they weren't a perfect fit—Bleu was his height but more slender. The fabric was taut around his muscular thighs. The T-shirt hugged his chest and biceps. He caught the scent of detergent, but not of Bleu. He was pleased but also disappointed. He wanted to wrap himself in the other man's scent yet at the same time needed distance to clear his mind.

After gathering up the soiled clothing and towels, he dumped them into the old washing machine. He added soap, then stood back and stared as steaming water filled the tub. Finally he looked up at the pinup-girl calendar on the wall. It was one of those sent out by a tire company. Like most auto shops, his walls were littered with them.

She was blonde and buxom and the wrong month. Nevertheless Blacque stared, trying to imagine such a creature in his bed, warm and flushed, her skin soft and perfumed.

Nothing.

He changed the month and stared at the brunette who now smiled from the pages. He liked her body better. Her breasts weren't as big, and her skin was as fair as porcelain. She smiled at him with vivid blue eyes that he suspected were Photoshopped to be that color.

Bleu's didn't need enhancement—his eyes really were that blue.

With that thought, Blacque's dick began to harden and lengthen. He closed his eyes, savoring the feel of the piercings as his skin stretched and went taut. He clasped it through the fabric of his pants—Bleu's pants—and got even harder. He imagined thrusting slowly into the tight warmth of the brunette's body, but when he looked up, he saw the lean muscles of a man, a strong jawline, and cobalt blue eyes under arched black brows.

He let his cock go and sighed. Blacque didn't even know why he bothered to question it anymore.

He needed to go home, shave, and eat. There was plenty to do to occupy himself for the day, though the hours would seem endless until sundown. The gutters needed to be cleaned, and he needed to paint the porch before winter. He tried to recall if the house laundry needed to be done. Then there was the grocery shopping...

The washing machine finished its cycle and began to spin, spitting fresh water on the soapy clothing. He stayed right there until the machine ground to a halt, and then he moved the load over to the dryer, ignoring his empty belly as time passed in small, measured increments.

Shit. This was going to be the longest day of his life.

Chapter Five

Bleu didn't have to find the werewolf when he woke—Blacque was right there next to him, leaning against the wall and reading a book by the small light of the bedside lamp. Bleu noticed first that he was warm. Second, he noticed he was rested. He didn't have the usual malaise that nearly kept him on his back upon waking. He felt surprisingly fresh—and not so surprisingly, hungry.

"Hello," Bleu whispered, aware that his fangs had emerged slightly.

He looked up into that dark, inscrutable gaze, and his arousal was instantaneous. After rolling to his knees, he knocked the book to the side and pinned Blacque in place. The big werewolf was delightfully compliant. With his free hand, the wolf reached out and gently stroked the rough patch at the corner of Bleu's mouth.

"It looks better."

Bleu leaned back and ran his own finger over the old burns. In a sense, he'd been lucky. If he'd lived on, he'd have been horrifically scarred, both inside and out. As it stood, he'd lived through most of his second life without a trace of the damage the gas had wreaked on his body.

He reached up and ran a hand over Blacque's head. He'd shaved, leaving a black haze over his scalp.

"Why do you keep it so short?"

"Don't like to wash the grease out of it at the end of the day." Blacque sat unflinching under his scrutiny. He was such a contrast—tough, dangerous, and mature, but surprisingly innocent in his inexperience. During the long night, his kisses had been clumsy, his touch a bit awkward. Bleu straddled his lap, his erection pointing in the general vicinity of the other man's navel. When Blacque's hands lowered to his bare thighs, the arousal transformed into intent. He leaned forward, coming in for a kiss…

"What do you dream about?"

The question killed the mood. Bleu's hands fell to his side, his head dropped. For a moment, he eyed his slowly wilting erection.

"Vampires don't dream." He knew that to be true. The body slowed to a stop, and brain function all but ceased. Dreams were simply not possible. But then, vampires also didn't suffer insomnia, and his long hours locked in a wakeful state during the day defied that rule as well.

"Then why did your adrenaline spike? You smelled like fear and pain." He continued to study Bleu's averted face. "Your skin…you had these awful blisters. All over."

Bleu shivered. That was where the scarring was coming from. When the night terrors took him, they took him completely—mind, body, and spirit. Without thinking, he reached up and brushed the site where the mustard gas had settled on his face and mouth. He remembered holding his breath, his eyes streaming and burning. He remembered the shrieking, the insane burn as he gasped for breath, pulling it into his lungs. His eyes began to water in reaction, and he blinked quickly.

"I don't remember the dreams, but they're probably memories of the trenches. The Germans starting using gas toward the end of the war." He sat back a little, letting his weight rest on Blacque's thighs. "Just because the cloud went away didn't mean the gas was gone. It'd settle in the mud. We'd wade around in it... The mud rose up to our thighs sometimes... We'd hit a pocket of gas. Or maybe a guy would take a leak, and it'd splash back onto him..."

His shoulders drooped a bit. So many memories, yet they'd stayed hidden and quiet for so long. Why had they returned? He covered his eyes with one hand, hiding the wave of despair that washed over him.

"What else is happening to you?"

"I can't sleep. I lie here all day sometimes. Can't move. All I can do is wait. Sometimes listen to the world outside." He smiled up at Blacque. "Funny thing, though, I slept today. Like a baby."

"You dreamed."

"Maybe for a while. But then I slept afterward. Hours." He arched his back and stretched, hoping to divert Blacque's attention. It worked. He watched the other man's gaze travel the length of his body. "Better than I've slept in years." He had the sneaking suspicion the werewolf under him was responsible. Whether it had been sexual exhaustion, the wolf's rich blood, or the warm presence in his bed, Bleu had slept in peace.

He'd be damned if he'd quietly take only a weekend. Literally and figuratively. He leaned forward and brushed his lips along Blacque's jaw. The big man had showered and shaved not so long ago. He nuzzled, feeling the drag of his lips along the wolf's smooth skin. He nipped and pulled slightly, sucking just enough to leave a small mark. He smiled against Blacque's throat when the wolf's big body flexed and the fragrance of his arousal filled the air. Blacque was so needy, so lonely. He was ripe for the plucking.

"You're wearing my clothes." And they looked damn good on him too. His biceps bulged, stretching the fabric to the limit. The bars through his nipples were clearly delineated.

"Had to wash mine. Needed to find something to wear." His cheeks went dark with blood, and Bleu remembered their messy, out-of-control sex at the Roadhouse. It was a bit embarrassing to have spilled in his pants like a schoolboy. On the other hand, it was probably the most memorable sex he'd had in...well...ever.

"I washed yours too."

He smiled at the confession. "Thank you." He settled a deceptively gentle kiss on Blacque's firm lips. He let his fangs play over the tender skin of his mouth, threatening to draw blood. Under him, the wolf's belly undulated from his heavy breathing, and his cock tightly filled the front of the twill pants that he wore. Bleu leaned down and nipped at the golden bars under the tight knit of the tee shirt.

"Why did you pierce yourself, Blacque?" He reached down and pulled the tight shirt free from the waistband of his pants. After pulling it up, he ran his thumbs over the golden bars.

"Don't really know," Blacque whispered. His voice was low and husky with arousal. "Just...nobody else was touching me there. Needed to remember I was a man, I guess."

"What happens to them when you shift?" He ran his tongue over the tan ovals of the wolf's nipples, letting the gold clink against his fangs. He was hungry, so needful, yet the seduction was so rewarding.

"Guess they stay put. I've never really checked." His hand came up tentatively and wrapped around the back of Bleu's neck. "Never thought... It feels so fuckin' good!" His hips bucked up, and he held Bleu in place over his chest. Obligingly Bleu teased first one nipple and then the other. Blacque's free hand came up and roamed his back, then slowly dropped to cup his ass.

"That's good, Blacque. Touch me any way you want."

That gave the wolf courage, and he explored, his fingers sliding into the crack of Bleu's ass. Bleu had to pause a moment to let the sensation sweep through his body.

Two nights. He had two nights to capture the shy wolf and to somehow find an answer to the dilemma that the alpha had dumped on his son. Bleu suspected the wolf would take his duty to pack and family very seriously. And the were would not relish the idea of being the main food source for an ailing vampire. He was amazed the werewolf had voluntarily given up his blood in the first place.

"There's lube inside the drawer there." The other man gave him a long look and then reached over and pulled the drawer of the cheap little table open. "Condoms too."

The wolf followed his instructions carefully. He set the items to the side. Bleu unbuckled the slender belt that cinched Blacque's pants, amused at the difference in the fit. Blacque was lean and muscular; his belly was ridged with muscle. He filled out Bleu's pants like a dream. Carefully he unbuttoned the trousers and lowered them, smiling to see his wolf hadn't bothered with underclothes. When Blacque's cock rose into view, he took a deep breath and let it out slowly.

The Prince Albert would drag through his passage, and Bleu's ass tightened with nervous anticipation. He reached down and lifted Blacque's testicles, then fingered the piercings that studded his scrotum. Heavy golden hoops dangled from the velvety skin, winking in the dim light. Three bars laddered from the base of his cock.

"You're going to wear a condom. I'm not sure if these will pull on you during sex."

Blacque's cock jumped, and he swallowed. A tiny bead of fluid welled from the slit on his cockhead.

"I thought...I thought..."

"You thought I'd take you?"

Blacque nodded.

"Is that what you want?" The wolf just stared at him. He didn't know what he wanted. Bleu smiled and stroked his muscled belly. "I figure the best way to teach you is for me to take you this way. You'll know what to expect." He traced his fingers down to brush over the other man's cock. He gently massaged his perineum and then trailed his fingers back farther.

"Take some lube on your fingers. Start working it into my ass. Gently!"

Blacque gave a short, surprised laugh.

"It's not like porn." He flinched when Blacque's slick fingers glided into his crack. "At least, it isn't yet." God. It had been years since he'd given someone his ass. He'd given men his mouth or hand, his cock when they wanted to fuck, but Bleu rarely bottomed. A rough, blunt finger pressed and retreated, returning seconds later with a fresh load of lube. In the past, he'd noticed wolves were possessive as hell. Once Blacque took his body, his primal self wouldn't want to let go of Bleu.

He moaned at the sensation of Blacque's hands on his body. Clearly seduction was a two-edged sword.

"That's it. Don't force your way in." He relaxed, taking a deep breath as Blacque's finger pushed through the tight ring of muscle. "If you clench, it hurts. If you push out, that makes it easier."

Blacque changed position a bit, and then a warm hand covered Bleu's balls even as the man's finger worked its way in and out. Bleu shivered at the sensation. "Good. Add a finger. Don't scissor. That's not safe." Within moments, he was being steadily finger-fucked. Glancing up at the wolf, he saw that his face was intent on his task. His cock had gone to half-mast. When Blacque brushed a finger over his prostate, he jumped.

"You okay?" Worry throbbed through Blacque's voice.

"Yes...do that again." He did, and Bleu groaned in pleasure. "Sweet spot. Use a light touch." As Blacque fingered his ass, Bleu buried his face in his chest and trailed his tongue up the jet-black tattoos that climbed his skin.

"You have a taste for pain, don't you, Blacque?" Those tattoos had to have been painful, and the piercings were clearly sexual in nature. It was a strangely kinky form of self-medication. Judging by the night before, the wolf could take it as rough as Bleu could deliver. That made him shiver.

The fingers withdrew, and before he answered, the wolf returned with a third lubed finger. His thrusts were shallow now.

"I didn't know it would be so tight." He didn't answer Bleu's question.

Bleu rocked back, seeking deeper penetration.

"I'll tell you about the tats...sometime."

Bleu's skin heated in warning. It was time to move on. "Stop now." He lifted from the wolf's body, and the fingers fell away. He rose high onto his knees and reached for the condom, then quickly tore it open. Blacque's gaze went hot and feral as Bleu smoothed the sheath over the wolf's cock. Next, he layered on a thick coating of lube. The piercings felt bumpy under the thin latex, so he added more.

"Just lie back. Let me drive." He moved into position, arrowing the tip of Blacque's dick into his ass. With a deep breath, he began to lower himself, an inch at a time. The lube soothed the burn, and goose bumps roughened his skin. Three fingers hadn't prepared him for the wolf's fat cock. Nor had they prepared him for the piercings; they caught on the edge of his sphincter, making him hiss at the foreign sensation.

Blacque cried out, and his hips thrust upward, pushing in faster than Bleu expected. One thrust...two...and he'd gone as far as he could go. Both men panted as they paused, taking a moment. Blacque's face was flushed, and sweat beaded his chest and trunk. With a groan, Bleu lifted his hips and began to move, riding the wolf slowly...deeply.

With his mouth open slightly, Blacque panted, his eyes wild. "I can't...I can't go long."

"That's okay, Lukas. We've got all night." If he was right, his partner would most likely have an impressive recovery time. He had a lot of years to make up for. Bleu ground down harder onto the other man's cock, grinning when a grip of iron came down on his hips, urging him to move faster.

Bleu had softened with the penetration. He reached down and tugged at his cock, jerking himself back to erection. A hand pushed his away, and Blacque's was there, stroking and pulling, then tugging his aching balls away from his body.

"I need to move, Bleu." Blacque's voice was breathless, as though he'd been punched in the gut. "Need to fuck you..."

Reluctantly Bleu rose and felt Blacque's cock slide from his body. He rolled onto his back next to the other man, legs parted and knees spread wide. Blacque wasted no time; he was on his knees and pushing his way back into Bleu's hole. This time the piercings were sheer, wicked pleasure.

Now Bleu was the one trapped. It wasn't a feeling he cherished, but it gave him the luxury of watching the wolf above him, seeing the flashes of need and lust flicker over his harsh features. Blacque let his eyes fall closed as he thrust deeply into Bleu's ass. He remained on his knees for several strokes and then moved lower, fucking him in missionary position. Bleu reached around and ran his hands up and down Blacque's back, then squeezed his ass to prompt him to move faster.

He turned his head, tucking his face into the wolf's throat, scenting…almost tasting the blood that pumped under his skin.

"Take it." Blacque sounded dangerously close to his limit. "Take what you need."

Bleu bared his teeth, found his spot, and bit hard, trusting the haze of sex to dull the pain for his partner. He wrapped his lips over the wounds and let the hot flow of blood pulse into his mouth.

Blacque groaned and thrust harder. True to Bleu's expectations, the wolf loved that blend of pain and pleasure. Their skin slapped hard, and with the weight of the other man's body above him, the stroking over his gland, and the rush of blood over his tongue, Bleu rose to climax, gasping, barely remembering where he was or who he was with. His back snapped tight, his balls drew up to his body, and his seed burst from him in a slick, heated pool that Blacque dipped into every time he thrust.

Bleu cried out with each spasm, white lights flashing behind his closed lids. Just when he thought it must surely come to an end, Blacque's cock changed position and hit his sweet spot over and over until Bleu came again, wringing every drop of seed from his balls. His body twisted, coming dry, and then coming some more, leaving him panting and exhausted.

Blacque was so wound up, so needy that he didn't know what the hell he wanted. He knew what he needed, though. He needed this man beneath him, taking his cock into his tight, hot body.

Another myth busted. The vamp might run cool most of the time, but during sex, his skin was so hot, he nearly melted Blacque into a puddle of man, lust, and fear.

Yeah, he was afraid. He was afraid that once he experienced sex with another man, he'd never be able to turn away again. He'd never be able to maintain the facade that kept his secret hidden from the pack...from his father.

Beneath him, Bleu's face had changed; his fangs were slightly distended. He guessed that for a vampire, sex and feeding were all rolled up into one big sensual package. He offered his throat, knowing as a werewolf, he was top of the food chain. He wasn't food, and Bleu wouldn't force him. But his skin burned for the penetration, for the sensation of teeth sinking into flesh, for the sharp tang of his blood to scent the air.

He craved the knowledge that he was feeding Bleu, giving him back just a tiny bit of health. Maybe—the thought that had begun to coalesce in his lust-addled mind dissipated as Bleu's teeth punctured his skin. After that was the sharp pull of his mouth as the blood began to flow. That tiny bit of pain was enough to roll Blacque over the edge, but he held on just a little longer. As the vampire fed, he climaxed, his slender body trapped under Blacque's. His muscles tensed, and Bleu released his throat, his cry harsh and desperate.

Blood smeared his lips, trickled down his chin. Blacque's blood was vivid against the pallor of the vampire's skin. His magnificent blue eyes went unfocused, and he held on tightly to Blacque as his body bucked and shuddered, finally expelling his cum between their bodies.

The fluid was warm, wet, and sticky, and that tiny push knocked Blacque completely out of control. He pumped and he grunted. He slammed into Bleu's ass, uncaring of how hard he thrust or what those damn piercings might be doing to the vampire's tender opening. His ears rang; when he cried out, he didn't hear his own voice. The spasms that rocked his body were so powerful, he wasn't certain if it was pleasure or pain.

His semen rushed from his dick, washing him in warmth. Though he lay perfectly still, he shivered as though he were freezing. He came in waves, unable to move anymore. All he could do was lie there and let the orgasm take him. He felt hands on his back, comforting and strong, and he slumped down onto his partner's body, mindless of his own weight.

He felt drained and powerless, helpless and overwhelmed.

"It's okay, Blacque. Let it go."

He wasn't sure what Bleu was talking about, but Blacque simply held on to him for life itself. When he finished shuddering and panting, he turned his head to the side, resting it on Bleu's wide shoulder. To his surprise, his eyes were wet, but he didn't remember crying.

Chapter Six

"So I told you about the dreams. You tell me about the tattoos."

Bleu hadn't thought the werewolf would be the sort to show physical affection, but here he was, head in Bleu's lap, calmly accepting gentle touches to his head and temples. He leaned back against the wall, enjoying the feel of the high cheekbones under his fingers. Bleu reached up and stroked the skin next to his mouth. It had smoothed out completely. It wouldn't last, but for now it was a good sign.

Blacque sighed. "It's a dumb story, really."

"Tell me."

He twisted and looked up at Bleu's face. "When I was a kid, still with my mom, I lived in Oregon. There were lots of blackberries up there. You ever see what happens when those things grow wild?"

Blackberries. That explained the spiny leaves and thorns of the tattoos.

"Yeah, I've seen them grow wild in a few different places."

Blacque's eyes dropped shut, and Bleu took the opportunity to run the tips of his fingers over his eyelids, then moved on to trace his heavy black brows.

"They can fill up acres of land if they grow out of control. I was maybe thirteen or so. Dru's a year younger. I'd just learned to shift not long before. I broke the rules, shifted during the day." He paused for a moment. "Guess I was an angry kid. Must have been tough on my mom."

"Most kids are tough on their mothers at some point in time."

Blacque's mouth turned up in a lopsided smile. "Yeah, but most mothers don't have a closeted adolescent werewolf to deal with. And I was pissed about my dad. I couldn't understand why he was there for his pack but not for us." He gave a small sigh. "I skipped school to hunt out in the countryside. I was flushing rabbits at an abandoned barn. Some old guy saw me and probably thought I was a coyote. He started taking potshots at me with his rifle. I thought it would be a good idea to run for the brambles, hide deep inside one of those huge berry patches."

"I take it that didn't turn out so well?"

The wolf laughed. "I was okay as long as I stayed on the little game trails that run through those things. But as soon as I got a little turned around, I ended up with vines wrapping around my legs and body, and thorns sticking into my feet. I got so tangled that I came to a dead stop. I was stuck there for hours."

"In the meantime, your mother…"

"She was frantic. When I didn't come home after dark, she had the few local shifters out looking for me. By the morning, the police had been called."

Bleu ran his fingers over the wolf's chest, once again idly playing with the golden bars through his nipples. "And you were trapped the entire time?"

"Oh, it gets worse. Since I couldn't untangle myself, I panicked and shifted back to human. I don't think I've ever experienced such pain in my entire life."

Bleu winced in sympathy. He'd got hooked up in rosebushes before. He couldn't imagine being entombed by blackberry vines.

"I was too deep into the patch to work my way out, but I did manage to shift back to wolf. I was so sliced up and bloody that even after shifting I didn't heal right away. It took days."

"And I assume you slunk back home with your tail between your legs?"

Blacque rolled his head to look up at him. "No, I collapsed just yards away from clear ground. We go back to human form when we're unconscious. A search team with a dog found me there, all torn up and bloody. Ironically it was the man who was shooting at me who spotted me first. They all thought I'd been attacked and raped or something. I had to tell my mother what really happened, but I just told the police I didn't remember anything. It was hard to explain why I was lying naked in a berry patch."

He gave a weak grin. "When I turned eighteen, I went to a tattoo shop. Thought I'd get a band around my bicep. Lots of other guys were doing it. I thought the berry vine was appropriate. Reminds me not to take stupid risks."

Bleu traced the trail of the original band on the wolf's upper arm, then followed it up his arm to the shoulder, and then down his chest. The vines twisted and coiled, looking both delicate and deadly. He knew what Blacque was telling him—their involvement was a risk. A stupid risk.

"You went a little overkill for just an armband."

Blacque's grin showed some embarrassment. "Yeah, well, he was my first crush, I guess. The fellow who inked me. He mentioned it would be cool to run it down my arm like a real vine, and I was so hot for him, I did it. After that, it was like an addiction. I'd need to see him, and the only excuse I had was to add to the tattoo."

"And you never let him know? Never approached him?"

"Nah, he was straight. Had a wife and a couple of kids. He liked putting his art on my body, and he liked my money. Maybe thought I was an okay guy. Nothing more."

Shit. His heart ached for Blacque. The guy had spent far too many years hiding what he was while never denying it to himself. He was closeted out of necessity, because Bleu honestly didn't think the man particularly cared what others thought. Unfortunately, being in a wolf pack, he'd risk a lot more than his pride if he came out without strong support behind him.

"What about the piercings? Did he do them?" Bleu felt and acknowledged a slight twinge of jealousy about the unknown man who first captured Blacque's heart.

"Nah, he just did ink. I had a girl do those. It seemed...I don't know...maybe a bit safer." His smile was slightly sheepish.

He could have exposed himself with a man. With a woman handling his genitals, any sexual response he'd have had would have seemed normal. Bleu sighed and resisted the impulse to hug the man in his arms, to hold him close and let him know that he understood. Instead he dropped a kiss on his rough knuckle, unwilling to risk frightening the skittish wolf in his bed.

"Have you eaten?"

Blacque stirred from the near-sleep state he'd fallen into. He pondered the question. He'd had lunch but no dinner.

"No big deal. I'll grab food after you sleep."

"No." Bleu moved him from his lap. Blacque felt unaccountably put out—he'd found a state of mindless comfort and resented leaving it.

"If you're feeding me, you need to increase your food and fluid intake." He slid from under Blacque's body and stood in the dim light, searching for clothing.

Blacque watched the vampire, studying the smooth flow of his muscles under skin. His body reminded Blacque of a swimmer—all lean and spare. The rough patches of scar tissue had faded away, leaving him smooth and ivory colored. His hair was unruly with waves that hadn't been there before.

Bleu stepped into a pair of briefs and then took a folded pair of jeans from the flimsy closet. Next followed a T-shirt—dark, maybe blue or black. He sure didn't seem permanent, considering how long he'd lived in Arcada.

"Come on, Blacque. Get dressed." Bleu tossed the borrowed clothing in his direction. Now that they'd mentioned food, he was hungry. He swiftly dressed, doing his best to watch the other man the entire time.

"We can get naked and dirty later." Bleu gave a grin that froze Blacque's heart in his chest. In all the years he'd known the vampire, he'd never seen him smile like that, all free and happy. Funny that you could know someone yet not really know them at all. His heart started beating again, almost as rapidly as it had when he'd been near to climax. Blood heated his cheeks. He'd do a hell of a lot more than ink his body for this man's smile! As he dressed, he felt an almost surreal sensation. The entire thing had happened so fast. Over the years, he'd had fantasies about the vampire, wild and improbable scenarios that had taunted his dreams. The reality was much more than he'd dreamed. The heat and lust hadn't been a surprise. What he hadn't counted on was the emotion and the sense of belonging. It was more than he'd allowed himself to hope for.

Without much conversation, they locked up and walked out into the moonlit night. Tomorrow—Sunday—he was to attend another pack meeting. Blacque pushed the thought away, knowing what he had to do and also knowing what he wanted to do. He wanted to tell them to leave him the hell alone, but that wasn't going to happen. He'd never say it, and if he did, they'd certainly never leave him alone. Not his father, and certainly not the pack.

He just didn't know if he had it in him to really go lone. Solitary as he was, that would mean leaving Arcada and the safety it offered, as well as his sister and his few friends. Hell, he'd hate to lose his father, even though the old man could be an overbearing SOB.

He automatically headed for his truck. Bleu walked easily beside him, matching him stride for stride. It felt good not to be alone in the dark.

"I think there's a diner that's open late."

"Mae Belle's. Good food there." Blacque slid the keys into the ignition. "You don't eat, do you?"

Bleu smiled, and his eyes went all sleepy and sexy. "Just for pleasure. It doesn't sustain me." He glanced over at Blacque. "Plumbing's all there. Doesn't make sense not to use it now and then."

That explained how he'd been able to drink at the bar. He'd been hunting that night, and Blacque had been fleeing.

He'd never visited that bar before. He knew its reputation. He knew there were men there looking for other men. Had he been unconsciously seeking that out?

Blacque moved the truck smoothly out onto the approach strip into town. It was only a mile or so, and they soon saw the neon lights of the diner up ahead. When they pulled in, there was brisk business going on. He frowned for a moment.

"High school football tonight. Musta been a home game." Briefly he let himself remember those days back when he played for the Arcada team. Those were good times, yet sometimes they'd been bad times. He'd look up into the stands, expecting to see his mother, seeing his barely familiar father instead. His father had always been surrounded by a crowd of children, some his, some not. Dane Blacque had never belonged to just his children. He belonged to the pack.

Pulling into the parking lot, he took another glance at Bleu, noting that under the lights of the parking lot, he looked pale but otherwise healthy. He was nearly a different person than he'd been just the night before. They'd have to talk about this, and soon.

But Bleu's health wasn't his business—not really. After tomorrow, they'd go back to being neighbors in an industrial park.

For a long moment, they sat in the cooling pickup truck, their gazes meeting in the darkness. Bleu leaned toward him slowly; his smile showed fangs glinting in the darkness. He rested those teeth right at the base of Blacque's throat, and then he licked him slowly. Without another word, he moved away and opened the door on his side.

"Shit." His hands were shaking, and Blacque had to stand for a moment to let his hard-on subside. Bleu leaned against side of the truck, his back to Blacque. His pose was a bit too casual.

It wasn't until they entered the noisy, brightly lit diner that Blacque realized how cold it was outside. He was running hot, and the vampire was probably impervious to the weather. They probably looked out of place, the both of them wearing nothing heavier than T-shirts. Meeting Bleu's gaze, he knew the vampire had noted their clothing as well.

"I've got a jacket out in the truck."

Bleu just shrugged in response. He was right; they'd probably stand out even more if they tried to cover their mistake. Instead they waited for the petite blonde waitress to take them to a booth. Blacque ordered coffee, and Bleu ordered hot chocolate with whipped cream.

"Hey, Lukas. Long time no see." Blacque glanced at the waitress quickly and then away. His gaze dropped to the tabletop, where he idly pushed his coffee cup around in circles.

"I asked Tiffany if it was okay to switch tables." She gave him a flirtatious smile, and then her gaze moved to Bleu. Her nostrils flared briefly, and she turned back to Blacque.

"Hi, Cin. How's your family?" He racked his brain for something else to say and came up empty.

"They're good. But you'd know that if you ever came around. On Sundays, that is." She smiled blithely at Bleu. "Our families like to get together sometimes on the weekend. Old friends." Her sharp blue gaze returned to Blacque. She was one of the few females in town who wasn't from the alpha's bloodline. He swallowed. In all the years he'd known Cindy Thompson, she'd never shown interest in him. Now she was inspecting him boldly from head to foot. The feeling made his skin crawl.

Bleu's smile unleashed all his charm, drawing her like a moth to a flame. In between appraising Blacque and peering at her own tables, she fell into the vampire's flirtatious trap. Soon she was giggling at his conversation. She swept away with their orders before Blacque could even gather his thoughts.

"I assume she's one of the women your father wants you to...consider?"

"Not consider. Fuck. There's a difference." Blacque sipped his coffee, watching Cindy warily as she worked her tables.

"Look, there's our esteemed mayor." Bleu nodded toward a table in the back. "He's an incubus, you know."

Blacque looked at him in surprise.

"And our town librarian descended from a long line of fae. One of our local mail carriers is a rather frightening witch."

"How do you know this stuff?" Blacque looked around the diner, wondering what else he was missing. "You never get out during the day."

"Yes, Blacque, but after nightfall, people let their true selves come out. I've witnessed more in this town than you can imagine."

"You lookin' in people's windows?"

Bleu grinned, and Blacque knew that was exactly what he'd been doing. After all, the vampire spent his day hours eavesdropping on his neighbor.

"Arcada is a wonderful, magical place. I'm so happy it found me."

He looked at the vampire in surprise. "*It* found *you?*"

Bleu was fiddling with his hands, pushing the saltshaker back and forth. "I needed somewhere to go. I was wandering, trying to keep my head low. I rode into town and my motorcycle broke down. From there, every time I tried to leave, something held me up. It seemed like a sign at the time."

They sat for a moment, Blacque letting the sounds and smells of the little restaurant flow over him. He caught a wild scent—a shifter who wasn't wolf—but he couldn't put a face to the scent.

"Are you still going to go through with this plan of your father's?"

He turned his attention back to the vampire. "Didn't say I was going to."

"And you didn't say that you weren't." Bleu stirred the melting cream into his chocolate. He took a sip, then smiled over the rim of the cup as a group of girls walked past their table. The girls giggled, and Bleu winked. Obviously he liked women as well as he liked men.

Blacque scooted forward on his seat just a bit. "Are you gay? Bi? Have you ever been with women?"

Bleu glanced away and then leaned in to speak quietly. "Maybe we should talk about this somewhere else?" Blacque leaned closer and looked straight into his eyes. They didn't have enough time together to put off important conversations.

Bleu looked at Blacque and sighed. "I was married. Married with a child on the way when I went to war. We didn't really label ourselves back then." He sipped the chocolate and set the cup down. "But by today's outlook, I was bisexual with strong leanings toward men. As a vampire, I'm less complicated than most humans. Feeding and sex are often intertwined, and I'll feed as readily from a female as from a male." He waited for their original server to refresh their water glasses before he continued.

"My marriage was arranged when I was quite young. I'd known my wife for many years. She was my friend first and foremost. I doubt she'd have been surprised to discover that I was unfaithful to her while I was away. Hurt, but not surprised."

Clearly the vampire still carried guilt for the transgressions of his previous life.

"Did you feel...different? Wrong in your skin?" Blacque asked.

"Yes, I did. If I'd stayed at her side, maybe it wouldn't have been an issue. I'd have slept with her and raised our children. In time, my libido would have waned. My attraction to men might have continued, but I'd have remained faithful to her." He shook his head. "I've thought of this often. Many men are unfaithful during times of war; that's always been the case. If I'd stayed in our small town, I'd never have met the men that I did, would never have visited the clubs of Paris..." His blue eyes held a sad look.

"We stumbled into a bar one night. I was drunk, and my companions... Once we realized it was oriented toward gay men, they were mortified." He smiled, no doubt remembering something amusing. "It was a cabaret, I suppose the equivalent of a drag club. There were soldiers there—French and British, even Americans. I saw an officer from my division. He saw me. My friends left in a hurry, but I lingered for a moment, completely wrapped up in the licentious freedom of the place.

"Days later, I returned to that place by myself, and the officer was there again. Yves took me to a small hotel room that night. We maintained a discreet affair for many months."

He lapsed into silence then, lost in his memories. Blacque felt no need to prompt him to continue. There had to have been love between the two, or Bleu wouldn't have been so deeply affected.

Their food was delivered. Both men had ordered burger platters and milkshakes. Blacque turned to his with vigor, while Bleu picked at his food, enjoying it but consuming little.

"Yves turned me without my permission."

Blacque looked up in surprise.

"He truly loved me. When I was in the hospital dying, he sat with me until the end. And then he took my blood and gave me his. Ironically, by saving me, he lost me. Once I was turned, I had to flee Europe. I was too raw and new to be able to pass as human, so he arranged for me to travel to the United States."

Blacque swallowed and then took a drink of his milkshake, his eyes never leaving Bleu's face.

"What ever happened to him?"

Bleu's expression became shuttered. "I'm sure he became someone else or was killed in the course of duty. He was in intelligence, which suited his need to avoid the light. He was very powerful, though, and could function during the day." The vampire seemed uneasy with the turn of the conversation. He didn't want to talk about his maker anymore.

"What about your family?"

"My wife remarried. My son grew up and had several children of his own. Thanks to the Internet, I've been able to track quite a dynasty of my descendants." He smiled.

"You ever want to go meet them?"

Bleu shook his head. "Never. And all the time." He gave a little laugh. "When I feel very old and alone, I go online and search for them."

They finished eating, and after a time, Cindy came and dropped off their check. She clearly wanted to linger and chat, but a crowd of high school students poured in, and she was off again, delivering menus and glasses of water. Leaving their money on the table, Blacque and Bleu made their escape out into the dark autumn night.

Chapter Seven

The breeze carried all sorts of information to Blacque's nose. He glanced up at the moon and noted it was about a week out from being full. That's why his senses were so acute. He smelled the trail of a bold coyote that had been coming down into town, plundering trash cans, most likely. He also scented a feral cat and the trails of dozens and dozens of people who'd come in and out of the diner.

He smelled Bleu and the scent of their mingled sweat and semen. If he smelled it, how could Cindy have missed it? His uneasiness surfaced once again.

"How would you like to see Arcada the way I see it?"

He looked over at the vampire curiously.

"Let's drive out to your place. We can go from there."

"How do you know where I live?"

Bleu slid into the cab of the truck and pulled the door closed behind him. When Blacque climbed in, Bleu just looked away with a smile. He wasn't going to answer, and really, did he need to know? He started the truck and headed out of town, feeling full, content, and oddly happy.

They didn't talk during the trip, and when Blacque pulled up in front of his house, both men stood next to the truck, partly to check for intruders and partly just to bask in the pleasure of the night. He'd never had trouble inside the city limits, but it never hurt to be prepared.

"You might want to shift." Bleu's eyes glistened in the moonlight. His hair ruffled in the breeze. Blacque waited a moment and then began to undress. No need to go into the house to get naked. He kicked off his boots and pants and then peeled off the tight T-shirt.

Bleu never looked away. Blacque enjoyed the lazy feel of his cockstand rising. Under the caress of the moon, he was comfortable in his skin, confident in his sexuality. His cock was heavy and thick. His gaze lingered on Bleu's face, and then his head dropped back in a moment of languid sensuality. Bleu was watching him, and it felt good. Bleu wanted him, and that felt better than good.

He inhaled, calling the change down, momentarily held in its grip as his cells shifted and his molecules danced. His muscles went taut, and fleeting pain shimmered through his vision.

When the pack ran, they took turns shifting, guarding the others during that brief moment of helplessness. Bleu looked away and scanned the house...the forest...and Blacque knew the vampire had his back.

Finally he was on all fours, and he shook vigorously, enjoying the feel of fur and flexing muscle. The wolf always felt good. It never questioned motives or intentions. It never worried about its sexuality. He bent down and bowed, stretching his long legs, casually inviting the vampire to play.

Bleu grinned and knelt on one knee, then reached out to run a hand over Blacque's massive body. "Is this okay?"

He shook again and gave the vamp a quick lick on the chin.

Bleu ran his hand down the length of his back, stroking along the long muscles of his spine. Blacque shivered with pleasure. He rested his chin on Bleu's broad shoulder, letting his eyes droop in pleasure as those wonderful hands buried themselves in the deep ruff of his fur and then down under his belly.

When those hands wandered between his hind legs, he automatically sat, protecting his most sensitive parts.

Bleu gave a husky laugh. "It's all there, Blacque. You are officially the first wolf I've ever met with body piercings!"

Blacque dived to the ground and rolled on his back, giving his belly to Bleu. When the pleasure became almost unbearable, he leaped to his feet and shook out his fur, looking expectantly at Bleu.

"Ready to go?"

Blacque panted, staring steadily up into his face.

"Let's go visit the good people of Arcada."

* * *

As a general rule, Blacque didn't notice much about the world around him when he was shifted. Yes, he was tuned in to the scents of the evening, to his surroundings—survival demanded his attention. But he rarely noticed the clarity of the sky or the beauty of the nightscape.

He loped next to Bleu, moving at an easy pace. Part of him worried about the vampire—was he moving too fast for him? Did he have the stamina for a long night of running? Bleu surprised him, gliding along at a steady run. They traveled in silence, never so much as disturbing a deer grazing in a meadow or an owl watching them solemnly from a branch above their path.

Blacque normally saw the world in black-and-white when he was a wolf, but this night he saw the dazzle of the stars and the feathery shapes of leaves and branches etched against the sky. He saw flowers that opened only after moonrise; their scent was light and magical on the breeze.

They came to a clearing where a small craftsman-style house sat. It was charming, landscaped with whimsical touches. A perfectly tuned wind chime sang in the darkness, and Bleu slowed to a halt.

"You know Kell and Pim?"

Blacque had seen the odd little couple around town several times. They were short, very nearly sexless, and tended to keep to themselves most of the time. They owned a small jewelry boutique, where Kell produced breathtaking works of art. Even Blacque occasionally gazed in the window of their shop, admiring his artistry with precious metals and gemstones.

He'd never spoken with them, though. His wolf was always a bit spooked by them.

Bleu stepped lightly onto the porch, gesturing Blacque to follow. The vampire glided in absolute silence; not even a whisper of a footstep testified to his passage. They moved to the side of the house, where a gentle light shone through a window.

"See what our little odd couple gets up to after dark?" There was a smile in his voice as he spoke, and Blacque peeked in through a gap in the lace curtain.

If he'd been in human form, he'd have gasped. He wasn't sure who was who, but the androgynous little couple was truly anything but!

"Kell is the male. He's an ice elemental." Pim was obviously fire. They were tall and elegant, magical and breathtaking. Normally Kell looked like a teenage boy with his pale skin and lank black hair. Now he was forbidding, naked, and muscular. His black hair cascaded in thick waves down his back. He was smiling, building ice sculptures in the air. Just as quickly as they formed, Pim waved her hand, dissolving them to mist. She laughed, her vibrant red hair dancing like fire around her body.

Blacque stepped back, unwilling to spy for much longer but reluctant to walk away.

"Magic, yes?" Bleu stepped from the elevated porch and landed lightly on the grass that rolled away from the house. "I know little about them, but they are young and unskilled still. Otherwise I wouldn't have risked showing you."

Young and unskilled. In spite of his age, Blacque felt the same way. He looked back at the couple, feeling the responsibility of their secret resting on his shoulders. Just days ago, his only responsibility had been to himself. Now he felt the weight of his sister and his father, Bleu, and now these two.

Oh yeah...the pack as well. Every connection was a bit more of a burden, and the pack was the heaviest of them all.

They eased away from the house, walking instead of running. Bleu's hand occasionally brushed his ruff, his fingers tracing through the fur. Blacque bumped into his leg, enjoying the contact.

He'd willingly spend his nights like this—walking and simply enjoying the world he lived in and the company of the man by his side. But he couldn't do it. He had one more night, and then Blacque's life would change.

It hurt a little, knowing he'd spent years just yards away from Bleu, years in which he could have lived this magical life.

But in the end, they'd have parted. He might not have known it would be like this, but the end would have been the same. He was the heir to the alpha. It was better this way, safer for his heart. He'd had this one weekend to learn who he was and what passion with another man could be. Now he knew he didn't want to let Bleu go. Ever. But he would.

He'd still keep an eye on the vampire, make sure he was safe and never hungry. Any more than that, he couldn't even consider.

In fact, feeding Bleu would prove to be a problem. Feeding meant sex with Bleu. If he did it, their affair would undoubtedly continue. If someone else did it? Even the thought had the wolf baring its fangs in anger. Fortunately the wolf had a very short attention span.

They walked into the dense forest, following game trails that were nearly invisible. Blacque led, picking up scents, discarding some, taking a moment to examine others. He came across the spoor of a fox—but it wasn't really a fox. He paused and considered the trail. Should he follow it and see where it led?

Until this night with Bleu, he'd never have considered that the fox might be something else completely.

In time they made a huge loop, coming back to the region near his house. They wandered into a yard that was slightly familiar. Blacque scented the air and tried to remember when he'd been here before. It must have been long, long ago.

"Move quietly. She's outside waiting." Bleu's whisper floated to him like the breeze, and Blacque looked up at the man's face. Bleu was intent, staring at the porch of the old house.

That's when he knew where he was—Mrs. Neville's house. She'd been his English teacher in high school. Over a decade had passed, and she'd been old back then. She must be elderly now.

They worked their way through the shrubbery and moved close enough for Blacque to see her sitting on a swing on the porch, waiting patiently, gnarled hands folded in her lap. Her glasses gleamed in the moonlight, and her hair was silvery white. She looked ancient yet oddly young.

Bleu knelt, and Blacque hunkered down on his belly, watching as the elderly teacher rose and moved stiffly to the door of the house. She vanished for a moment, and then soft strains of music floated out onto the air.

When she returned, she was wearing a long-sleeved sweater over her soft, feminine dress.

"Watch!" Bleu rested a hand on Blacque's shoulders. Anticipation had them straining to see through the bushes.

The man came to her like a dream, a misty cloud that filtered in from thin air. As Blacque watched, the mist slowly took shape, whirling and shifting until a man stood there. He was formed of gray and white, indistinct, yet his features were plain to see. He wore a uniform, one from another era. His light-colored hair was neatly cut and combed. With an exclamation, she rose to her feet and met him as swiftly as she could.

They radiated joy, an elderly woman caught tightly in the arms of a young man. As Blacque watched, they remained in their embrace, moving slightly to the music in a ghostly dance. They kissed, and Blacque glanced away, feeling like an intruder on their stolen moment.

An incubus? He glanced up at Bleu, looking for answers.

"Ghost," he whispered. Bleu continued to watch, swallowing hard before turning away. "They get one dance, maybe two, and then he loses form."

Bleu rose, and Blacque followed him from the garden. They didn't speak again until they returned home and Blacque returned to his human shape. Even then, they didn't speak of what they had seen in old Mrs. Neville's garden.

Chapter Eight

"It's getting late. I should probably go back to the shop."

They sat in the warm little kitchen of Blacque's house, each man cradling a beer. Blacque drank his while Bleu only sipped. They'd pulled the curtains tightly closed and kept the lights down. Bleu glanced at the clock. He had plenty of time to run back if he left soon.

"You don't have to go. Not yet. I can drive you."

Bleu shook his head and took another sip, savoring the fine flavor of the dark ale. "You need sleep too. And I can actually run much faster than I showed you tonight."

"That takes energy, doesn't it?"

It did, and frankly, Bleu didn't have the reserves to flash-run home. He stood, stretching his arms.

"Bleu, you can stay here." Blacque's cheeks went slightly pink. How odd to see someone so tough be so shy.

"I'm just not comfortable sleeping in a house, especially one I'm not accustomed to. Too much chance of light." He smiled gently. "I can think of nothing better than falling asleep in your arms again, Blacque."

The wolf stood, still looking a bit awkward. "Downstairs...I have a basement. It's not finished, but there's a bed down there.

It was started as an apartment, so it's not too bad. I checked it earlier, put fresh bedding on..."

"Are you offering me a place to stay, or are you asking me to stay with you?"

"Asking." He looked uncomfortable but was able to meet Bleu's gaze.

"Cool." He rose and leaned over the table, then kissed Blacque gently. "Show me."

The shifter stood, facing him from the other side of the table. Bleu studied him in the warm light. Since he'd shifted, his hair had grown a bit, and his skin glowed with an inner light. Funny, Bleu had never noticed how beautiful the shifters were when they were this close to their magic. That's what it had to be, because he could think of no science that would explain their ability to become something else completely.

He exhaled, realizing he'd been holding his breath.

"This way." Blacque turned away and led him to a door at the back of the kitchen. He could see there was an outside entrance to the basement, and as they descended the stairs, that the door to the outside was also the entrance to the kitchen. If Blacque ever decided to rent the basement, he could lock the kitchen door for privacy.

At the bottom of the stairs was another door, and Blacque pushed it open, then flipped on an overhead light.

He'd been right; the place was half finished, with exposed beams on the ceiling and unfinished drywall elsewhere. There was a kitchenette and a bathroom. Not a window in sight. Bleu relaxed a bit.

It was surprisingly spacious and much bigger than the tiny storage room he'd been sleeping in at work. The floor was covered with industrial carpeting, and Bleu could see that

Blacque used this space as a gym. A weight bench and a large punching bag took up one end of the room; a large bed dominated the other.

"I wish we had time..." His thought was half formed. He wanted time tonight, time forever. Blacque's face didn't change expression. He waited for Bleu.

"Take off your clothes, Lukas. I want to see you naked."

Blacque was wearing nothing but Bleu's borrowed clothing, and he quickly undressed, leaving the garments discarded on the floor. He stood patiently, hands at his sides. His cock was thick and heavy, slowly reaching arousal. He was beautiful, and Bleu's stomach twisted with a feeling he'd forgotten years ago. Decades ago. Suddenly a beloved face that used to haunt his dreams was difficult to recall. Anger and grief knotted in his gut.

"Damn. Damn you anyway, Blacque!"

Bleu was on him then, pulling their faces together, nipping and biting hard at the other man's lips. Blacque didn't resist, letting the vampire take the lead. Bleu gripped his head and then forced him backward toward the bed. They crashed down onto the mattress. The frame groaned ominously, yet Bleu didn't back down.

In a test of brute strength, the werewolf would break him easily, but vampires are cunning creatures, fast as well as strong. In spite of his weakened state, Bleu had the other man pinned and helpless under his body, his mouth taking Blacque's fiercely. His hands stroked and explored freely. He grunted in satisfaction as the wolf shuddered, his skin going rough with gooseflesh. Bleu fumbled at the waistband of his trousers and impatiently jerked them down his hips.

He didn't have the time to take what he wanted. The sun was rising, and in just moments the blood would begin to slow in his veins. His thinking would become sluggish, and his body would prepare for the long day ahead. His hands shook, and he cursed as he covered Blacque's body with his. Bleu felt his rough hands on his back, then gripping his ass, pulling him down to his body as they ground together at the hips.

It was insanity. Bleu couldn't think. He could only feel, gasp, pant as they began to thrust together. His cock tangled with Blacque's and then slipped up to his sweaty belly. They were a tangle of limbs and bodies, his fully clothed, Blacque's naked and vulnerable. In the midst of all this, hunger flared, and he shook it off. He bowed down to the shifter's body, caught the golden bars in his teeth, and tugged hard, watching Blacque's back arch in ecstatic pain.

They rolled, and Blacque was on top of him, pulling away his clothing, tugging off his boots and pants. Naked, they slipped together into a sweaty tumble until Blacque straddled him, clasped their dicks in one hand, and used the other to support himself as they finally caught the rhythm that carried them to that plateau that moments ago had seemed impossible to reach.

Bleu arched his head back. His fangs had dropped, and he hungered, though he shouldn't have—not this soon. Blacque caught his jaw in a muscular hand and looked down at him from inches away.

"Do you need blood?"

Bleu tried to shake his head. Once a day was enough. Any more would be a drag even on Blacque's recuperative powers. Blacque gripped tighter, and his body went still.

"Shit!" Bleu bucked up fruitlessly, deprived of the werewolf's body.

"Do you need blood?" His voice had dropped to a growl. His hand circled Bleu's throat. He choked against the grip.

"Yes," he rasped out.

"Take it, then."

This wasn't the time to argue. He'd have Blacque for one more night, and then he would be alone again. Bleu reached up and swept the other man's hand away, then rolled him to his back. Blacque lay there, nude and lovely, his engorged cock jutting from a tangle of black curls. Wild brambles cut through his skin, and metal gleamed from improbable places on his body.

Blood hunger took away his caution. Bleu crawled off of Blacque and prowled around his body, bending in to scent the hot blood flowing under his skin. He buried his face in the wolf's groin, scenting sex and food, and under that, he scented himself. He pulled Blacque's cock deeply into his mouth, sucking roughly on his pierced testicles. He felt a tug on his own dick and moved, allowing the other man to get a good grip. He arched and flexed as Blacque pumped him hard.

He sucked, and he thrust into that rough hand, growling his satisfaction as Blacque's body went tense. The other man's cock was hard as stone, precum salty in his mouth. He tugged at the Blacque's balls and then reached up to grip the base of his cock. At the moment of crisis, right as his own climax was cresting, Bleu broke away and sank his teeth into the wolf's thigh. Blacque cried out. His hips thrust as he spilled, semen spitting over his belly, over Bleu's hands, dribbling down to mix with the blood he was gorging on.

Blacque's grip tightened painfully, forcing Bleu into a shattering orgasm. His balls and ass were gripped, and he froze, mindless of the blood spilling into his mouth. He shuddered through spasm after spasm, his face buried in the other man's muscular thigh. When the storm passed, when he was no longer locked in his bliss, Bleu opened his mouth and dragged his tongue along Blacque's inked skin, cleaning the blood, sweat, and semen from his thigh.

His cock still rested in Blacque's fist, and he finally rolled away, too spent to crawl back up to the top of the bed. He lay gazing at the other man's knees, wondering how God had managed to make such a mundane body part so completely beautiful on this man.

He sighed, and his eyes grew heavy. He wasn't sure if it was the sex or the approaching sun, but Bleu was weak and drowsy. He didn't stir until there was a tug on his arm.

"Bleu. Come on." Blacque used brute force to haul him up to the pillow. He fumbled around, adjusting his hips so that the were could drag the blankets over his body.

"Sun coming?"

Bleu looked up at him and smiled. "No, just fucked out." He was drunk on sex, drunk on blood. Maybe even on happiness too. And sweet despair.

When Blacque smiled, Bleu felt himself drift off, and for once he didn't worry about what the day would bring.

For the moment, all was good in the world.

The bite marks on his neck were gone, and the one on his groin was rapidly fading. Blacque ran the soap over the wound a second time and then a third. Even though hours had passed, he knew Bleu's scent would linger. In addition to feeding, the bites were most likely some primitive means of marking his property. Other vampires would smell Oliver Bleu in his very blood and know that Blacque was claimed. Unfortunately so would the pack.

Blacque rinsed one final time, letting the water run over his freshly shaved face. His hair was still bristly, but he didn't feel like messing with it right now. Shifting made it grow faster, and he might end up changing form at the Sunday pack meeting.

If he opted to attend. Fuck. Who was he kidding? That last conversation with his father had caught him—hook, line, and sinker.

After shutting the water off, he stepped out of the shower and toweled off. He'd be working around the house and would eventually need to shower again. Hopefully he'd sweat the smell of the vampire from his body.

He didn't want to. He enjoyed the fact that he smelled of Bleu and that the vampire carried his scent as well. It made him feel like he belonged to someone.

He dug out a pair of old jeans from his closet and dressed quickly, then laced on a pair of rubber-soled work boots. He was doing gutters today, and though he'd survive a fall, he didn't really want to take that chance. Showing up at the pack meeting with a busted arm wouldn't do much to boost his credibility. Somehow Blacque knew his future hinged on the impression he'd make today.

Soon enough he was up on the roof in the late morning sun, scraping the leaves and autumn detritus from the gutters, enjoying the simple, mindless task. He paused, looking out over the rise of trees to the east. Did someone go to Mrs. Neville's house to take care of her gutters? Her place looked neat enough, but he didn't know if the teacher had someone to do her heavy chores. He could ask Bleu. The vampire seemed to be pretty current on everyone's business.

Or he could simply call her and offer.

He finished the gutters and climbed down the ladder to gather up his yard tools. He raked away the leaves and dirt that had fallen from the gutters and bagged it up, then hauled it out to the compost pile.

He now remembered why Mrs. Neville's property seemed familiar. When he first moved to Arcada, his father used to take him and some of the other boys there to help with yard work. He remembered that Mrs. Neville was a widow with no children. He'd felt bad for her living there all alone.

Clearly she wasn't as alone as she'd seemed.

What was it about this town? Sometimes it seemed too good to be true, and Blacque was certain he'd find something evil and ugly lurking beneath the surface of Arcada. Yet if there was something bad, it hadn't yet emerged, not in the years that Blacque had lived here. It was a normal town. The crime rate was low but not too different from other communities. There was unemployment, and some folks seemed to have more than others, but the houses were all neat, and neighbors helped one another. He'd never seen any racial divides or overt discrimination in the community.

He grinned, wondering who the town council was sacrificing to.

The whisper of a car's engine broke into his reverie. Blacque shaded his eyes and watched as his sister's hybrid SUV came rolling up the drive. He appreciated the economy of the vehicle, yet was relieved it wasn't likely to be coming into his shop any time soon. He needed ongoing education, with auto technology evolving so quickly.

He began to stow his tools in the little lockup shed at the side of the yard, continuing to watch as Drusilla made her way around the house.

She still looked stunning. In fact, she was rarely anything but beautiful. But today she was wearing torn jeans and some T-shirt thing layered over another shirt. The sun glinted off her hair, and she smiled, her eyes hidden behind trendy sunglasses.

"Hey, Bro."

He was very aware of his sweaty, dirty skin and clothing. Blacque wiped sweat from his brow.

"Hey, Dru. What's up?" Meaning, what the hell was she doing coming by unannounced on a Sunday? Not that she wasn't welcome, but a phone call would have been nice.

"Pack meeting today. Came by to see if you wanted a ride."

That meant the alpha had sent her to personally see to his attendance. He slipped off his leather gloves and tossed them on a shelf inside the shed. He closed the doors and locked them, then turned to the side stairway up the porch.

"Looks good out here, Lukas. You've done a lot of work."

He grunted acknowledgment and held open the door to the kitchen for her. She headed for the fridge, surveyed the contents, and then grabbed a pan from the cupboard and began boiling water. She pulled a pitcher from another cupboard and found his stash of cheap teabags.

"You're a bit early. Meeting's not for another couple of hours." His stomach rumbled, but he ignored it. There'd be food at the meeting. There was always food at Dane's house.

"Dad wants you there early." She found sugar and began putting together simple syrup for sweet tea. It always surprised him how efficient she was in other people's houses. She stared at the water on the stove for a moment and then turned.

"So you're going to do it?"

"What?" He collapsed into a kitchen chair, wondering if she could smell the vampire on him.

"Do the baby thing."

He sighed in resignation. "He didn't tell you what's behind all this, did he?"

"There's more?" Drusilla leaned against a counter, watching him steadily.

"He's worried about his mortality, I guess. Wants to make sure things are all in order."

"He's not sick, is he?"

"No, not sick. That attack a while ago… I guess it scared him." He looked up at his sister and then down at his hands. "Nobody told me how bad it was till after."

Drusilla crossed the room and sat across from Blacque. "No one told me either. His inner circle…" She looked at him with a frown on her face. "Why should we be any different from his other kids?"

"Firstborn. And our mother, I guess. He said he loved her."

"Damn." She pushed back her thick hair in a gesture that Blacque realized was the same habit as his. In fact, they looked similar enough to be twins rather than just siblings. That made him feel a bit odd, as he was a rough-looking man and she was a beautiful woman.

"He doesn't just want grandchildren. He wants to see our mother's grandchildren."

"That's kinda sweet, isn't it?" She smiled and reached out to clasp Blacque's dirty hand. "Pretty sad too."

"There's more." This was the hard part. He cleared his throat. "He told me that Mom was his mate. His true mate."

"Oh Lukas." She spoke in a broken whisper. She covered her face, hiding the tears he knew she was shedding. They all knew there was nothing so bleak as life after the death of a mate—a *true* mate.

"How'd he hide it all these years?" She looked up at him, her eyes red and swollen. "How'd he manage to leave her in the first place?"

"Ambition. He said he figured they'd eventually get back together." When his sister reached out, he took her hand and held it tightly in his.

"He wants me to... He wants an heir of his own blood."

"You?" She dropped his hand in surprise. "You aren't an alpha!"

"Yeah, well, I'm not too thrilled about it either." Her reaction stung. "I did suggest you'd be better. Or Mallory. Even Michella has more respect in the pack."

"No...no, Lukas, it's just... You haven't even been involved with the pack in general. Ever. You've always stayed on the outside."

He lifted his hand to scrub his scalp, and then, self-consciously, Blacque lowered it. "Yeah, well..." He shrugged a shoulder. "This is the alpha's thing. Not mine."

"And you agreed?" She folded her arms, a skeptical look on her face.

"In case you hadn't noticed, saying no to him is easier said that done. He's a manipulative bastard." He leaned forward and propped his chin on his fist. "And he also pointed out that I have an MBA. The pack's business interests aren't too healthy. I can at least get that shit straightened out." He stared out the window, refusing to meet her eyes. "I've managed employees, and I'm pretty good with finances. If we start this small…kinda work up to it…maybe they won't react too badly."

"Come on, Lukas, you know him. He'll just dump it on everyone at the meeting."

She had a point. Once their father decided on a course of action, his utter confidence swept everyone along. He'd never have that sort of charisma. Blacque sighed and rose. "Look, I've got to shower. Then we can head over. Try to limit the damage."

"That reminds me…" She crossed back to the counter and emptied the tea and sugar syrup into the pitcher. She then pulled a couple of ice trays from the freezer and emptied them in as well. She stirred and turned back to him.

"Why does this place smell like vampire?" She dipped a finger into the tea and tasted it. "Perfect."

Perfect. That's exactly what Blacque was thinking.

Chapter Nine

Blacque slipped his feet into a pair of boots and leaned forward to lace them up. "So he's been living in a storeroom at the industrial park. Figured I could let him crash here for a night or two. Seemed the decent thing to do."

"This is Oliver Bleu, your neighbor?" He nodded. "The cute one that does car interiors?"

"Cute?" He raised a brow.

"Well, he is a little frail-looking. Those blue eyes of his, though…" She whistled. "And he does have that dangerous vibe. Like he'd bite hard and make sure you wanted it."

He stifled a groan.

She had her back to him and was rifling through his closet. After pulling down a couple of items, she turned and surveyed her brother. "Chuck the crappy clothes. Put this on." She tossed him a black T-shirt and a pair of brand-new jeans. He caught them with a scowl on his face. When the black boots came at him, he ducked.

Grumbling under his breath, he stripped down to his briefs while Dru prowled the room.

"I quit wearing this shirt 'cause it's too tight."

She turned and smiled at Blacque. "That's what we're going for, muscle boy." He stepped into the unadorned cowboy boots and straightened his pant legs. Blacque caught sight of himself in the mirror. His biceps and chest stretched the thin fabric of the shirt, and the denim molded itself to his thighs and ass.

"Leave your hair the way it is."

After his shift, it had grown out just enough to cover his scalp without sticking up. Normally he'd buzz it off.

"Yes, *Mother.*"

A wet towel pelted him in the back. "And pick up after yourself!"

He laughed and shut the bathroom door behind him. He didn't know why she was worried about how he looked; no one paid any attention to him, whether he was in greasy denim or in a suit. Rather, they avoided him. Blacque wasn't an outcast, but he was out on the fringes of the pack. He wiped a clear spot in the foggy mirror and ran his hand over his damp hair. After that, he brushed his teeth, taking a moment to wonder what Dru was worried about. She'd taken the story about Bleu at face value, so it was most likely something that Dane had dumped on her. He sighed and cleaned up after himself. On the way out of the bedroom, he glanced at the bed and realized that it was neatly made and obviously unslept in. Crap. Would she just think that maybe he'd already straightened it? He picked up his discarded clothing and put them away.

"You ready?" He walked into the kitchen to find Drusilla at the window, gazing out at the yard. She had a glass of sweet tea and was just finishing it. She smiled, and it made him feel a bit sad. His sister looked like the weight of the world was on her shoulders.

"Yeah, let's hit the road." She set the glass in the sink and headed out the door, slipping her sunglasses on. "We can take my car. I'll just drop you off on the way back."

Never mind that his place was out of her way.

* * *

Dane's house was a huge Victorian farmhouse that had been built in 1902 and then added on to over the years. It was quaint, homey, and decorated for comfort rather than style. Dane kept his private rooms on the bottom floor. The various other residents and visitors lived on the top floor. Right now, he had Alice Mitchum living there. She was an older widow who'd recently retired and handled much of the pack's social affairs. He also had the Quinlan family, who was new to town. A couple of teenage boys were bunking in the basement. One was a young shifter who'd run away from foster care in Nevada and had made his way to Arcada and to Dane. The other was a kid who'd left home to keep the peace in his family; his human stepfather was beginning to suspect something was off about the boy.

Judging by the neatly trimmed lawns and piles of leaves, Dane was keeping them busy.

They gathered around the spacious kitchen table, taking Blacque back quite a few years. Back then, the three of them had spent hours here together in the days after he and Dru had moved in. Every day, Dane had fixed their meals and had sat and watched them eat. Drusilla had lost a drastic amount of weight, and in his grief, Blacque had forgotten what hunger felt like. More went in the trash than in their bellies, but Dane had seen them through.

They sat in the huge kitchen, which was now conspicuously empty. Alice and Sharon had fixed snacks early in the day, and steaks were marinating in the fridge. The rest of the meal would be potluck.

"Dad, have you even discussed this with your betas? Your enforcers?" Drusilla was pale with distress.

"No. They're due to show in a half hour or so. I'll warn them beforehand."

Blacque listened as he idly caught the sweat on the outside of his water glass. Cool liquid trickled down his callous finger. His mind raced over the implications of what was to come.

"Who do you suppose will challenge me first?"

"Challenge?" Drusilla leaned back in her chair. "I suppose you're right. That's bound to happen."

Dane took a long drink from his glass. He was probably taking time to think about what to tell his oldest children. "The lieutenants will be upset that I excluded them from this. But honestly, I don't think there'll be anyone who'll step up to the plate and challenge you today."

"That's why you announced that you're opening breeding—to keep the males' minds off Blacque."

Dane smiled and glanced over at his daughter. "Drusilla, that's part of it. The two of you won't be caught up in the general stampede, so that'll help." He shrugged. "It's just all the same process. We're well into another century. I'm not ready to step down, but I'm within my rights to announce and prepare my heir." He reached out and clasped her hand. "And frankly, Dru, look at him. What wolf in his right mind would challenge that guy?"

Blacque leaned back in his chair, arms folded defensively. His sister looked at him and then back at their father. "There's more than one, and you know it."

"I do, but I'm confident Lukas can handle anything that comes up."

Blacque sighed heavily and gazed out the huge window, appreciating the way the lawn fell away to acres of orchards. He'd never felt completely comfortable in this house, yet in a way it was more his home than the little craftsman he lived in now.

"Travis will try and catch me alone. Maybe Michella too."

"Unless he does some major growing up, your half brother is nowhere near ready to consider fighting you."

"That's why he'll try and fight dirty. He doesn't need an excuse, but this'll make him feel justified."

Blacque didn't hate Travis Feris, but he didn't particularly respect him. The younger man had some major anger issues. When Blacque came around, jealousy came to the fore as well. Maybe it was time his little brother received a good ass kicking.

"You will want to watch out for Michella. She's tough and ambitious." Dane followed Blacque's gaze out the window, smiling when he saw a doe at the edge of the orchard. When the full moon came, his smile would be completely different.

"She's a good fighter. Otherwise she wouldn't be in your inner circle." Blacque pushed back the chair and crossed the room, then watched as a car made its way up the long drive. It was immediately followed by another. "What are you going to tell them?"

"For now, I'll let them know you'll be stepping in to oversee the pack businesses. Which is what I'd like you to do."

"Do you suspect someone's been embezzling?"

Dane sighed heavily. "I don't know. I just know that profits are down and expenses are going up. I don't have the business sense to judge whether it's the economy or mismanagement."

Blacque nodded. There were going to be some pissed-off wolves in the next few hours. He watched as four adults got out of a tan sedan. A small family unloaded from a minivan. He fisted a hand, closing his eyes against a vision of the future he'd neither expected nor wished for. As he was pulled deeper into the pack, he was increasingly aware of his differences. How much longer could he hide his indifference to the females? Until Bleu, he'd felt about as sexual as a eunuch. Now he felt alive, and need boiled through his body. Need for Bleu. Starting now, he'd need eyes in the back of his head.

"That other thing…" Blacque turned and faced his father, locking gazes with the older man.

"I've thought about it." Dane turned his attention to Drusilla. "You aren't in a good position to consider a child right now. You wait until you're ready."

"Dad, I've thought it over. It's not completely out of the question…"

Blacque turned back to the window, letting them hash this out between them.

"You've got too much on your plate as it is. I didn't know you'd been accepted into the doctoral program. I'm really proud of you."

There was a moment of silence, and Blacque kept his back turned. This was their moment. He felt a small smile cross his face. Dr. Blacque. He shook his head slightly. Not bad for a bunch of rowdy wolves.

* * *

Blacque sat in the love seat, his ankle crossed over his knee, a glass of tea cradled in his hand. His sister sat next to him, and they exchanged glances, both uncomfortably aware of the fluctuating emotions in the room. There was tension and anger…a touch of fear. And an overwhelming fog of lust filled the room. The alpha's strategy had worked well—most of the pack was preoccupied with the lifting of restrictions on breeding. Dane had announced Blacque's new position in the pack after he'd given them that little nugget to chew on. That had successfully split the focus in the room, defusing what could have been a hostile situation.

He hadn't been able to home in on the fear, but Blacque suspected it came from members of the alpha's inner circle. They would feel the most threatened by his interference in the pack businesses. He gazed at Mallory and Michella, Dane's two main betas. They worked together as a flawless team.

"Before you have any thoughts of choosing a partner, you'll want to consult Alice. She has the genealogy of the local pack and will be able to prevent you from making a rash decision. I know many of you have ongoing relationships. If you choose to formalize those unions by mating, we will be glad to celebrate as a pack." Dane smiled with utter and complete charm. Few children had been born over the past five years; this action would benefit the health and happiness of the pack.

"What about Lukas? Is he available?"

Blacque's gaze dropped to his hands. He barely recognized the woman who'd asked the question.

"Because of his close relationship to me, the restrictions will remain imposed on my eldest son. We will be hosting females from outside the area, and he's free to consider any offers from our guests. However, please speak to Alice if you are interested, and we'll take your request under consideration."

"I assume you're putting the same restrictions on me?" Travis's comment was bitter. Blacque didn't need to look at the young man to see the glare directed at him.

"You're barely legal, Travis." Drusilla's voice was kind but firm. It was her vice-principal voice. Their half brother stifled an angry growl. "Lukas is over a decade older, a college graduate, and a successful business owner. He's proven himself."

"Not against us." Michella lounged back on the sofa, lazily gazing at Blacque. She was blonde, pretty, and athletic in appearance. Mallory sat at her side. He was Dane's second in command. As his name suggested, Sean Mallory was Irish in appearance, with a pugnacious face topped by golden red hair. His smile wasn't friendly.

Blacque took a moment to survey the room. Some faces looked curious; others were overtly hostile. A few were carefully blank.

Blacque reached to the table next to his seat and carefully set his glass on a coaster. From the pull on his T-shirt sleeves, his muscles were stressing the fabric. He allowed his gaze to settle on Michella's face.

"Whenever you're ready, Shel."

She went slightly pale. Suddenly Blacque remembered those days when he had been blocked from the hospital room where his father lay so gravely injured. Michella had often been the face at the door sending him away. He didn't growl, but his wolf did, sending power washing through the room.

He was so stunned that his own skin went rough with goose bumps.

"Shit, Lukas!" Dru's whisper carried through the silence of the room. He nudged her with his elbow.

"Well, if that's all, I'm sure everyone's hungry. The grill's ready, the steaks are seasoned, so let's get to it." Dane's voice broke the spell, and at his words, it was as though a well-oiled machine purred to life. Men and women dispersed to the kitchen. Others swept outside to round up Dane's youngest plus the children of human-shifter matings. Some broke off into small clusters, excited conversation carrying through the air. The games had begun.

Blacque stayed in place, feeling the tension leech from his body. Dru scooted forward on the seat and turned to face him. "I apologize for saying you aren't an alpha. Other than Dad, I've never felt someone unleash that much power." She studied his face, her own slightly pale, her eyes bright. "You were made for this. I know you don't think you are…"

He rose to his feet and picked up his empty glass. "Yeah, well, I don't really want to talk about it now. It's just gonna be shit for me from here on out."

He headed toward the kitchen, weaving his way through small clusters of women who eyed him speculatively. He wondered if Dane had any idea what forces he'd unleashed in this room today. He'd held Blacque out like a carrot on a stick and then had pulled him away. He took his glass to the sink and filled it with water.

No alcohol was allowed at pack meetings; having this many wolves in one space was volatile at the best of times. As the full moon grew closer, the window for disaster opened even wider. Many planned to shift and run tonight, and drunkenness upped the chance for mayhem.

"Hey, Allie, anything I can help with?"

Alice wasn't his grandmother, but he sometimes wished she was. She'd moved into the alpha's household when she'd retired from her job as the town librarian. She managed his household with a gently administered iron hand. She fed the hungry, comforted the lonely, and had once forced Blacque over her knee when she caught him stealing a pie she'd baked for dinner. He'd laughed as she paddled his ass with a wooden spoon, but had respected her authority ever since.

His mother's family loved Drusilla but were uneasy in Blacque's presence. Like their mother, they had mainstreamed as much as possible, and their big, tattooed grandson just didn't fit their notion of harmless. He had no doubt they felt bad about not missing him. Dane's parents were long gone. They'd passed before he'd been born. He smiled down at the older woman, hoping there were no traces of his earlier snarl on his face.

"Thank you, sweetheart. If you could help me set out those platters…"

He glanced into the refrigerator and saw the trays she pointed to. Meat, meat, and more meat. A bit of cheese and mustard. He carried the food to the table and swiped a slice of turkey. The next shelf in the industrial-size refrigerator held bowls and plates of salads. Fruit, macaroni, potato, and green salads were soon arrayed on the table.

"Dessert stays out of sight until supper is over." Alice stood, hands on hips as she looked over the spread. The mouthwatering aroma of grilled steak began to drift into the kitchen.

"Oh my, that does smell good…" Alice was out the door in a flash, undoubtedly to lay claim on an extra-rare piece of meat. Blacque stepped out onto the deck and stood back, watching the milling pack. Some hovered around the grill, while others returned to the house, filling plates to capacity. A group ranging from preteens to young adults played under the basketball hoop, breaking every rule of the game.

He felt a tug at his leg and looked down. A little girl had crawled up to him and was pulling herself unsteadily to her feet. Bright copper hair and too young to be one of Dane's. She blinked big blue eyes at him, reminding him just a bit of Bleu.

"Hey, ankle biter." He knelt and picked the baby up from the deck. "Someone's gonna step on you, for sure." The baby was much happier to be up high. She reached out a sticky little hand and clasped his nose. He was grateful he'd opted against facial piercings.

His stomach growled, reminding him that he'd skipped both breakfast and lunch. After doing double duty with Bleu, he should probably fuel up. "Wanna grab something to eat?" What did a kid this size eat? Or did they eat? Maybe she still nursed. He wandered around with the little girl in his arms, looking for a likely woman to hand her off to.

"Oh, there you are..." A red-haired, blue-eyed woman approached Blacque hesitantly. She reached for the baby. "Hannah, you go so fast now! I can't keep up with you."

He lowered the child into her arms. "I found her climbing up my leg." He tried another smile and was relieved when the woman smiled back.

"Well, thank you. I'm Joetta Mallory." She nervously gave him her hand, and he shook it. He didn't recall having seen her before, but he hadn't been around much over the past couple of years. Odd that Mallory had married and he hadn't even known about it. Or maybe not so odd, given that Blacque had been lone for so long.

"Lukas Blacque."

"I understand we'll be seeing more of you."

He felt his smile slip and fought to keep it on his face. "Yeah, I'll just be nosing around in the businesses for a few weeks, see if we can shore up finances a bit. Times are pretty hard right now."

She looked incredibly grateful for the small talk. He wondered what she'd heard about him from Sean Mallory and the others.

"It is hard. Sean's hours have been reduced this month. But at least he's still working." Once she relaxed a bit, she talked. By the time he moved on, Blacque had heard about the financing on their home, the shaky state of the company Mallory worked for, and her suspicion that she might be pregnant again. What she didn't say was shadowed in her eyes—her worry that her husband was spending too much time away, and there just never seemed to be enough money to get them to the end of the month.

He managed to move on and was cornered by a pair of young women who flirted with him shamelessly. If nothing else, it was flattering. He escaped and then found himself listening to a play-by-play recitation of Friday's football game from a young man whose name he couldn't recall. He was fairly certain the boy wasn't a half sibling, but in all honesty, he wasn't sure.

He was finally rescued from social hell by his sister.

"You're doing good. See? If you smile now and then, they get over being afraid of you." Dru handed him a plate covered by an enormous steak. "Helping Alice was good. Carrying the baby around was better."

He sighed. "I'm not playing games, Dru. Just trying to be helpful." He headed for an empty picnic table. A few minutes later, his sister joined him with a plate of her own plus an extra loaded down with side dishes. She set the plate between them. He noticed she didn't seem to have much of an appetite. He focused on his meal until she was ready to speak.

"You fell on your sword for me."

"Hmm?" He looked up at her, swallowed a bite of steak, and cleared his throat. "What's that?"

"You know what I mean." She cut into her steak with a sharp knife. "I come to you griping about the alpha's demand that I give him a grandbaby. You have a discussion with him, and suddenly you're stepping to his tune and I'm off the hook." She glanced around, checking to see if anyone was within hearing distance.

"I could have taken care of it myself, Lukas."

"Dane probably just came to his senses. As for me, he was right. It's long past time for me to get involved." He set his fork down and caught his sister's gaze. "You were right too. I'm not an alpha. The only way to make Dad understand is to do what he wants me to. Besides, I don't see him stepping down anytime soon. He'll have plenty of time to change his mind about me."

Her laugh held disbelief, but she turned to her food, pushing it around her plate.

They ate in silence for a few moments, but Blacque knew she wasn't finished with him. When an older couple sat down at the table, their discussion was effectively ended.

* * *

"You sure you don't want to stay for the run?"

It was still a few days out from the gibbous moon, and an early run would help take the edge off some of the younger wolves. He almost agreed and then thought of Bleu waking up alone. Had he slept through the day? Had he dreamed?

Not his responsibility. Blacque had to shake the odd protectiveness he felt for Bleu. He was, after all, a vampire.

"No, I ran last night. I'll be here for the pack run next weekend."

"And Sunday for dinner. You too, Drusilla." Dane walked with them to the car, then stood at the driver's door. In the late afternoon sun, he looked vibrant and powerful, ready to go on forever. How old was Dane anyway? In his fifties? His sixties? He looked like a man just entering his thirties. Some unknown tension inside Blacque loosened a bit. Werewolves lived much longer, more robust lives than humans. Dane would outlive all of them. This was the least he could do to make the old man feel a bit safer in his world of pack politics.

"The first Sunday is family only, just us. The third Sunday is the inner circle, and the last Sunday is pack. I expect you to be here."

"Yes, sir." Blacque thought he'd succeeded pretty well at muting the sarcastic tone of voice, but Dane's glance told him he hadn't done well enough. Laughing, Dru slid into the driver's seat and started the engine. Blacque folded down into the low seat next to her.

"Seat belts."

"Yes, Sheriff." Dru slid sunglasses onto her face. She turned to look over her shoulder. "All clear back there? No rug rats?"

"All clear." Dane stepped back, watching as she smoothly maneuvered the car out of the driveway. As they reached the end of the lane, Blacque twisted around in his seat to look back.

His father hadn't moved.

"I was wrong about you." Drusilla glanced over at him. Blacque didn't have anything to say to that. "I said you weren't an alpha. You are. But I don't think I've ever encountered another like you before."

"What do you mean?" he asked, truly puzzled.

"You're awkward with people, but they confide in you. I heard Mallory's wife telling you all their dirt." She gave a slightly wicked smile. "Then the Bartons told you about the problems their grandson is having in school." She paused, and he smiled, shaking his head. "When Michella challenged you, you met aggression with aggression. And frankly, you put out enough juice to have forced some of our people into a shift if it had been directed at them. That isn't beta power, Lukas."

He looked out the window, watching the wall of trees as they passed.

"I don't want to do it."

She sighed. "Train as alpha?"

He shook his head. "Any of it. Audit the businesses, spend every hour at his beck and call...."

"Breed the women?"

He stifled a dry laugh. "I don't like the idea of a command performance any more than you do."

She slapped his thigh. "You are just unnatural, you know that?"

Blacque rubbed the sting from his leg and forced a grin. She had no idea just how unnatural he really was.

Chapter Ten

Bleu faded into awareness. He lay absorbing the sounds and scents of his resting place, knowing immediately that he wasn't in his room at the shop. He was...

Blacque. He was at Blacque's house, down in the basement. He was warm and wonderfully comfortable. For once, hunger didn't gnaw at his gut, and he wasn't weak from exhaustion. As sensation gradually returned to his limbs, he felt a warm presence at his side and the weight of a quilt over his body.

God! He could get used to this. Only he wouldn't get the chance. Not if the big wolf stuck to his decision about this being their last night together. He pulled the first full breath into his lungs and let it out slowly.

"Morning. Or evening, I guess." Blacque's voice. He felt a smile coming on.

He blinked, and his vision filled with Blacque's rough, handsome face. His hair was longer than Bleu was accustomed to seeing it. He reached up to sample the texture. It was surprisingly soft to the touch. As his heart began to pick up its pace, blood rushed through his body, bringing him back to the sharp awareness of life. Usually he hated the helplessness of the few minutes before he broke from the torpor of the day, but this time it felt unexpectedly good.

He stretched and laughed to feel his cock rise for the morning as well. He smiled at Blacque.

"Like the look. It's almost civilized."

Blacque's obsidian eyes told him nothing. He looked steadily down at Bleu, an odd expression on his face.

"Drusilla's idea. She didn't want me scaring the pack."

That's right. He'd had his big meeting today. "How'd the meeting go?" He dragged himself upright and propped himself against the headboard. He piled the quilt over his lap, hiding his inconvenient erection.

"It went…okay. No challenges."

"But there will be."

Instead of replying, Blacque reached out and gently stroked the side of Bleu's mouth. He stifled the urge to turn, to catch the finger between his lips. Instead he remained still, not wanting to spook the wolf. Blacque's other half was close to the surface.

"The scars are gone."

He reached up to feel the skin on his face. "Soft as a baby's butt."

Blacque nodded. "Good. It's good that you're better."

His relief was palpable. Bleu's health would be one less obligation in Lukas Blacque's overburdened existence. Sudden irritation flared through him. He pushed back the covers and got out of bed. Glancing around the room, Bleu located his clothing. There was no point in hanging around, taunting himself with what he couldn't have. Blacque had made up his mind, and this mistimed affair was not his priority. Bleu had lost the game before it had even started.

But they had one more night. He had to try. Blacque might be an adult man, but in the world of love and sex, he was a babe in the woods. Surely he'd fall to Bleu's seduction.

"I need to shower." He stumbled into the small bathroom, turned on the hot water, and waited as it heated. He braced his hands against the wall and leaned forward, shaking his head. He couldn't leave yet, though his gut was telling him to flee. Blacque was the key to his recovery; he knew that. The werewolf's blood was restoring him to health. In just another week or so, he'd be recovered enough to hunt.

He didn't fool himself. The damage to his body had been a long time in the making, and he wouldn't recover overnight. But another week could save him. Another week of having Blacque in his bed, chasing away the dreams… Another week, and then another…

He pushed away from the wall and checked the temperature of the water, then stepped in. There was a small bottle of shampoo on the floor. It was almost empty, but he salvaged enough to wash his hair. A tiny bar of soap from a hotel sat on a ledge, still wrapped in paper. He peeled it open and lathered up.

Bleu wished the damn wolf would join him. He knew he wouldn't. Regardless of whatever else Lukas Blacque might be, he was a sexual submissive, and at this point he lacked the confidence to make a move that might displease Bleu.

Amazing that someone as physically powerful and as disciplined as Blacque would be a submissive. Amazing and wonderful. He idly rubbed a hand over his chest, trying to soothe the discomfort there…deep inside his heart. Damn, but it'd been a long time since he'd felt anything there. Should he celebrate the reawakening of his heart when it was so likely to be broken by this man?

Bleu rinsed his hair and sighed, then shut the faucet off. He grabbed a towel and dried himself, considering how to go about seducing the wolf for another few days. He had to think of something—his life could very well depend on it.

Bleu dressed and unwrapped a toothbrush, then brushed his teeth carefully. When his fangs dropped a bit, he grinned. They reacted to hunger, fury, and lust. He wondered what was bringing them forth right now, because he was starving, pissed, and horny as hell.

He didn't see Blacque when he stepped out of the bathroom, but heard the rhythmic sound of fists on leather. He glanced over to see Blacque focused on the huge practice bag, punching and jabbing, pushing the bag into a frenzied dance. Bleu moved to the far side of the bag and grasped it to hold it in place as the wolf worked out his frustrated rage.

There was a light sheen of sweat over his brow, and he grunted with every powerful blow. Blacque was so contained and quiet that it was difficult to read him. Bleu studied his face. Even as he let loose, the wolf was still rigidly disciplined, still controlled. He'd controlled his emotions and anger for so long, it was amazing he hadn't snapped.

Blacque gave a final, powerful blow that nearly rocked Bleu off his feet, and he dropped his raw, bloody hands to his sides. He panted, looking around as though he didn't know where he was. Instead of taking a break, he moved to the weight bench and brought down the bar to bench press an inhuman amount of weight. But Blacque wasn't human.

Bleu stood back and admired the straining muscles, the flex of his powerful body. He probably didn't need a spotter, but

Bleu stood by anyway, shaking his head at the werewolf's strength. After working himself to a standstill, Blacque returned the bar to its stand, and he sat up, wiping sweat from his brow. He was still wearing a tight T-shirt and new blue jeans. It had looked good on him before, but now that he was pumped, the clothing clung to his powerful body.

Bleu backed away and leaned against a wall. "Do you want to talk about it?"

The werewolf shook his head and moved into the small bathroom. The water in the sink ran, and then he returned, water stains splattered across his shirt.

"Let's go upstairs, Lukas. You should drink something." He climbed the stairs ahead of Blacque, then turned the light on in the dark kitchen. He opened the refrigerator and found a pitcher of tea. He held it up. "This?"

Blacque nodded and sat at the table, his head in his hands. Bleu opened cupboards until he found a glass. He poured the tea and remembered belatedly that people usually liked ice in their ice tea. He poured a bit back into the pitcher and found a bag of ice in the freezer. He carried the glass to the table and sat across from the wolf. Out of curiosity, he tried the stuff, wincing in reaction to its sweet taste. Not bad. Too sweet, though. He pushed the glass across to Blacque, who was watching.

"Never tasted sweet tea before. It's quite different from the tea I drank...before."

Blacque picked up the glass and drained it quickly. Without speaking, Bleu rose and retrieved the pitcher, then set it on the table. Blacque refilled his glass and sipped at it this time.

"I just feel...snared." He kept his gaze lowered to the table. Initially Bleu thought it was a submissive trait, but now he knew Blacque hid his feelings this way. He remained quiet, letting his friend work his way through the tangle of his thoughts.

"I expected challenges. Fights. Instead they embraced me, took the alpha's words at face value." His distress and confusion radiated from him. Bleu fought the urge to reach out and touch. Right now, that would not be a good thing. He was too hungry, and Blacque was too jumpy. He kept his hands on the table.

"The betas?"

"Oh, that's different. They'll probably take me on in a formal challenge. It was the families...even the kids." He scrubbed at his head in a gesture that Bleu was beginning to expect when Blacque was distressed.

"So you weren't the bogeyman."

Dark eyes flashed as Blacque looked at him in surprise.

"You thought they hated and feared you. Instead they were more than willing to accept you. But you understand, Blacque, that's how it is with an alpha. A good alpha is not a bully; he doesn't need force. An alpha is a leader, a father or a mother figure. They nurture and protect, and sometimes they use underhanded tactics to do what is right."

"You think Dane manipulated me into this? Agreeing to be his heir...breeding females?" The expression on his face was speculative rather than angry. Bleu had expected anger.

"Why did you finally concede to his wishes?"

"Drusilla. She's got so much in front of her, Bleu. What he wanted her to do... It's tough enough for a man, but for a woman?" He sighed. "And my mother. He'd never told us she was his mate."

He looked up and met Bleu's knowing gaze. "Shit." He leaned back in his chair, an expression of wry amusement on his face. "He knew my weak spots and played me like a novice."

"You are a novice, Blacque. You are very young still."

The wolf's cheeks darkened a bit. "That's how you see me? A novice? A kid?"

"No, Blacque, I see you as a man. But in the world of werewolf politics, you are very inexperienced. Your father knows you are a nurturer. He knows you would do anything to protect your sister. He knew that if he shared his greatest pain, you'd feel sympathy for him. Those are good traits that you will someday extend to every person in your pack. He knows it, and your pack senses it as well."

Blacque's amusement had faded as abruptly as it came. His gaze dropped to the table again.

"I don't want this, Bleu."

"Your father has many years left, my friend. You have a long time to adjust and ready yourself."

When the wolf looked at him, his eyes were bleak. "How can I live out those years...after you?" He pinched the bridge of his nose. "I'm a homosexual, Bleu. I didn't choose to be gay, and I sure as hell didn't choose to be the heir to a werewolf pack. I'm going to have to watch my back every minute of every day. And if they sense this..."

"Weakness? Is that how you perceive it?"

Blacque went still.

"Does your love for your sister make you weak?"

"No."

"Then why should your sexual orientation make you less a man?" Bleu waited for an answer that didn't come. "Yes, it might make you a target, but does it make you less able to defend yourself? Less able to be a good leader?"

"I don't know." Blacque stood and carried the glass to the sink, then washed it and put it in a rack to dry. "I do know that from now on—after tonight—I can't be gay. I might be odd or eccentric, but it's time to step up and do what I promised to do."

Bleu gave a little laugh. "Saying it does not make it so, Lukas. But I understand survival. I understand protecting those we love. But it breaks my heart for you."

"It sucks."

He stood magnificent in his despair, and all thoughts of seduction left Bleu's mind. The man was already suffering. If he pushed him, he might break Blacque's heart.

No wonder he was starving to death—as vampires went, he had no balls. Pathetic.

"Would you like me to leave?"

Blacque looked up at him in alarm. "No!" He took a deep breath and gathered his control. "No. I owe this to myself. I owe it to you."

"Yes, I think you are correct. You owe it to yourself." Bleu continued to watch him as he paced the small kitchen. Blacque stopped and then turned to face him.

"There's something between us, isn't there? More than just hunger...lust..."

There it was. Bleu felt an unexpected twist in his chest. He remembered his earlier anger and the need to flee. He could deny it, but Bleu knew that honesty was always less painful in the end.

"Yes, Blacque, there is something between us. I'm very sad we did not have the chance to let it play out as it should have."

He rose and crossed the room, and he clasped one of Blacque's hands in his. "If it helps, I'll have your back. After dark, anyway."

Blacque's mouth quirked into a lopsided smile. "I'll keep feeding you as long as you need."

Bleu let his eyes drop closed. "No, Blacque. I don't think that's a very good idea." He forced a smile, barely able to believe his own words. "Once more...tonight, and then I will be fine. I'm very nearly healthy now." It was a lie, but a necessary one. He didn't want the wolf distracted by a misguided sense of obligation.

"You're probably right. Feeding and sex seems to be pretty much the same thing with you." Blacque squeezed his hand and then picked up the other. Bleu opened his eyes and looked at him.

"They are very much the same thing." He glanced down at their linked hands. "Right now, I am hungry."

"Good." Blacque's voice was harsh. "I'm really hungry for you too." He reached out and caught Bleu's head, pulled it close, and rested their foreheads together. "I'm not sorry this happened. Not in the least." He leaned back and looked into Bleu's face. "I'm just sorry..." He sighed, catching the contradiction in his words.

"I know, pup." He was sorry to find happiness and then to have to push it away so quickly. He was sorry to leave Bleu alone again. He was sorry for himself.

"Remember, Blacque. I'm a vampire. I've lost before. Besides, we're still neighbors. I'll be in the next unit over. If you need me for anything...well..." He lifted one shoulder.

"Where'd you grow up, Bleu? France?"

"A small village inland of Nice. It was—is called Sisteron." He smiled a bit, remembering so very long ago. "I understand it is still very beautiful. My father was a wealthy tradesman. We had a good life."

"Until the war."

He reached up and cupped Blacque's jaw in his hand. "That is the past. I already spend far too much time there." He slid his hand back behind the wolf's strong neck and pulled him close. He feathered his mouth over Blacque's, not opening his lips, just teasing.

"Let's do it, then."

"Yes, Blacque. Let's do it."

Chapter Eleven

Blacque expected balls-to-the-wall, dominant sex from Bleu. There had been too many emotions in the air. Anger had flared and receded in his scent, keeping the wolf on edge. He was ready to roll over and submit, to bare his throat to the vampire. Instead Bleu gently led him to the bedroom. They undressed slowly, using the light from the bathroom to illuminate the room.

Uneasiness prickled his skin, and Blacque glanced at the windows, making certain the shades were pulled tightly closed. Once he was confident they were safe, he turned his attention back to the vampire.

Bleu looked better, almost back to the way he looked when he'd first set up shop next door to Blacque's garage. His thick hair waved back from his face in a style that was oddly old-fashioned, but that was probably just the result of neglect. Like Blacque, the vampire didn't seem to spend too much time on his appearance.

His eyes had become richer in color; the intense blue reminded him of the crystalline depths of the Caribbean. He looked at Bleu's mouth. The scars had smoothed away from those generous lips, leaving his face looking fresh and youthful as he must have looked before the war destroyed him.

There was still so much he wanted to know about the other man. What had his chosen profession been? What had he done in the years following the war? Most importantly, Blacque wanted to know what brought the vampire to Arcada, and why had he fallen so ill?

But for now, he didn't want to talk. Maybe in the weeks ahead, when the sting of their premature separation wasn't so sharp. Now he wanted to touch. He reached out and trailed a hand down Bleu's lean torso, smiling when the vampire gasped. His heart beat faster at the passion that was etched so openly on his face.

Boldly he ran one hand over a rosy nipple, then leaned in to nip and bite it to erection, feeling another erection down below rising to greet his hand. He cupped the silky cockhead in his rough palm. When Bleu groaned, Blacque's arousal hit him like a tidal wave.

He ran his tongue down the flat, hairless planes of the vampire's belly, teasing at the navel and then dipping into the nest of silky black curls that nestled his cock. He held it at the base and licked the head, laughing as Bleu's hips jerked.

He could imagine what felt good to the other man based on what he liked, but he was fairly certain Bleu didn't appreciate pain to the degree that he did. Not this early in, at least.

He nuzzled the space between cock and balls, letting his wet tongue trail down to Bleu's velvety sac. He gently sucked his balls into his mouth one at a time and reached up to stroke Bleu's muscular buttocks.

Giving in to impulse, he rubbed his face in Bleu's groin, gathering every bit of the vampire's scent, letting it settle on his skin and in his hair.

"Damnation, Lukas!" Bleu gripped his head to hold him steady. Reaching up, he fisted the vampire's rigid cock and returned to his effort, bobbing his head, trying to take him a little deeper each time.

Blacque tasted sweat and musk and the unique flavor of Bleu's body. He moved faster, pumping at the base of his shaft with every deep swallow.

"Okay...okay...enough." Bleu's voice was harsh and breathless. "Bed, Lukas."

He wanted to growl in disappointment but obeyed, letting Bleu's cock free and rising from the floor.

"Get on the bed. Lie on your back." He followed Bleu's instructions, lying back as the vampire covered his body, pinning him to the bed. "Hold on to the headboard. Don't let go until I tell you."

He reached up and held on. It was every bit as effective as if the vampire had chained him to the bed. He growled in protest but found himself unable to let go. Where had this willing obedience come from?

"Are you glamouring me?"

Bleu gave him a wicked smile, then shook his head. "No, pup. You just happen to have a very special character trait, one that I cherish." He leaned down and kissed Blacque fully on the lips. He lingered for a moment, letting the tip of his tongue probe and tease, and then broke the kiss. "You have the gift of submission. For someone like me, that is the ultimate aphrodisiac." He bent down again and kissed Blacque deeply this time, his tongue sweeping into his mouth.

For a creature with a pair of razor-sharp fangs, Bleu sure loved to kiss. He was damn good at it, as far as Blacque could tell. He lay back, enraptured by the sensual dance of lips and tongue. He felt a surge of arousal when Bleu nicked him, drawing blood from his lip. When he sucked Blacque's lower lip into his mouth, Blacque fisted the headboard, hearing it give an ominous groan.

Bleu broke away and laved a wide path down his shoulder, following the trail of tattoos on his arms, ending up at his inner elbow and then dropping to his wrist, feathering kisses over his pulse point. A nip brought a gasp from Blacque, and his hips bucked, but he didn't let go of the headboard.

Bleu clasped his hip and trailed strong fingers along the line of his groin, then teased at the juncture of his thigh. He ignored Blacque's aching cock and forced his leg to bend at the knee. Dropping hot kisses on the back of his thigh, Bleu leaned in and nipped his exposed ass, then caught a single golden ring between his teeth. Blacque felt the tug on his balls, and a spasm ran through him, so violent and strong that he thought surely he'd climaxed.

He felt warm saliva trickle down to his hole, and then a finger played there, pressing and teasing until he submitted, relaxing into the pressure. He strained to look down at Bleu and could barely see the man down there under his raised leg. The vampire worried at the golden hoops in Blacque's testicles even as he played with his ass. The realization of what the vampire intended sent another surge of twisting arousal through Blacque. His body arched off the bed, but his hands kept him anchored.

Blacque's heart slammed in his chest, and he closed his eyes, divided between raw, adrenaline-fueled fear and sheer bliss at the primal invasion of his body. He held his breath and then released it in a harsh gasp. Sweat trickled down his forehead, and he had to blink to keep it from running into his eyes.

"Get your lube, pup."

His hand felt fused to the wooden headboard, but he loosened his grip and fumbled at the bedside table. He handed the bottle to Bleu with a hand that was not particularly steady. Bleu sat up, gazing at him through sensual, half-closed eyes. He smiled slowly, obviously enjoying the effect he was having on Blacque.

"I love what this is doing to you, Lukas." He stared for a moment longer and then looked down at the container in his hand. "Do you want this? Do you want me to fuck you?"

"Yes. Please." Blacque heard his voice, broken and pleading, but shame and embarrassment no longer existed in his world. Now there was only Bleu and the bliss he was lavishing on his body. He was desperate, not for the climax, but for the journey that would take him there.

"Hands back on the board, pup."

Like magic, they were back in place. He heard the snap of the bottle's lid and opened his eyes. He watched as Bleu knelt between his legs and slicked up his shaft. He looked up and smiled.

"I want you on your hands and knees so I can fuck you hard. But more than that, I want to watch your face as I fuck you the first time."

Blacque swallowed and nodded. He didn't care. He just needed Bleu to keep doing what he was doing—weaving an erotic spell that took them out of the harsh world of their daily lives. He dropped his head to the pillow. The overload of sensation had him resting on a cloud rather than a mattress in a bedroom. Bleu adjusted his hips slightly, and then the pressure came, building until Blacque felt his body reluctantly give way.

He remembered entering Bleu's body and forced himself to relax, letting the vampire guide and control his penetration.

His hands fisted the headboard, but his body went loose; he barely felt it when Bleu bent his legs and looped them up over his arms. He watched, seeing the play of expressions on Bleu's face. He frowned fiercely and then let his head fall back in ecstasy. He stroked Blacque's legs and then looked down into his face. "So tight. So hot."

Bleu's shaft was a cool, heated presence invading his body. He drew back smoothly, then paused to add more lube. He pressed forward and drew back again, lubing up each time he withdrew. Finally he groaned; his face almost looked pained. He thrust and slid in all the way to the root, and Blacque's body arched against the burn. His softened cock suddenly filled at the painful invasion. Bleu thrust again, and he slid over Blacque's prostate with dizzying speed.

They fucked. Blacque lay helpless under the vampire's onslaught, and it became completely necessary for him to grasp that headboard. With every thrust, Bleu sent a shock wave through his body. Pain and pleasure mingled, and his cock was hard and alive, rolling across his belly every time the vampire pounded into his ass. When he thought he could take no more, he prayed that it would never end.

Bleu dropped his legs and lunged forward, his face inches from Blacque's. He shifted position, and the penetration wasn't as deep, but Blacque looked up into his face and lost himself in the depths of Bleu's eyes.

"Will you come when I tell you to come?" Bleu stared at him with unnerving intensity. "If I stop…" His body went still, and Blacque fought not to writhe and plunge in protest. He took a breath and held it until he reclaimed control of his body.

"Very good, Lukas. Very good." Bleu lowered more of his weight until Blacque's cock was trapped between their bodies. "Such beautiful control." He kissed Blacque gently, and his hips began to pump slowly. "Am I hurting you?"

Blacque nodded. "It's good hurt, though."

Bleu reached up and trailed a finger down the side of his face. "I rely on you to tell me if it's too much. Will you promise me that?"

Blacque nodded, dizzy from the slow, smooth glide of Bleu's cock in his body.

"What do you want, Blacque? Do you want to come?"

He nodded.

"Tell me what you want, Blacque."

He panted, looking up into Bleu's face. "Fuck me. Hard. Make me come."

Bleu came back for another kiss, this one not so gentle. "Let go of the headboard, Lukas. Hold me."

His arms felt stiff and numb, and they tingled as he let go, but Blacque reached down and placed one arm around Bleu's shoulder and the other around his ass. Bleu let his eyes drop closed again, clearly savoring the contact. "Soft first, and then hard." He opened his eyes and looked down at Blacque. "Is that all right?

"Yeah." Blacque licked his lips, desperate to continue, desperate to fuck and be fucked, to be completely and totally possessed by the vampire. Bleu nuzzled his neck and shoulder and slowly picked up his pace. They writhed together. Blacque tightened his arms around the other man, urging him to take him harder and deeper. Slow and sensual gradually gave way to hard and fast. Their hips churned, their skin slapped, and

Blacque felt it rising, a pressure building in his body like the waters of a tsunami. His eyes snapped open, and Bleu was watching him.

"Soon?" Bleu asked. He nodded, losing the last tendrils of control over his body. "Come, then, Blacque." The vampire whispered in his ear. His teeth bore down on the skin of Blacque's neck. Blacque shouted, angling his head, giving Bleu the permission he needed. Right at the moment that Blacque teetered on the precipice, pain lanced through his neck, firing his climax. He shouted again and again, too overwhelmed to feel the cum spilling on his belly. Blacque's world fractured into shards of pleasure laced with pain. His back arched, his muscles clenched and released, and too soon he was unable to shout, unable to buck and meet the thrusts of Bleu's body.

In a fog, he heard Bleu gasp and swear in French. He felt his body shudder, felt his warm breath against his skin. Bleu's seed flooded his ass, cool and foreign and so very welcome. He held on to Bleu through the climax, rubbing his big, rough hands over the silken skin of the vampire's back. Bleu didn't try to move off his body, and if he had, Blacque wouldn't have let him go. He never wanted to let him go.

* * *

Bleu lay in the darkness, his attention divided between the man who was sleeping at his side and the rustling breeze outside the window. It was three in the morning, the afternoon of his day, and he was wakeful. He rolled onto his side and studied Lukas Blacque as he slept. He wanted to touch but didn't want to wake the wolf.

So this was it.

Inside, his soul cried, his body grieved for the loss of the companion who offered so much. The shifter had proven to be so much more than food and a body to slake his needs with. He was a friend, a selfless companion who saw the man who Bleu had been before he'd died. He was frightening in his feral strength and heartbreaking in his lonely determination.

He was a fucking martyr, and Bleu bit back anger at the needless loss.

He took a deep breath and blew it out. No, Lukas was right. If he tried to maintain a relationship with a vampire—another man—he risked the contempt of his pack and the challenges of the wolves. Hell, they'd be on him enough without adding this particular fuel to their bloodlust.

Even this last night had been an unacceptable risk. If a single wolf scented them on each other, the secret would be out.

If only things were just a little different—if only Dane Blacque hadn't stooped to emotional blackmail.

Hell. If only Blacque were even slightly bisexual, he wouldn't be facing such a shitty future. Oliver Bleu would move on as he always had, hunting blood where he found it, taking sex when he could. Blacque would be locked into a lie. Perhaps he'd make a grandchild for Dane; perhaps he'd even take a mate. But like countless other closeted men and women, he'd always know he was living a false life.

Finally he rolled out of the bed and padded to the bathroom, where he turned the shower on, the water as hot as he could bear. He couldn't run the risk of carrying Blacque's scent on his body. He soaped off and rinsed his hair under the hot stream of water, then opened his eyes to see Blacque's razor on a shelf and a bar of Lava soap in a soap dish. The scent of the pumice soap quickened him once again, but he didn't have the heart to maintain an erection.

He stepped out of the shower and chose a freshly laundered towel to quickly dry off. He dressed and ran his fingers through his wet hair.

When necessary, Bleu could move in near complete silence. He stood for a moment, wishing he could say good-bye but knowing it was silly. They'd probably see each other tomorrow or the next day. They'd talk about business and cars and maybe the pack. Life would go on. Their friendship would still be there. All else would be unspoken.

Briefly he thought about leaving, about packing up his equipment and driving to another city or state. But Arcada was his home now, and he'd found a measure of safety here. If he'd remained on the road, he'd be dead for real by now. He wasn't ready to give up his sanctuary.

He looked down at Blacque to gaze at the face of the big wolf as he slept. He closed his eyes, committing this night to memory. He savored every touch, every sigh. Blacque had held him through his climax, soothing him as he plummeted from the heights to the near death of the orgasm. Blacque had held him in near desperation, not allowing him to move so much as an inch. When he thought that Bleu had fallen asleep, he'd let him go with a soft curse.

Blacque wasn't the sort to lose himself in angst, but Bleu had sensed his wolf had suffered a world of hell in those moments when he'd forced himself to surrender his wants to his duties.

Bleu turned from the bed and left the room, moving swiftly into the kitchen. He lingered for a moment, looking around the homey space. It didn't look like the sort of house Blacque would live in. It was warm and comfortable, as far from Bleu's spartan lifestyle as could be imagined. He even had magnets on the refrigerator.

Bleu slipped out the kitchen door and blended into the shadows, where he remained motionless. He scented the air until he located the watcher at the edge of the wood. It had already started. Blacque had enemies, and soon enough they'd show their faces.

He moved quicker than thought, feet barely touching the ground. In seconds, Bleu was within striking distance of the young werewolf who crouched behind a tree, doing his best to catch a scent on the wind. Bleu stayed downwind, memorizing the young man's scent and appearance. He was too young to be a serious threat to Blacque, unless he pulled something dirty. Bleu moved just feet from the young man and reached out a hand to run a phantomlike finger down his spine.

The youth whipped around, only to find empty air and not a trace of the vampire that had just touched him. From the branches of a tree, Bleu laughed silently, his wicked fangs glinting in the moonlight.

Chapter Twelve

Blacque started the engine on the late-model truck and smiled in pleasure. He gunned the powerful engine for a few moments, satisfied that the truck was running smoothly. One more job out the door.

He turned off the engine and climbed out the vehicle, admiring the big quad cab. Too fancy for his needs, but still, it was damn nice. The owner had purchased it to haul his daughter's horse to and from shows. It had needed some minor work, but nothing too complicated. It had brought him a new customer as well—the owner was bringing in his wife's little sports car the following week.

He slammed the door closed and tossed the keys in the air, catching them and heading into his office.

"Hey, Lukas. I'm heading out."

He waved to Jason, the newest mechanic on staff. He hadn't been joking those weeks ago when he'd told his father business was good. It was too much for him and Davey, so he'd brought in another guy. Jason gave Lukas the chills, not because he sensed a potential danger in the guy, but simply because of his aura of otherness. The kid looked like any other twenty-something man around Arcada, but there was something in his pale blue eyes that he hadn't yet learned to conceal. He wasn't fae, but he was something.

He was certainly a miracle worker with an engine.

Nights were coming early now that fall was moving in, and when he glanced outside, the security lights in the parking lot were beginning to illuminate. He heard the gunning growl of a motorcycle engine, and for just a moment, his heart beat a little faster. The engine wasn't the throbbing roar of a hog, but the purr some something Japanese. Automatically he surveyed the shop, locating possible weapons.

He'd been jumped once, just a couple of weeks ago. The young wolf had apparently taken Blacque on at the urging of his friends, who'd gathered in a loose circle around the two of them. They'd scattered after Blacque dangled the pup in the air, letting him down after several long moments. He was being watched as well by one or more wolves. Something would be coming down soon.

His sharp ear caught a catch in the sound of the engine, and he relaxed a bit, standing back and watching as a leather-clad rider coasted into the bay. It wasn't Bleu. It wasn't even a man, but it was certainly a vampire.

The rider pulled off her helmet, revealing chestnut brown hair in a neat braid. Her leathers were built for function—chaps over jeans and sturdy boots. She wasn't out to play the femme fatale in that outfit. She was tall, lean, and for a woman, damn intimidating. Pretty enough, he supposed, but he'd think twice about pissing her off.

Bulging saddlebags were mounted on the sides of the bike, and her helmet had a smoked visor. Did she ride during the day? Her leather jacket was battered and worn and nearly perfect to his eyes.

"Hey...wolf." She gave a sly grin and winked at him. Her clear blue eyes were full of mischief and good humor. Her skin was as parchment pale as Bleu's, but her lips and cheeks had a healthy glow. She'd eaten fairly recently.

"I was riding into town, and my engine started giving me problems. I spotted your shop, thought maybe you could give me a hand. That is, if you're still open." She kicked the bike onto its stand and dismounted, giving the bike a rueful glare.

"She's almost new. I haven't had a moment of grief with her till now."

Blacque gave her a smile. She reminded him of Drusilla with her cocky assuredness. Of course, Dru would never be caught wearing engineer boots. "Arcada has that effect on vehicles sometimes." He wiped his hands on a rag and stepped up to the bike. "I'm not a motorcycle mechanic, though."

"Damn. Is there someone in town who is?"

"No. Back a few miles in Southport. There's probably a dealer." If Blacque had to guess, if she continued into Arcada proper, the bike would run just fine. If she tried to leave, it'd give her problems. The town must like her.

"Well, I know a bit about mechanics if I could borrow some tools."

"Have at it. I'll give you a hand in a sec." He ducked into the office, wrote up the paperwork on the truck, and then called the owner. All the while he kept an eye on the vampire out in his shop. No matter what they did, they'd find nothing wrong with the bike. It was simply a quirk of the region. She might be a vampire and more dangerous than a shark in the depths of the ocean, but instinctively he trusted her.

Nevertheless, he watched carefully. He wasn't certain how vampires interacted with one another. This was Bleu's territory, and he'd be up soon.

He knew exactly when she scented the other vampire. Walking out to join her, he saw her head come up. Her nostrils flared. For a moment, a feral gleam flashed in her crystalline eyes.

"I see that I've blundered into someone's territory." She rose cautiously, scanning the shop.

"He owns the shop next door." Blacque squatted next to the sleek motorcycle and reached up to turn on the engine. It turned over and sputtered.

"You planning on staying around awhile?" He started the engine again.

"Well, no, I wasn't planning to. But it looks like I don't have much of a choice now." Unlike Bleu, she didn't try to feign being human. "This place is...different."

"Yes, it is." He revved the engine, paying more attention to the vampire than to the bike. "It's a good place...peaceful. We pretty much leave each other alone."

"Live and let live, eh?" She squatted back on her haunches and glared at the engine of the bike. She shot a glance at Blacque. "I don't think your vamp's been honoring that pledge, wolf. He's fed off you. He left his mark in your blood."

Dull heat stained his cheeks. "It was voluntary."

She lifted a brow and grinned. "Yummy. That was probably fun." She straightened and stood, hands on hips. "Well, since I'll be here for a while, can you suggest a place I can stay? A place with heavy curtains?"

"Yeah, there's a motel down closer to town. There are a few mom-and-pop kind of places too." He stood, staring at her. "I've got a kid just starting here. He's pretty good with machines. Bring the bike back here tomorrow, and I'll have him take a look." He folded his arms across his chest.

"Anything else I should know? Territory…local customs?"

He shrugged. "Don't hunt inside the city limits. No aggression toward locals. There're a couple of other vamps around, but I don't know 'em. You can leave a note for Bleu if you want to let him know you're in his territory."

"Bleu? Oliver Bleu?" A slow smile spread across her face.

Blacque stifled his alarm and didn't look away from the woman. "Blue for blue eyes. It's a nickname." He could see she didn't believe him. "So, you have a name? A way he can contact you?"

"I'm April. No last name. If your *Blue* wants to talk to me, he can come and find me."

The vampire straddled the bike and turned the engine over. "Hmm. Smooth as glass now." She steadied the bike as she started to put her helmet back on. She'd swapped with a spare; this one had a clear visor. "I never caught your name."

"Blacque."

She threw back her head and laughed, but the dangerous edge gave way to good humor once again.

"Blacque and Bleu. Doesn't get any better than that!" She pulled the helmet on and fastened it, then rolled the bike backward out of the shop. Within moments, she was on the highway, riding into town.

Blacque went back into his office to search for a sheet of paper to write a note for Bleu. A warning, he suspected. He folded it neatly and headed next door to the darkened shop. He slipped it under the door, hoping Bleu would notice it when he left…or returned. Blacque hadn't seen the vampire around lately.

He scanned the empty parking lot, hoping to see Bleu's motorcycle parked in the shadows somewhere, but it wasn't there. Didn't mean anything. Bleu usually pushed it into his shop when he returned for the night. He went back to his office and shut down for the night, all the while wondering what it was with vampires and motorcycles anyway.

* * *

Someone had been prowling on his turf.

Bleu shut off the engine of his Harley and removed his helmet, then glanced at the pink streaks of dawn on the horizon. He didn't have much time. He slid from the back of the machine to the shadows like a great cat, watching, listening, and scenting the air.

He smelled werewolf, but that was to be expected. Blacque was there as well as the young male who was stalking him. There was another scent, wild and magic. That wasn't a new scent, nor was it danger. It was Jason, the new mechanic.

There was the scent of a vampire.

In all his years in Arcada, the others had never bothered him. Those who'd hunted him had never successfully assailed him within town limits—that was the only reason he'd survived as long as he had.

He ghosted to the front of the building and then back to the rear door. The vampire had been here just hours ago. He'd never scented this one before, but the smell resonated through him. He rubbed his forehead, pushing back the fatigue that was settling over him. There wasn't anything he could do at the moment, so he unlocked the door to his shop and grimaced at the unfinished job that was sitting in the middle of the workroom.

His foot struck something on the floor, and he looked down, frowning at the sheet of paper. He picked it up, closing his eyes as Blacque's fragrance rose from the paper. He sniffed the note as though it had been perfumed and then headed through the darkness to the hidden entrance to his room.

He locked up behind himself and kicked off his boots, letting them lie on the floor where they would. He flipped on the light and rolled his eyes at the mess in the room. He'd dropped clothing on the floor, clean mixed with dirty. A dirty glass, its sides hazed with dried blood, was left near the bed.

Lovely. Just the sort of place you'd bring a date.

He collapsed onto the bed and stretched out his long, leather-clad legs. It wasn't his usual kink, but when hunting, it was helpful to wear camouflage. He struggled out of the short leather jacket and tossed it to the foot of the bed. He'd pick up the room once the sun went down.

Tiny spots of blood spattered the white tank top he wore, and he frowned at them. If he didn't soak the shirt, they'd stain. Since when did vampires worry about bloodstains on their wifebeaters? He shook out the paper, bracing himself to see what Blacque had to say. His stomach gave a tiny lurch.

Bleu, new vamp in town. Said her name's April, acts like she knows you. Blacque.

Well, not much to say. There was a postscript.

She's dangerous. Be careful.

Bleu folded the paper and set it to the side. Yves and his bounty hunters. He shook his head. They'd never managed to track him this far. When he'd moved to Arcada, it was as though they'd lost his scent. Obviously this April creature had picked it up. He'd been spending too much time outside the shelter of Arcada, haunting neighboring towns and cities, aggressively searching for food. He didn't want to lose the little healing he'd gained with Blacque. Unfortunately he must have left a trail.

Before the dreams had started, he could skip a day or two without a problem. Now he needed to feed every day, sometimes more than once. The sleeplessness persisted, so he compensated by consuming more blood to bolster his strength. He'd found it necessary to range even farther out of the area. If he hunted too much in one location, he'd alarm the locals. That would be a bad thing indeed.

Bleu arched his back, intending to slip out of his leather pants, but the torpor of the day washed over him. Outside the sun had crested the horizon. For a moment, he fought the sensation, struggling to undress, to get covered. Finally surrendering, he exhaled, his eyes fluttering closed.

The lamp. He hadn't turned off the lamp. He reached out and fumbled until he yanked the cord from the wall. He had a morbid fear of fire, and while an electric lamp didn't have the same dangers as gas, it was still worrisome.

He drifted off, the scent of Blacque in his nostrils, the image of his face on Bleu's mind. He slept, and his dreams were not of war.

Chapter Thirteen

The attack wasn't unexpected. Nevertheless, Blacque was not prepared. He'd come in early for work, just minutes after dawn. Scenting Bleu at the back entrance of the building, he'd lingered by the vampire's motorcycle, drawing a deep breath and holding it. He exhaled in relief and started for the service entrance of his shop, only to spot a shadow to his left.

The blurred figure vaulted the bike and launched toward him almost before Blacque registered its presence. He clasped the wolf's ruff and rolled with it, coming up on top. He pinned the wolf and snarled, letting fangs drop in his human mouth. Not many wolves could do a partial shift, but he and his sister had the ability. Their mother had as well. That realization set off an alarm at the back of his mind, but Blacque had something else to attend to first.

"Damn it, Trav—"

It wasn't Travis. The wolf had gone passive in his grip, staring at him with eyes glazed with fear. Blacque looked at his hands. Long claws grew from the beds of his nails. Blacque gave a final snarl and then let the small changes fade. The figure he straddled shifted back to human. It was a young male Blacque vaguely recognized from the pack. In his human form, he looked nearly as terrified as he had as a wolf.

"Jeremy?" He shifted back so that he was resting on his heels, keeping the other man's thighs trapped in place. "Mind telling me what the ninja attack is all about?"

"You know."

"Remind me." He glared at the surly face below him.

"Let me up first." Blacque didn't move, and he didn't say anything. "Listen, I'm not gonna do anything else. I'm getting gravel in my ass."

"You're lucky you don't get my boot up your ass." Blacque rose easily and stood with one foot to either side of Jeremy Powter's knees. He stared at the man's naked body, automatically cataloging the muscular torso, the light dusting of hair over his lower belly. He avoided looking any lower.

Blacque slowly stepped away, blinking at a sudden thought. Was this to be the rest of his long life? Wanting yet never allowing himself to indulge? By all rights, he could take the younger wolf, dominate him, assert his authority sexually. He could take what he wanted and then walk away.

But that wasn't really what he wanted. He wanted Bleu. He wanted the vampire, and not just for a short-term fling. He couldn't think of that right now, even though Bleu's cool scent still tickled his nostrils. He leaned back against the locked door, his arms crossed over his chest. Jeremy eyed him uneasily as he rose from the ground. Blood trickled down his skin from gravel burns.

"You're all she talks about now." The young wolf stood, staring at Blacque's boot-clad feet. "What color hair will the baby have? Will it be a boy or girl?" His skin was red with embarrassment—or anger.

"Who are we talking about here, Jeremy?" He rested his head against the metal door, wondering when the next pissed-off wolf would show up on his doorstep.

"Debbie Sears. My fiancée." He frowned and fisted his hands. "What's wrong with me? Why would she pick you over me?"

Blacque wanted to groan. He wanted to pound his head against the door. Instead he turned and dug his keys from his pocket, opened the door, and led the younger wolf into the darkened room. He flipped on the lights and then unlocked the heavy bay doors. "Grab a pair of coveralls. I don't need to keep looking at your naked ass."

He rolled up the doors and headed to his office, listening to Jeremy dressing behind him.

Blacque flopped into his office chair and turned on his computer. As it booted up, Jeremy hovered in the doorway, the anger in his face burned away without fuel to keep it going.

"Has she talked to Alice?"

"No."

Blacque frowned, trying to recall the girl he was talking about. Was she an offspring from Dane's predecessor?

"You know, Dane's not going to approve me for many local women, if any at all. The point is to add new DNA to the gene pool."

Jeremy snorted in disbelief. "He'd be an idiot, then. Nobody else can do what you do."

"Partial shifts? Drusilla can do it to. My mother did it as well."

And that was the little message his brain had tried to warn him of. His mother wasn't European—she was Native

American. A chill ran up his skin. Dane wasn't acting on sentiment—he was working on cold practicality. He and his sister were the last of their line. They weren't the only shifters of their kind left in the world, but they were rare.

"I'm not interested in making trouble for committed couples." He leaned back and propped his boots on the desk. So many issues were swirling through his brain right now, but at the moment, only one had any import at all.

"You attacked me." He gazed steadily at the younger man.

Jeremy remained standing, trying to keep the advantage by remaining higher than Blacque. Like he cared? He rocked the chair back a little farther.

"Didn't know what else to do."

Blacque laced his hands behind his head, knowing that the muscles bulged in his bare arms. "You could have gone to Dane. Me. Even Alice. Nobody wants to break up families. You're engaged, so that's a family, far as I'm concerned." He lazily studied the wolf before him, watching Jeremy's unease mount.

"You owe me, kid."

"I know." He stood uneasily. He knew pack law. Blacque could challenge him, fuck him, even claim his woman as penance. But there were better uses for sneaky young wolves.

"You aren't the only one who's coming after me."

Jeremy's eyes went wide, and a panicked look crossed his face. "I'm not turning you loose on anyone else!"

"Did I come after you? Did I rip your skin from your hide when I had every right to do so?" Blacque stood and leaned forward, knuckles resting on the surface of the desk. Even from across the small room, he dwarfed the other shifter.

Deliberately he pushed power over Jeremy, grunting in satisfaction as the younger wolf fought the urge to shift.

"From now on, you're my ears and my eyes. You understand?" He watched Jeremy swallow hard. His jaw clenched, and then he jerked his head in assent. "Who else?" He settled back into his chair, nodding for the other man to sit as well. The young wolf sat, looking stiff and uncomfortable. He completely lacked the grace he'd shown earlier.

"Travis. He's been watching you and that vamp next door."

"And...?"

"Michella. She hasn't said anything, though. She's just pissed. Mallory too, but he's got other problems."

Blacque didn't answer.

"There's a couple of other males who figure you're gonna get babies on their women. Gabriel and Sam. They won't come after you unless they can get a group together."

Well, it was nothing he hadn't figured out already. Blacque chewed the inside of his lip and gazed steadily at Jeremy, who sat uncomfortably in his chair.

"Okay, the plan is to lure you out of town, maybe on a run or something. Maybe for drinks. They're gonna take you on as a group. You just won't come back."

He barked with laughter. "Are you serious? What do you think Dane will do when a bunch of pups show up smelling of my blood? Hell, what do you think my sister will do?"

"I know." Jeremy shook his head. "That's why I came on my own. I just..." He looked at Blacque. "I don't know what I was thinking. It just seemed a little more honorable this way."

Blacque continued smiling. "At best, you'd take me down, prove yourself the better man. At worst, I'd beat your ass. You'd go limping back to your fiancée, and I'd be the villain. Not a bad plan, son."

"I love her."

"I can tell." Blacque dropped his feet to the floor and sat up straight, then leaned forward. "So are you willing to fight for her?"

Jeremy went pale, but he nodded.

"No, not me. There're other ways of fighting."

The young wolf looked at him, surprise in his brown eyes. "How?"

"Tell her how you feel. Tell her you love her. Let her know how it hurts your wolf when she talks about having another man's baby."

He couldn't believe those words were coming out of his mouth. The biggest hypocrite in Arcada was telling others to be honest. But he didn't take it back. Jeremy sat silently, looking at the battered surface of the desk. They sat there in Blacque's office, listening to the ticking of the clock on the wall. In another hour, Davey and Jason would be coming in for the day. He scratched his chin, realizing he'd forgotten to shave.

"You think that'll work?"

Blacque didn't answer, because he truly didn't know whether or not it would. It just seemed to be the approach that women appreciated.

Jeremy stood up and then sat back down. He hadn't been dismissed, and his wolf was reading Blacque as dominant.

"Go home. Talk to her. Let her think about it." He stood, and Jeremy rose to his feet as well.

"If that doesn't work?"

They started out to the bay, and Blacque couldn't help looking out at the early morning light. Had Bleu received his message? Tonight he'd hang around, try to catch the vampire before he left for the night. He pulled his thoughts away from Bleu and his worry, and focused on the very real problems that faced him within the pack.

"It will. Besides, she hasn't even talked to Alice. If you need to, talk to the alpha. He doesn't want to see families broken apart."

But he did want to see Bianca's line continue. Come hell or high water, Dane was determined to see Blacque's children within the year.

"You check in with me if you hear anything important."

Jeremy turned, and the morning light caught the angles on his face. He slipped out of the coveralls he'd snagged earlier. "How will I know if it's urgent enough?"

"Use your common sense, Jeremy."

He laughed a little and then walked with Blacque to the service entrance. "I haven't shown much of that lately, have I?" He pushed open the door and stepped out into the chill morning air. He shifted before Blacque could answer and dashed out across the parking lot as a small economy car rolled in. Alice stepped out, a folding portfolio clutched in her arms.

Shit, shit, and double shit.

"Morning, Lukas! I have some names I want to run past you." She was bubbling with enthusiasm that Blacque didn't share. "Was that Jeremy who just ran out of here? What a coincidence. I just spoke with his Debbie last night."

He held the door open to the building and let her precede him. "Yeah... Alice, we're going to have to talk about those two."

He didn't even bother trying to smile as he escorted her into his office.

* * *

In resignation, Blacque looked at the stack of papers on his desk. Alice had drafted a genealogy that was far past his comprehension. She'd patted his hand and set it aside, then drew his attention to a stack of papers. She sorted through them quickly and divided them into two stacks.

"These are the women who have expressed interest in you. This stack is of the applications I've determined are not appropriate for one reason or another." She pushed the thicker stack to the side. "These are the ones I think you should consider." He looked at the pile, which was much less intimidating than the other. He didn't even bother to sort through that one.

The first name he saw was Debbie Sears, the fiancée of Jeremy. He lifted it and put it on the other stack.

"Is there a problem with Debbie?" Alice peered up at him, her blue eyes curious.

"She's in a committed relationship, according to Jeremy."

Alice sighed deeply. "She is wearing his ring. So you won't consider them if they're married, mated, or engaged?"

Hell, he wouldn't consider them if they were going steady.

"Don't want bad feelings in the pack. No more than can be helped, anyway."

Alice retrieved the stack and sorted through it, setting three more to the side. "I know your father won't agree with your scruples, Lukas, but I appreciate them." She gazed at one of the applications. "This is my granddaughter. She's been married to a human for nearly ten years, and they've had no luck with children." She set the paper down on the reject file and carefully aligned its edges with the others. She looked up and met his gaze. Lately he'd noticed that few of the wolves were willing to meet his eyes until they'd spent time with him.

"As much as I'd like to see a grandchild, I'm afraid her husband wouldn't understand our methods."

He gave a short laugh. He wasn't sure he understood their methods either. What was the problem with donating sperm and doing it in a doctor's office? Granted, if they bred while shifted, the wolves required a tie. But in human form ties rarely happened. *Very* rarely. In fact, a human-to-human tie was probably a myth. So why was the sire expected to have intercourse with the mother-to-be?

It just didn't make sense. He could only chalk it up to the innate lust of their species. Dane had certainly had no issues with it, and he hadn't been gunned down by an irate husband. Yet.

He picked up the remaining papers, scanned them, and set them down. "I suppose I'm old-fashioned or something. It just kinda rubs me wrong."

Alice didn't comment; she simply gathered her papers and tucked them back into the portfolio. "Should I contact these three?"

He swallowed hard. "They have to meet me for an interview first. Let them see what they're getting into." She looked at him curiously. "This is more than genetics, Alice. If I father a child, I'm the father forever. These women need to know that, and they might not want someone like me in their lives."

"Nonsense. You're a perfectly pleasant young man, and anyone who knows your father will expect your involvement as the father."

Great. Another avenue of escape shut off. Scare tactics probably wouldn't work either. He rose to see her out. The mechanics would be here soon, and he hadn't spent any more time with the audits of the mail order business he was reviewing. Some of the pack members had opened a small side business, making and selling jam, jelly, and fruit butter from the orchard. But since it was such a small business, he should be able to review it all before lunch.

As Alice drove away, he noticed a skip in her engine. He'd have to take care of that.

He leaned against the wall of the building, pinching the bridge of his nose. He gazed at Bleu's big black motorcycle and had the most ridiculous impulse to cry.

Chapter Fourteen

"Lukas?"

Blacque jerked, nearly slamming his head on the hood of the Studebaker. The voice was so unexpected that it startled him. How had he allowed someone—anyone—to take him by surprise? Especially Bleu.

He looked good. Hot. His black hair waved away from his face, revealing the graceful lines of his cheekbones and jaw. His sensual lips curved up in a smile, hiding the fangs Blacque knew had dropped. He stood up, taking in the leather pants, the blunt-toed engineer boots. Bleu was looking him over as well, and Blacque heated at the arousal in his eyes. The excitement was edged with hot, dangerous anger.

"Don't you think this has gone on long enough?" He moved toward Blacque, pinning him against the car. He stood inches away, invading his space, overwhelming Blacque with his presence. "You know this isn't going to work. They want more than you have to give, and it's eating you up inside. Isn't it, pup?"

He looked away, trying to escape the intensity of the vampire's stare. He had nowhere to go; even if he escaped from Bleu, he still couldn't change the truth.

He watched in fascination as Bleu's face came closer to his. Those blue eyes held his gaze, and his lips parted slightly. His skin was flawless—he literally glowed with health and strength. For the first time ever, Blacque knew he'd never be able to overpower the vampire, not when he was at full power like this. He felt helpless, and he liked it.

"I need you, Blacque. I'm...hungry."

His heart skipped a beat as cool lips brushed against his throat. Bleu moved forward, pressing Blacque back against the car. Their hips brushed closer. He felt the heat of the vampire's erection against his, and he reached down and clasped that iron-hard rod in his hand...

"Boss?"

Blacque opened his eyes and looked down at the wrench he clasped in a too-tight grip. The engine of the truck he was working on was grimy with decades of old oil and dirt. He straightened up and pushed away from the vehicle. He turned to find Jason looking at him, a trace of anxiety in his mild blue eyes. Thankfully the coveralls he was wearing hid the fact that his dick was still immersed in the daydream.

"Davey said you wanted to talk to me?"

He tossed the tool into a rolling box and leaned back against the old Ford. "You know motorcycles?"

"Yeah, I'm pretty good with bikes."

The kid had hair the color of straw and freckles across his short nose. Wearing a raggedy hat and biting a piece of grass between his teeth, he looked like he belonged in another century. But this wasn't a kid—age fairly radiated from him. What in hell was he? This was a game Blacque played a lot lately when he meeting various residents of Arcada.

"Look, can you stay after closing? A client is bringing a bike in tonight."

"The vamp next door?"

Blacque paused, taken aback by the kid's casual mention of Bleu. Was there anyone not clued in to his true nature? He was uneasy for his friend.

"No. She's new in town. Her bike died just down the road."

"Let me guess, it started up fine when she headed for the motel."

"Right."

Jason just laughed and shook his head. "Guess it won't hurt to check it out. She's a vampire too?"

"Yeah. Don't see any for years, and then they're coming outta the woodwork."

"No problem." Jason turned back to his brake job. "I'll just take a long lunch."

Speaking of lunch… Blacque glanced at the clock and grimaced. Between the drama of the morning and the pack audits, the day was slipping away. He needed to finish some actual work here today, bring some money in. He was finally in the black and wanted to stay that way. His stomach rumbled, and he headed to his office, ready to take a working lunch. If things kept rolling like this, he'd need to hire someone just for the books.

The sound of a smooth-running sedan brought an unspoken curse. He glanced up to see a black-and-white pull up outside the bay. His father climbed out, food bags and sodas in hand. Well, at least he was paying for lunch. Blacque tossed his day-old sandwich back into the little dorm cooler he kept behind his desk.

"I was hoping to catch you before you ate." Dane shouldered his way through the door, then pushed it closed with his foot. Great. That meant he wanted to talk. After setting the food and sodas carefully on the desk, he settled into the chair across from Blacque and adjusted his gun belt. He looked good, vital and alive. It seemed ridiculous that he was so worried about his mortality. The thought made Blacque a bit uneasy, but he didn't smell illness on him.

"So what's up?" He tore open a bag and inhaled the aroma of fried burgers. The other bag was bulging with French fries and onion rings. Good thing werewolves ran so hot; otherwise they'd all be dying of heart disease. He unwrapped a burger, took a bite, and chewed it slowly, watching the alpha steadily.

"Nothing really. Just wanted to come by and visit." Dane popped the lid off his cola and drank without a straw. It surprised Blacque, because that's exactly what he did. Dane set the cup down and started into his first burger, letting his eyes drop closed a bit. "No one does them like Mae Belle's. All the other places fry them till they're like jerky."

Blacque grinned and kept chewing. His father liked his meat rare.

"Heard you had visitors today." He paused and scented the air. "Vamps, gremlins, wolves…"

"Gremlins?"

Dane jerked his head back out toward the shop. "That kid you got working? He's probably centuries old. I recognize your neighbor's scent, but not the female vamp. She's new."

Damn. He was good.

"What's a gremlin?"

"They're sidhe. Old magic. There probably aren't many left nowadays. Closer to brownies and beggars than the fae and elementals."

Blacque swallowed his food and took a drink. "They're dying out?"

"That is possible, but I suspect they just retreated to their realm. This one's getting too crowded with humans for the Fair Folk to cope with. Too much metal and technology. In fact, you remember when scientists were dropping acid and mescaline back in the sixties and seventies? Calling it research?"

Blacque hadn't been around then, but he was familiar with the experiments.

"Well, they claimed to see these magical creatures. Called them mechanical elves. I figure they accidently crossed over somehow. Anyway, they were discredited. Who can take that sort of data seriously?" His dark eyes twinkled in humor. "So a gremlin is a sidhe with mechanical inclinations. They get pissed off, and they meddle with things. You keep 'em happy, and everything will keep going your way. For a business like yours, it's like having good luck personified."

"And what keeps a gremlin happy?" He darted a glance out to the shop. Jason was next to Davey, leaning into an engine compartment.

"Well, it depends on the particular gremlin. But in general, they don't like the typical human failings—greed, dishonesty, and unkindness."

"Well, I guess it's good for me that I'm the only mechanic in town." He grinned and started eating again.

"Good for you that you pay these guys too much. And you aren't a bad guy."

"Gee, thanks."

Dane grinned and balled up the wrapper of his second burger. He started on the fries. "So back to your visitors. What brought Jeremy around?"

"He was trying to fight me for Debbie."

Dane paused, his face growing dark with anger. "You took him down?"

"I pinned him, then brought him in for a little talk."

Dane sniffed the air. "No blood." He stared eating again.

"No blood. Just talk." Blacque threw away his trash and watched his father's face. "I told him I didn't know anything about Debbie and that she needed to go through proper channels." He paused. "Then I told him I wasn't interested in busting up families."

Dane sighed in frustration. "Of course the men aren't going to like it, Lukas. That's why we used to have challenge fights for women. It happens, and they need to deal with it."

"We live in a human environment. Wolves like Jeremy view their women as theirs. They get married, make the commitments to monogamy and faithfulness. If couples in agreement come to me, or if he agrees to artificial insemination—"

Dane snorted in disgust.

"I agreed to this, Dane. If you want me to be a stud, it'll be on my terms." He stared evenly at the alpha.

"Lukas, that's not how we do it. If you want to be alpha—"

"That's your thing, not mine. If some of the wolves think I'm weak, they can take me on. I'd rather deal with that than cause tension in families."

Dane shifted in his chair. "Jeremy and Debbie aren't married."

"But five of the other females who made requests are. A couple of them are married to full-blooded shifters who would be much better fathers than me."

The room was silent for a long moment as Dane processed that information. "Have I been wrong all this time?"

"Not for you. You're the alpha. I'm not."

"You aren't like other wolves, are you, Lukas?"

He gave his father a grim smile. "Same thing can be said about Drusilla. And my mother."

Dane returned his smile and shook his head in frustration. "Figured that out, did you?"

"Yeah, that bit about loving her...wanting to see her face—"

"All true. But yes, you're the end of her bloodline. I owe it to her—and to us—to see that your line continues. If I hadn't forced the issue, you'd never have done it on your own."

"I'm not an alpha, Dad. I'm happy in my life."

"Bullshit. You're always alone. How often do you date? Take lovers?"

Blacque felt a jolt of pain run through his entire body. Odd that his emotions carried their own brand of pain. His gaze dropped to his hands.

"Oh God. Blacque..." Sudden understanding laced his father's voice. "You lost someone."

"I gave someone up. For you. And the pack."

Dane slumped back in the chair. "I had no idea." He rested his hand over his eyes, clearly distressed. "Not pack?"

"No."

"I'm sorry."

Blacque said nothing. What could he say? Deny the feelings that had been growing against his better judgment? Tell his father that not only was his lover a man, he was a vampire? No, the less said, the better.

"It's best, then. Someday, when you're ready, you'll find a mate."

"You had a mate. That didn't make you happy."

Dane looked away then, pain shadowing his eyes. "I did. I walked away from her for my own ambition. Now it's too late, and I'll never have that chance again."

What a mess this family was!

"What am I? Me and Dru? Nobody else can do a partial shift like we can."

"You're like the rest of us. Your mother's bloodline goes back to precontact times. Some clans have gifts that others don't have. Some have a half form, like a wolf on two legs. Others have traits that are bad, like moon madness. By the time your mother was born, most of her pack had died out or had been assimilated into other packs."

"So is this the real reason you want us reproducing? To pass that trait into the Arcada pack?"

"I made a promise." Dane looked away uncomfortably. "Before she told you kids she was sick, she contacted me, made sure that I'd step in when she was gone. I promised her I'd do whatever it took to make sure the two of you had offspring."

Whatever it took. He stifled a laugh. Even if it meant ruining lives.

Blacque was numb. He glanced over at his computer and watched the screen saver lazily build tubular bridges that faded away into nothingness. Much like his life.

"So far, nothing's come up in the business audits. Nothing bad, anyway. Just fiscal carelessness."

"Good. What have you cleared so far?"

"The produce stand and the Internet preserves business. The gym is running in the black. The nail salon isn't making a profit, but it has in the past. I'll get a report put together for you."

Sharing time was over. Blacque fished out a stack of papers and handed it to his father. "Here are some suggestions on how they can tighten up their fiscal management and maybe bring in some business."

Dane took the papers and set them down, barely glancing at them. "Thank you. This is a big help."

"Well, it's good to use my degree." He gave a tight smile, trying to hide the bitterness that was welling up inside. "I haven't started on the larger end of the produce company." He looked speculatively at his father. "Is there something you suspect? Something I should be watching out for?"

Dane shook his head. "Cops call it a hinky feeling. Instinct. I'm just getting an odd vibe lately, and if someone in the pack is up to no good, it'll most likely have to do with money."

"Or power." Blacque remained seated as his father rose to his feet.

"You watch a real wolf pack someday, son. You'll see battles over food and over bitches. That's pretty much it. Once an alpha takes firm control, the hierarchy remains stable. Once he dies or weakens, that's when chaos breaks out."

Dane turned and faced Blacque before he opened the door. "That's why I'm getting you ready now. If something happens, you'll be prepared. The pack will be accustomed to the idea of you taking over for me."

He watched from the office doorway as his father waved at Davey and Jason while he sauntered out to his cruiser. Though reluctant, he had to admire the old man; he was working so many angles right now, a normal-thinking person simply couldn't keep up. There was a reason he was a hell of a chess player. He was even better at solving crimes than playing games.

Blacque started to leave the office and then turned back, closing the door again. He stood facing the wall that adjoined Bleu's secret bedroom. "Don't know if you can hear me, Bleu. Just wanted to let you know I'm close by." He hovered awkwardly, embarrassed by the impulse to speak. Guilt gnawed at him; he should be checking on the vampire during the day, making sure he wasn't lying there locked in his nightmares. But to do so would be disastrous. As it was, he could barely get through a minute without remembering…

And just like that, he was hard again. Hard and aching, his skin craving Bleu's cool touch.

He huffed out a breath and turned to the music system, then popped in a stack of CDs. He toggled the switch so that it played in his office as well as in the shop, and then pulled his coveralls back on. He had a truck he needed to fix.

* * *

Damn Yves for doing this to him!

Damn him to hell.

Bleu lay in his bed, powerless to move, pain searing his body until his brain could no longer process reality. He knew it was a dream, yet that knowledge mattered little.

Please let me die.

He opened weeping eyes and looked up at that once beloved face. Yves had been gazing at him, agony in his expression, indecision written large upon his countenance.

Please, don't do this to me.

His weakened heart fluttered as death crushed his lungs. Infection raced through his bloodstream, shutting down his organs, bringing him to the edge of peacefulness. He thought briefly of Yves and the long, lust-filled nights they'd shared. But inevitably his mind went backward, lingering over images of Stella, embracing her with love. Not the love of passion and lust, but of a lifetime of friendship. He loved her with his body and loved her with his mind and—Oh! He had failed her so completely!

He let his eyes drop closed, savoring the memory of a child in her arms. His son, a baby boy he'd met only once. Now he'd never know the child, and perhaps that too was a blessing. The little one would not grow up seeing his father with a mass of scars brutalizing his face and body. Oliver wouldn't be faced with seeing the horror on Stella's pretty face when she first saw the scarred wreck of her young husband.

He opened his eyes to see Yves lean closer, tears running down his face.

Don't do this, Yves! No!

He hadn't known for long what Yves really was. He'd found out quite by accident when he followed the older man from his flat early one morning. He wondered why Yves always went wandering alone in the darkness. He knew his lover was a spy, but when he saw Yves lure a teenage boy to an alley, fondle him before feeding at his neck, he knew he'd fallen in love with something much more sinister. Something...evil.

He was food, my darling. Nothing more. I did him no harm. He still lives.

Oliver had accepted those words, yet their relationship changed subtly, becoming more dangerous as he flirted with the lethal, perverse side of Yves' nature. He fed him from his neck, from his thigh. He discovered the seductive joy of dancing with danger. Oliver found himself addicted to the ecstatic pain of feeding...of dancing in the arms of death. The vampire was like a drug, alluring and deadly, and so very, very beautiful. But in the end, Oliver wanted nothing more than to be free of him. He was desperate to escape, yet saw no way out.

Oliver felt the brush of fangs at his neck. No matter how he protested, he was unable to speak, to beg the vampire to release him to death.

No!

A flare of pain so minor compared to the brutal burns that covered his body. Weakness...darkness...the gossamer touch of nothingness...and then the taste of bitter wine upon his tongue.

No!

The bloody face of his lover hovered above him, the silken drag of the vampire's blood slipped over his lips, bringing unwelcome life to Bleu's ravaged body. His eyes grew heavy, and the last thing he saw was Yves, eyes misty with tears, lowering his face for a bloody, unwelcome kiss.

No!

And then he had died, only to wake again, wrapped in the cold arms of Yves. Yves, who had loved him so very much that he gave Bleu eternal life.

Oliver had never forgiven him for that.

* * *

Bleu's eyes were open, yet he saw nothing. If Blacque had been here, he'd have left the small lamp on. A night-light.

The humor of the idea brought a reluctant smile to his face, pulling at the fading burns next to his mouth.

Damn Yves!

Bleu let the fury boil for a few moments, but as he was unable to throw punches or kick furniture, the anger ebbed until he could hear and smell and make sense of his surroundings. He was on his bed. He hadn't managed to fully undress before collapsing. His leathers weren't particularly comfortable, and the stained white tank top he wore would be ruined by now. He'd have to remember to buy more black shirts.

He overheard the murmur of voices and recognized Blacque speaking to his father. Earlier he'd had a revealing conversation with a pack member right after Bleu had awakened the first time. He focused, not hanging on to the words so much as the intonations of Blacque's voice. He squeezed his eyes shut against the pain that voice brought to him.

Yes, another layer of pain had entered his life. How foolish of him to play with fire as bright as Lukas Blacque and expect to avoid being burned. He'd assumed the wolf would be so hungry for his love that he'd set aside his obligations to his family and pack. What arrogance. All he'd accomplished was extending his life by a few months and bringing heartache to a truly good man.

He closed his eyes, listening to the conversation, letting Blacque's voice soothe him back to sleep. There was a pause, and he opened his eyes, listening.

Yves had meddled with his life, turning him into a vampire out of his obsessive love. He'd seen the fear in Bleu's eyes and assumed it was fear of death. Oliver had meddled with Blacque's life out of desperation, uncaring of the impact it would have on the wolf, oblivious to the pain he'd bring himself. He damned Yves for delivering him undying torment, yet what he'd done to himself and to Blacque was so much worse.

How could he say he was sorry when he couldn't even move his lips to speak?

"Don't know if you can hear me, Bleu. Just wanted to let you know I'm close by."

Damnation. He squeezed his eyes shut at the sound of the muffled voice on the other side of the wall. The weight on his chest had nothing to do with terrible dreams and memories or with grinding hunger and weakness. It was pain he'd known only once before, when memories of Stella washed over him at the moment of his death. It was regret and the bittersweet taste of love that could never be reclaimed.

He blinked and listened, desperate for Blacque's voice. Instead he heard music start, Blacque's favorite mix of southern rock and Texas blues. He'd turned on the speakers so Bleu would have music during his sleepless day.

Stella was dead, long gone and buried. His son as well. His grandchildren were lost to him, but Blacque was only feet away, just on the other side of the wall.

He might have screwed up royally by seducing the big wolf, but it was done and behind him. Blacque liked things simple in his world, and he'd just been handed a whole plateful of complications. Best thing Bleu could do would be to steer clear of him, keep away.

But he knew he wouldn't do that. Someone needed to watch the big guy's back. Maybe he could make Blacque's life a little safer, a bit simpler.

Then he remembered April, the new girl in town. April, who recognized his name and might be working for Yves.

Maybe he just needed to get out of Dodge before all hell broke loose. Lukas had problems of his own; he didn't need to deal with Bleu's as well.

Chapter Fifteen

It was still early by the time Bleu made his way back to Arcada. To evade Blacque, he'd slipped out the back door when the wolf was occupied with the new vamp and her motorcycle. He'd left the Harley behind in the parking lot, feeling good enough to flash-run his way around town.

He'd encountered Hancock, who worked night shifts at the post office. They'd nodded in passing, and he'd felt a twinge of jealousy. Hancock had a small stable of willing donors right here in Arcada. Bleu had never felt comfortable about treating humans in that fashion. He'd kept lovers in the past, people who shared their bodies and blood, but they led lives independent of him. When the relationship ended, they moved on, just as he and Blacque had done.

He'd been lucky. After only a short time at the local watering hole, Bleu had connected with the pretty young thing who was stupid enough to walk out back with him. She was legal but not yet old enough to drink, so he'd fed and planted an eerie warning in her mind. Hopefully she wouldn't be so eager to walk into trouble in the future.

After feeding, he'd wandered the town, watching the residents of Arcada as they threw the cloaks off their closely guarded secrets. He perched in a tree at the edge of the alpha's property and watched as pack members came and went. One young man played basketball under the lights of the security lamps, depression clear in his body language.

From there, he visited Drusilla Blacque's condo and grinned when she came to the window and flicked the curtain to cautiously watch the street. She was sharp as a tack. Seeing that all was well with Blacque's loved ones, he headed out to the wolf's house, feeling melancholy as he stalked the perimeter of the property, searching for intruders. Satisfied that it was clear for now, he headed back for the shop, ready to begin his workday.

He came to a stop at the edge of the parking lot. Someone was sitting on his motorcycle. Not sitting—reclining. She leaned against the backrest, her booted feet on the handlebars. He stifled his irritation and walked into the parking lot, not bothering to hide his approach.

Her sleek Honda was parked just a few feet away, its cooling engine ticking in the chilly air.

"Can't believe you ride a hog."

He looked at her sitting there on his classic motorcycle, and she sat up, dropping her feet to the running boards. She gave him a grin, brought one leg over the side, and easily hopped off. She played casual, but her underlying tension showed in her posture. He thought he saw a flicker of fear behind her smile.

In the moonlight, he saw that her hair was dark; her eyes were light. Like her scent had earlier, her appearance shot a bolt of alarm through him.

"You must be April."

"I must be." She was still grinning, looking him over. She looked about his age, maybe a little older. In spite of her apparent youth, he decided she wasn't a baby, but she wasn't too old either. She radiated power and vitality. However, he was the elder; his depleted strength was more than enough to take her down if need be.

He sighed and continued to study her. "Tell Yves I will not return."

"You think Yves sent me?" Her arched brow lifted. She tilted her head a bit, listening to her surroundings. She then turned her attention back to Bleu.

"The wolf seems to be a popular guy."

"Pack politics."

"Oh." Her look of distaste mirrored his. "Funny, if you watch the movies and such, they always show the vampires with these rigid hierarchies. The wolves run around in lawless packs. Yet that's not the way it is at all."

"No, it isn't." He crossed his arms over his chest and let his weight settle on one leg.

"Well, he seems to be an all right guy for a big ole wolf." She glanced up at him. "You two have a falling out?"

He didn't answer.

She cleared her throat. It was a very human habit. She was nervous. "Okay, then. We aren't talking about the mechanic." She moved a bit closer. "I always thought you'd be older."

"I am old."

"But you weren't when you were made." For a moment, he saw a look on her face... Compassion? But then it was gone.

"I was twenty-five. I was walking on the campus after dark, heading back to my flat." She shook her head. "It happened so fast. I'd never known anything could move so like that."

He shifted uncomfortably. It'd been years since he'd spent any extended time around another vampire, and this trip down memory lane was just a little too poignant.

"So you might be older than me, but in an odd way, I'm older than you." She looked pleased with her reasoning. "It's odd that we're frozen in time like that. I was made in the seventies. I was a product of the mash-up time between hippies and disco. I still want to look like Farrah Fawcett. You seem a little old-world, in spite of the leather."

Bleu felt a smile starting. She certainly had charm. He studied her, taking in the elegant lines of her cheekbones, the full lips and luminous eyes. Like his, they were blue, but light blue, framed by thick, dense lashes. She was uncommonly beautiful and uncomfortably familiar.

"You aren't one of Yves' hunters?"

"Lord no. I want nothing to do with that crazy bastard. In fact, I'm curious about why he's hunting you so desperately. It's hard not to hear about the reward he's offering. The idiot even posted it on some Internet forums." She shook her head in disgust.

A reward? And he'd posted it on the Internet? No wonder there'd been so many hunters these past years. It was amazing Yves hadn't outed vampires to the public at large.

"He's my maker and wants me back at his side."

She looked away, an odd expression on her face. "Funny. He's my maker too. But he's not nearly as interested in me." She looked at him. "Does that make you my brother?"

Cold began to creep into Bleu's limbs, stretching its tentacles to his heart.

"Yves was your maker? He stalked you on a college campus? He turned you without your knowledge?"

That's when he saw it—the subtle uptilt to the eyes, the hairline. Small things he saw in the mirror every day. Small things that still lived in his memory.

"What is your family name?"

"I was taking a year abroad, studying art. My family was from France. My father spoke with such a beautiful accent. He was so happy when I got the chance to go to his home. I met my grandfather and my cousins. Many have a look of you about them."

"April. Louisa April Bleu." He nearly staggered at the knowledge. "Yves hunted you…turned you…"

"Because of you. I suppose he was getting some sort of revenge. Or maybe he was trying to find a replacement. He always talked about you…about the wonderful times in Paris. He would talk for hours about the joy you shared and the love you made." She lapsed into a haunting imitation of Yves' aristocratic accent.

Unable to prevent his reaction, Bleu clapped a hand over his mouth. His own great-granddaughter stood before him, a victim of Yves' insane love for Bleu. He moved that hand to his heart, trying to soothe the pain there.

"I am so sorry."

She studied him for a long moment. "You are, aren't you? Most of the vamps I've run into have been pretty self-involved. I didn't expect an apology."

Unable to remain on his feet any longer, Bleu turned away and unlocked the door to his shop. He returned to the bike and rolled it inside. April followed, looking curiously around his business. She wandered over to a bench seat he was almost finished with.

"Nice work." She shook her head. "A blue-collar vampire. Who'd have thought I'd find you someplace like this?"

"Have you been looking for me?" He found a folding chair and sat down, feeling numb from head to foot.

"Not consciously. When I first escaped him, I tried to find you. I thought you must be in Europe. Yves was always so sure you'd go home. He watched the family for years, certain that you'd show up. Instead I went back to visit family. He saw you in me, I suppose." She dragged another chair over and set it just feet away from Bleu, then straddled it and rested her chin on her arms.

"Tell me." He didn't have the heart to question her, but he needed to know. He needed to know it all.

"He grabbed me, managed to exchange blood in the shrubbery, just feet away from a sidewalk filled with students. Afterward he took me up into the Pyrenees Mountains. He had a quaint little love nest up there." She rolled her eyes up to look at him. "He's insane, you know."

"I know. I…" He shook his head. "When we were together during the war, he had lapses. I didn't know what he was. I assumed it was the stress of the war. He'd sit for hours, saying nothing, seeing nothing, and then he'd suddenly return, unaware that any time had passed. He'd become furious when he saw that the night had gone by." He'd also had his dangerous moments, times when he flew into a rage at Oliver. Often savaged bodies would be found in the back alleys of Paris after one of his furies. Love had slowly fused with fear, yet Oliver had been unable to leave Yves behind. Not until he'd found himself dying in a hospital.

She looked down at the floor. "He was...what he was, I suppose. A vampire. He taught me to hunt and hide. He taught me to control my wildness early on."

Bleu shook his head sadly. "He turned me against my will also. Unfortunately I couldn't remain in Paris. I was boarded into a coffin. Yves paid a servant to accompany me to the United States. He fed me and did his best, but in the end, the poor man fled in fear of his life."

"Shit. How did you survive?"

"Sheer dumb luck. The influenza pandemic came at the same time. Chaos and death were all around. I stayed in large cities and moved often. I lived in alleys and in the basements of abandoned buildings, finding shelter as best I could. One day I woke, my mind clear, and I remembered all I had once been and what Yves had done to me." He looked at her miserably. "Did he...? Were you...?"

"Yes. Yes, there's no avoiding sex when feeding is involved, especially at the beginning. But I had a pretty solid awareness underneath all the early insanity. He was also foolish enough to have kept my passport and everything I had in my travel pouch. One night when we were hunting in Nice, I escaped. I stole a motorcycle, of all things." She grinned and shook her head. "Managed to make it to Italy. I don't think he followed me too hard. You were the true love of his life."

"Make that the object of his obsession." He looked up at her. "I have followed the family as best I could. I was saddened to discover you'd vanished. Yet you're here."

"Yup. Here I am." She studied his face. "I'll just be around till my bike is working. Then I'll get out of your hair."

"Don't count on it. Arcada has taken an interest in you."

"Huh?" She sat upright. "Arcada? That's the town, right?"

He grinned and stood up, stripping out of his leather jacket. "There's something to the town...a presence... I don't know how to say it. Just something. When I arrived over the city boundary, I knew it was my home. I immediately purchased this building complex and set up a business. In all, I've had few problems here."

"Well, I didn't feel anything. My bike just gave out." She stared at him suspiciously. "It runs fine when I'm not planning on going anywhere out of town."

"Then you should stay put for now." He slipped a work shirt on and stepped into the storeroom, then pulled out a length of expensive upholstery for cutting. He laid it out on the broad worktable and began taking measurements. "There are many houses here that have basement apartments. I'm sure you can rent short-term."

"Well damn." She got up and leaned on the table, watching him. "You own these buildings?"

"It's not widely known. I wanted an income property without dealing with homeowners and the problems that come with residential tenancy."

She turned away from him and leaned against the table. She was angry. That didn't surprise him at all—he was the source of her current life, and now she was trapped. She turned back to look at him.

"How do I get out of here?"

"You can walk. Hitchhike. Push the bike until you're out of town. It's not holding you captive, April. It just likes you."

She relaxed a bit. "Okay, I can deal with that. So, the big guy told me no hunting inside city limits."

"I'm afraid if you feed from any but a willing donor, you'll become quite ill. If you attack or assault, you'll be rendered unconscious." He looked up from his work. "I learned that the hard way."

She laughed. "So you aren't such a gentleman after all."

"No, I am not a gentle man." He began his first cut. "There are bars outside the city limits. The shifters have places outside where they hold their pack challenges. There are also some good-size cities within driving distance. It's an inconvenience, but one grows accustomed."

"Is the werewolf yours?"

For the first time, he felt primal, predatory hostility toward her. He looked up, knowing the beast was in his eyes. She was no longer his great-granddaughter—his kin. She was a trespasser. He straightened, and she took a step backward.

"Okay...okay, message received. He's yours." She continued to back off. "Damn. I'm sorry, Oliver."

It took a moment to cool down, and he leaned on the table, feeling his heart return to normal. Bleu squeezed his eyes shut.

"So it's like that." Slowly she returned and rested her hands on the cloth-covered table. "I'm sorry. It didn't end well?"

"It didn't have time to begin. I waited...too long."

"Look at me, Oliver." He swallowed and then looked over to where she stood. She was beautiful and so like Stella. In that moment, he realized that even when death took one person, that person lived on in others. Even though he'd been taken from his family, he'd lived on, as had Stella.

"You look so much like her. You behave like her too."

"You loved my great-grandmother?"

He nodded. "Very much. I cheated, though. When I died, my last thoughts were not happy ones. I wished I could undo all the harm I'd done." He gazed at her steadily. "I thought to lure

Blacque into my life as...food. And for convenient sex. I meant to use him until I no longer needed him. But his character... I misjudged my feelings and the strength of his character. He is noble and selfless, and in spite of his appearance, he is the gentlest soul I've ever met. He's suffered because of me."

"You ended up hurting as well. That's pretty obvious." She leaned over and ruffled his hair. "Sucks when the spider falls for the fly." She dropped her hand and looked up at him. The hungry expression on her face had nothing to do with food.

"You are *so* damned handsome. I've seen photos...heard stories about you. Nothing could have prepared me for meeting you in person."

"You mean—" He broke off, overwhelmed by emotion. "I wasn't forgotten?"

"Never. You were listed as missing in action. Great-grandmother Stella told my grandpa that she knew exactly when you died. She said she woke up unable to breathe. And then you were gone." She reached out and touched his cool fingers. "She never stopped loving you, even after she moved on and remarried. She said you were her best friend ever."

"And I betrayed that friendship."

She sighed. "You were a boy. You were a boy thrust into hell. Then you fell in with a predator like Yves." She looked down, unable to meet his eyes. "He told me he thought you were much younger...perhaps seventeen. He saw your sexual curiosity and took advantage, Oliver."

"If I hadn't been forced to leave Paris, he'd have eventually tired of me."

"And then he'd probably have killed you for real." She slipped her hand over his and squeezed. "Then I'd never have met you at all." She raised an arched brow. "Being a vampire isn't what I'd have asked for, but in all, it's not so bad. I look pretty damn good for a middle-aged broad!"

He smiled and turned his hand over, clasping hers. "For all the danger, I am grateful you've come here. I want to know you. I want to know about your family."

"Your family." She slipped her hand loose. "Where are you hunting tomorrow?"

"I rotate. I'm thinking about the Roadhouse. It's a run-down place a few miles out of town. Ladies' night on Tuesdays, gay night on Thursdays."

"Right. I'll head in the other direction, then." She flushed slightly. "No offense, but you know...hunting brings on other appetites—" He laughed quietly. "You look like my little brother rather than my great-grandfather. Either way, it'd just be too awkward."

They walked outside together, and she gazed up at the sky and then out to the forest that rose into the hills. "This place is different. I have no idea how to go about life in a place like this."

He scented the air, letting it tell the story of the night's surroundings.

"You're welcome here when I'm working. Sometimes when I'm not hunting, I just go out and run the night." It would be nice to have her company. She *felt* like kin. He'd never have dreamed that was possible. Not with another vampire.

She mounted her motorcycle and sat with the helmet resting in her lap. "I used to live in the desert. Sometimes I'd ride out as far as I could go and then just lie out there, looking at the sky. The next night, I'd paint what I saw."

That's right. She'd been in art school when she'd vanished. Perhaps she'd stay here for a while and paint what she saw in Arcada. Bleu was fairly certain she wouldn't be around long.

Her motorcycle started up quietly, and she rode away, skimming around the corner of the building and into the night.

* * *

He's out there.

Blacque looked up from the bare wood of his kitchen table. The wolf whispered to him gently, urging him to get up, to shift and run with Bleu as they had weeks ago. The wolf didn't have his self-imposed constraints. It wanted to be at the side of the vampire. It wanted Blacque to pull out of his funk, to live and be happy.

He finished the beer and set the empty next to the other five that were lined up in a neat row. He'd been doing this a lot lately—coming in from work, killing off a six-pack in hopes that he'd be able to sleep. Then when he did finally drift away, it was usually in his battered recliner or stretched out on the couch.

After that last time with Bleu, he'd stripped the bed, laundered it right down to the mattress pad, yet he still smelled the vampire in his room. He hadn't changed the bedding downstairs. He spent hours down there pumping iron or working his fists bloody on the bag, letting the smell of Bleu sink right into every pore.

He pushed back his chair and headed to the bathroom to piss out most of what he'd just drunk. When he returned, he jolted to a halt.

"Damn. Why does everyone just come and go around here?"

Drusilla sat at the table. She'd found the other six-pack and had started in on it. She smiled sweetly. "Your light was on. Thought I'd drop by for a visit."

He glanced at the clock. "A little late, isn't it?"

She shrugged and leaned back in her chair, surveying him openly. "I don't smell the vampire anymore. Thought I caught a whiff of him outside, but it's gone now."

Bleu was really here? His heart perked up and then slowed down again. There was no place for hope in his life, not when it came to Bleu.

"He likes to wander around at night, check things out. No harm intended."

"It's harm if he's the one who hurt you so badly."

He froze, facing her from across the room. "We got into a fistfight at the bar. It escalated. We fucked, and then we went our separate ways."

Step by step, he forced his feet to carry himself to the table, to the chair he'd been sitting on. He lowered himself and looked down at the open beer in front of him.

"You went your separate ways because Dad called you in and unloaded all that garbage on you."

"No, it ended before anything ever began. End of story, Dru."

He didn't look at her. He kept his lashes lowered, praying she didn't see what was there in his eyes. He'd seen it when he looked in the mirror—the bleak, hopeless expression of the truly brokenhearted.

"I haven't seen you like this since you were a kid. Maybe fifteen or so. You scared me then. Momma too."

He didn't answer. What could he say?

"I remember...there was a game...a home game. After it was over, I was leaving with Mom. I forgot my jacket in the bleachers, so she waited for me in the car. I was running back when I saw two people down by the locker rooms. It was dark, but I could tell... I saw it was a couple of guys. They were...they were making out. I thought it was pretty funny—"

"Till you realized who it was." His voice was harsh and raspy.

"Yeah."

"You told Mom?"

She shook her head. "No. I figured it was your issue. I thought..." She let out a big sigh. "Look, I've been with girls. Usually just silly stuff, and almost always another pack member. We're too sexual not to blow off steam. It happens, and you move on. But I watched you afterward, and I could tell you were really sad. Like you are now."

He reached up and rubbed his face, then pinched the bridge of his nose.

"Mom talked with me eventually. She told me you might end up being like her older brother. He never felt a mating compulsion. Not with women, anyway."

Shocked, he looked up at her. "She talked with you? About me?" More to the point—he had an uncle who was like him?

Dru flushed slightly. "How would you have dealt with it if she'd come to you back then to talk about your sexuality?"

She had a point there. "Why the hell would she talk to you about it?" He didn't know what was burning through him—rage or humiliation. Either way, he burned. His skin prickled with the need to shift and run. To run until he couldn't go on. He closed his eyes, covering them with his hand.

Drusilla swallowed hard. She sat stiff and upright in her chair, hands folded in her lap. She looked like a schoolgirl. "She told me because I complained about you all the time. You were moody and rude. You never did your share of the chores, yet you were out all the time and you never got into trouble. She wanted me to understand and have a little compassion." She reached out and brushed the back of his hand. "She wanted me to keep an eye on you, make sure you didn't do something stupid."

"Like become an alpha. Or agree to breed."

"No. You are an alpha, and in all honesty, you probably should have offspring. Momma didn't want you to die on the vine, denying who and what you are."

He rolled his eyes. "A gay werewolf. Now just how well is that gonna play out here, Drusilla?"

"Not well." She let his hand loose and brought hers back to her lap. "Mom said… Before she died, we talked about it again. She told me the native shifters believe that when a pack grows stable, reproduction becomes less important, and that's when alternate sexuality begins to emerge. She thought maybe it was a form of population control. Or perhaps it meant the pack had evolved to the point that it wasn't so dependent on traditions that are rooted in survival. But she said it wasn't uncommon."

"Why didn't she tell me? Why, Drusilla?" He was confused, truly and genuinely distraught. If he'd known these things, life would have been different. Better, at least in terms of his self-perception.

"Would you have heard what she had to say? Or would you have been crushed that Mom thought you were gay? Honestly, when did you admit it to yourself?" She caught his hand again and held it tightly. "She told me so I could tell you when the time was right."

"And when was that to be?"

"Now. Now that you aren't denying it. Now that you've grown comfortable enough with yourself to accept that you are what you are."

His laugh was wild. "Now that I finally admit what I've been hiding from, and I want it so badly yet I've made it impossible? Now that it's too late for me?"

She didn't let go of his hand, though he pulled. He pulled until he was free, and then he shoved his chair back and backpedaled to the kitchen wall. Dru rubbed her hand and then covered her eyes, but she didn't cry. No, Drusilla was made of tougher stuff than that.

"I'd have done it, Lukas! I'd have had all the damn babies Dad wanted me to have! I knew it would be a disaster for you. I just didn't anticipate him dragging you in so deeply...making you his heir." She looked up at him. Now he saw tears, and they made him feel like hell. She was crying for him. "Why'd you have to be so damn noble?"

He was leaning against the wall, panting like he'd run miles. Slowly his mind began to process her words, and he began to calm down, bit by bit.

"Mom knew I was gay?"

"Yeah, Lukas. She knew."

"Dad?"

She shook her head. "It's so far from his nature, he just can't see it in others. And face it—you aren't really too obvious."

He shook his head, clearing all the tangled thoughts. He could hurt, he could regret, but he'd chosen a direction, and his path into the future was clear. Except for giving him the knowledge that he wasn't the only one, Drusilla's revelations really didn't change anything.

Who was he kidding? He needed time…time to think about this whole mess. Time to figure out if there was any chance for a modicum of happiness in his miserable life.

But then, his life wasn't really so miserable. Yes, he missed Bleu fiercely. His body ached with the need to touch the vampire, to feel him deep inside his body once again. Mostly he just missed him. In all honesty, he enjoyed the extra tasks the alpha had dropped in his lap. On weekends he was hauling a few of the youngsters around town to do chores for people like Mrs. Neville. On Sundays at the main house, he spent hours with Alice, going over pack history. He spent time with his father or just hung with the kids who were just as lost and sad as he and Drusilla had been when they first came to Arcada.

He enjoyed the posturing of the lieutenants and even the occasional scuffle when a male decided to test him. He was running with the pack again, turning himself over to the moon when it was full.

Just last weekend, they'd announced the first pregnancy since Dane had made the momentous decision that had changed all their lives.

Life was good, until he thought of the empty nights to come. Years—decades of the lonely nights that he faced. Sometimes during the day he paused, automatically wondering if Bleu was sleeping, if he was regaining his health. He lapsed into fantasies he had no business indulging in. He tried to lock it all away, but the pain had an evil way of slipping those bonds.

"Lukas, are you all right?"

Drusilla was looking at him anxiously. He took a deep breath, gathering his self-control, wrapping it around him like armor.

"I'll be fine. In a way, it's good to hear it."

"A little too late for you and Bleu." She sounded truly regretful. Blacque realized that if he decided to renounce it all, to throw everything away for Bleu, Drusilla would stand behind him. It firmed his resolve.

"It never would have worked out for us. Vampire and werewolf—not gonna happen. One of us would end up killing the other."

She stared at him as though she didn't believe him but kept her opinion to herself. "I'm sorry this was so hard on you."

"My whole life has been hard, Dru. This…this makes it a little easier." She looked unconvinced. "Honest. When I get a little time, I'll go to Oregon and visit Uncle James."

"How'd you know it was him and not Jesse or Matt?"

He paused, running her question through his head. "I don't know. It just seems…" He called up memories of his uncle. The man was big and brawny, as he worked in construction. Blacque recalled him as a quiet man—always kind but rarely talkative. He was serene.

He looked at Drusilla and shrugged. He wasn't sure how he'd known it was James.

Blacque glanced at the clock as he followed her outside. If he hurried, he could make it to the Roadhouse well before closing. He didn't want to hang around the house tonight, wallowing in memories and regrets and amorphous fears of the future. He wanted to be someplace loud and rowdy. Someplace he could lose himself for a while.

When the taillights of his sister's car faded in the distance, he dug into his pockets, checked his wallet and keys, and then climbed into his truck.

He just didn't want to be alone tonight.

Chapter Sixteen

The parking lot was full, and the music seeped from the building, spiking when the door swung open. Blacque stood next to his truck, scanning the parking lot, looking for a big black Harley Davidson. There were several, all parked in a row next to the building. None of them were Bleu's. He felt a quiver of disappointment combined with a wash of relief. He knew this place was on Bleu's regular route, but he went to other places too.

His sharp ears caught the sounds of sex; someone was around the corner in the same spot he and Bleu had come together for the first time. He felt a pull of nostalgia and wanted to return to the darkness, to lean back into the bent corrugated metal and let the memory of that night wash over him.

He smelled the wet heat of a woman and the musky release of a man, and then they laughed together, slightly drunk and completely satisfied. He kept to the shadows until they emerged and returned to the bar. Even though he'd come to a place overflowing with people of all sorts, he felt separate and alone.

"Fuck." He shook off the self-pity and pushed his way through the door, letting the smell of bodies, booze, and sawdust smack him in the face. There was a fenced-in smoking area outside. Every time the door to the patio opened, smoke rolled in on the chilly night air. He bypassed the tables and booths and took a seat at the bar, then gestured to the barmaid. It was the same young woman from the night he and Bleu had their argument. She plunked a sweaty bottle in front of him, eyeing him mistrustfully. He gave her what he hoped was a reassuring smile and twisted off the cap.

The music changed from honky-tonk to Stevie Ray Vaughan, which made him think of Bleu. What kind of music did the vampire like? He never really wondered about it before. His knowledge of Bleu's life was spotty at best. He was French, had lived in the United States for nearly a century, and while he was from an upper-class, well-to-do family, preferred to make his living using his hands.

He liked to be on top. He liked it when Blacque bit down gently on his nipples and traced his navel with his tongue. He loved the clinking sound that Blacque's piercings made when he fucked his ass.

This wasn't doing any good.

He turned from the bar and speculatively surveyed the roomful of men and women. No matter where his gaze settled, it always moved on, unsatisfied. A pair of laughing men hoisted a pretty blonde onto a table, where she shimmied and swayed and lost her balance, then fell into their arms. He smiled, took a drink, and then froze.

He wasn't sure how he missed the scent, but there was Sean Mallory, huddled in the corner of a booth, engaged in discussion with a woman Blacque had never seen before. They leaned close, hands roaming, the occasional kiss exchanged. He turned away, anger spreading through his gut. He had to fight down the need to get up, take the man by the scruff, and toss him outside. Idiot had a wife and children. No wonder he couldn't make his fucking mortgage!

Heart pounding, he faced the other direction, only to sway in shock as a familiar long, lean figure slipped from the front door. How in God's name had he managed to miss Bleu as well? All thoughts of Mallory vanished as he stood, then dropped a ten on the bar. He sat back down and finished his beer.

Following the vampire would be sheer idiocy. Complete self-destruction. Stupid.

He got up and started toward the door, his feet moving as though he had no control. He was going to regret this. Nevertheless he was unable to stop himself.

She was a sweet young thing.

Bleu hid an ironic smile. She was years older than he'd been when Yves had deprived him of death. But still, her skin was smooth, and her hair felt long and silky as he fisted it, smiling down into her pretty brown eyes.

"What do you want me to do?"

She giggled, hooking one leg up over his hip, drawing him closer. "I want what you brought me out here for, baby." She ground her mound against his cock, bringing it to reluctant erection.

He stroked the soft skin of her cheek and smiled into her eyes. "Whatever it is you want, that's what I'll give you." Immediately she lapsed into her own version of bliss, allowing Bleu to find her vein, hovering over her to feed. He studied her for a moment, watching her moan in pleasure, her hips grinding air. Her arousal scented the air, and he was tempted...so very tempted.

She fell back against the wall, framed by the outline of the indentation Blacque had left in the corrugated metal, and temptation fled. It wasn't a matter of fidelity. No, it was simply a lack of desire. He just didn't want to take from yet another anonymous human. But he needed to feed—that was simply not an option.

"Oh Blacque. What have you done to me?"

He leaned in and made the wound, then drank deeply as the girl bucked and thrust, her hands digging into his back. The need to drink blinded him, and he bent to catch the drops before they reached the collar of her shirt.

"What have I done to you?"

He thought his heart would cease to beat. He swallowed, automatically willing the punctures in the woman's neck to close. "Go back to the bar, darling. You had a wonderful fling tonight. He was a stranger... He looked like..." Bleu drew a blank. "He looked like Kenny Chesney."

She smiled and giggled, pulling away from the wall and walking unsteadily back into the bar.

"Kenny Chesney?" Blacque was behind him, just inches from his body.

"She kept putting his songs on the jukebox. She thinks he's cute." He didn't turn to look; it was enough to feel his warmth, to indulge in his scent.

"To each his own, I guess."

Bleu closed his eyes and soaked up Blacque's presence.

"You didn't fuck her." He was close enough that Bleu felt the whisper of his breath on the back of his neck.

"My heart wasn't in it."

"Oh."

Taciturn as usual. Bleu smiled. "You sound relieved."

"Not used to feeling jealous. I was near to hurting the both of you." He crowded closer to Bleu, pushing him against to the wall. A burly arm came around and looped Bleu's waist. It wasn't an embrace...not really. It felt like heaven after so many weeks of craving his touch. With a groan of frustration, Bleu let his head fall backward and rest on the wolf's broad shoulder.

"I *miss* you, Lukas."

Blacque's head came forward. He nuzzled Bleu's hair, and his arm tightened slightly.

"Same here."

They were close enough that Bleu felt the swelling of Blacque's erection grinding into his ass. He was hard as well. Somehow that wasn't important. The needs of his body had been eclipsed by the needs of his heart. He started to speak, to say the words, but then stopped the impulse. This was a moment...just a stolen moment. Détente.

It changed nothing.

Blacque kissed his ear, then buried his face into the bend of Bleu's neck and inhaled deeply. Without another word, he let loose and stepped away to fade into the night. Bleu remained where he was, leaning into the indent in the metal wall of the bar. He heard the sound of Blacque's truck start, heard the crunch of gravel and the whine of tires as he sped down the freeway.

He laid his cheek against the frigid wall and felt the heat of Blacque's body slowly fade from his back, and then he turned to stare out into the night. The bushes that bordered the parking lot rustled as a couple sought solitude. He heard the muffled groan of a woman and the whisper of clothing as it was discarded. Moments later, he caught the scent of arousal and semen spilling on the dirt

That's when the realization hit Bleu. His need wasn't for blood or sex or even companionship. His need was for his soul mate—the person who justified his very long existence.

Lukas Blacque.

He might not ever have the big wolf again, but he'd never be able to leave him either. He turned and looked out into the night, wondering if this was some sort of karmic retribution for cheating on Stella. He'd tried to take advantage of Lukas Blacque and had fallen for him instead. Bleu laughed and pushed away from the building, then fished for the keys to his bike from his pocket. Something cold kissed his cheek, and Bleu looked up at the sky. Snow swirled and danced through the beams of light that illuminated the parking lot.

Time to stop feeling sorry for himself and get his shit together.

* * *

Never in his life had Blacque come so close to hurting a human—a female at that.

When he saw her in Bleu's arms, saw their bodies undulate against each other's, he'd assumed the worst until he realized their clothing was still in place. She was making love with the air and Bleu's glamour. He'd stood watching as Bleu murmured into her ear, glazing her mind with pretty promises and glittering temptation.

To touch him again! His body ached with a need he had no rational explanation for. His skin burned to touch. He couldn't ignore that need. His wolf had agreed, sighing in happiness as he'd slipped his arm around Bleu and held him close. If he'd looked Bleu in the face, he'd have lost all his resolve. He'd have begged him to forget, to forgive, and take him back. If he'd looked into Bleu's eyes, he'd have had to kiss him. From there, the outcome would have been inevitable.

He steered the truck toward home, briefly considering going into the shop and working some more on the puzzles of the pack finances. If he was there, he might intercept Bleu on his way in. He gritted his teeth and kept driving, blinking as the snow skimmed through his headlights. He glanced down at the cell phone that Drusilla had forced on him. He carried the damn thing but rarely turned it on. With a sigh, he hit the Power button, noting that there were messages waiting.

Well, they could keep waiting; he was driving. He snapped it closed and turned onto the two-lane highway that led into Arcada. The pack finances were as he'd expected—funds were drawn by Dane, Michella, or Mallory. There were disbursements for school expenses and the occasional mortgage assist for families who were in difficulty. There was a leak, and as he looked objectively at the various accounts and businesses, Blacque was beginning to see a pattern. That pattern made him feel slightly ill.

His truck bumped onto the dirt road that led to his house. He steered carefully, as the snow had settled a couple of inches deep now, obscuring the driveway. As he coasted to a stop, his headlights illuminated a figure lounging on his porch.

He sighed. Blacque had the feeling that peace was a thing of the past. Instead of getting out of the truck, he checked his messages. Most were routine, but one text made him pause.

Tomorrow during the pack run. J.

So the plan to ambush him was going forward. He grinned. They could just bring it on. In fact, he'd take it to them.

He stepped out of the truck, his breath fogging the air, powdery snow crunching beneath his boots.

"So did you ever you manage to meet up with Bleu?" He approached casually, not allowing his stance to show his caution. She seemed pretty benevolent, but April was a vampire, and though he might be lusting after one, vamps weren't all warm and fuzzy.

She was sitting on the steps, her back to the large column, her booted feet stretched out across the stair. Snow frosted her black clothing and dark hair. Her smile seemed friendly enough. She'd left no footsteps in the snow. He shivered, but it wasn't from the cold.

"As a matter of fact, I did. You did too."

He stepped over her legs and opened the unlocked door. "Do I need to invite you in?"

She laughed. "That's an old-world myth that hung on." She preceded him into the house. "It was rooted in the idea that if evil was to enter your soul—or your home—it was only because you invited it in."

"Makes sense." He headed into the kitchen, wincing as he saw the time. Well, it was Saturday morning. He could sleep late if he needed to. "Can I get you anything? Bleu likes—liked—hot chocolate."

"Funny. So do I."

He glanced at her, and she was smiling, just slightly.

"Do you mean him harm?"

"No, Blacque, I mean him no harm. Unfortunately I might have led someone to him who *does* mean him harm."

He growled, feeling hackles rise on his neck.

"Whoa! Not on purpose. Honest!"

He backed off only slightly.

"Look, you dumped him, so I don't understand the attitude."

The growl died away. "That's true, but it doesn't mean I don't care." He turned to the refrigerator and took out the milk, then poured it into a small saucepan. He set out cups and waited for the milk to heat. "Explain."

"It's a long story. First off, do you realize just how close to fading Bleu is?" She slipped into a chair at the table. In the warm light of the kitchen, he once again noted that she was unusually beautiful. The severity of her hairstyle suited her, revealing sculpted cheekbones and full lips. Her eyes were clear blue, surrounded by heavy lashes. She was bare of makeup and clearly didn't put herself out to appear seductive, as so many vampire females did.

She reminded him of…Bleu.

"Fading?" He busied himself with the chocolate and milk. He tried to ignore the slight trembling of his hands.

"Slow death. Sometimes it's caused by starvation, sometimes illness or age. While we are no longer human, we aren't dead. Our bodies are surprisingly fragile."

Fading. The idea made his gut tighten, yet it was apt. For the past few years he'd watched Bleu fade from the vibrant hunter who had moved into Arcada to the frail man he'd fallen hard for.

He turned to face her. "He was ill, but he's better. I can see it in his face. He's able to hunt. I…" He trailed off, embarrassed to finish the thought.

"You fed him."

He nodded.

She sighed. "The damage is extensive, Blacque. It took years to get this bad, and it'll take years for him to fully recover. Even so, he's pretty old and still has a lot of juice. I wouldn't want to take him on."

"How do you know this?" He set the cup in front of her and sat at the other side of the table. Oddly this was how he and Drusilla had faced off just the day before.

She shook her head. "You can smell illness and fear in others, right?" She looked at him and continued. "I guess we can sense vitality in other vamps. It's like he's a big battery, only he's been drained. I need to know if you have any idea what's behind it."

"Why? Why do you care, and why should I trust you?"

"He's kin."

Kin? Was she from the same maker? He studied her face, and then saw it. Kin, as in family. She was a relative. Blacque felt the blood leech from his face.

"Does he...did he know?"

"He does now." She sipped her hot chocolate, toying with it much the same way Bleu tended to. "I'm his great-granddaughter. Which brings me to the cluster fuck I just might have brought to this town." She took a deep breath, inhaling the scent of the chocolate. "Has he told you about his maker?"

"Yves? A bit. Not much." He wrapped his hands around the warmth of the cup. Cold was beginning to wrap around the house, and he hadn't started a fire. He got up and raised the thermostat, then returned to the table.

"Well, ole Yves is crazy as a bug. Loony. From what he told me, Bleu began to figure it out just before he was turned—against his will, incidentally."

"He told me Yves did it to save him."

"Yes, well, sometimes it's better to die when it's your time. Oliver went through the horror of one of the most brutal wars in history. He saw death at its most grisly and then was burned by mustard gas. He earned the peace of death. If Yves had been rational, he'd never have put Bleu through the change. It's amazing he wasn't a complete rogue. And it might be the root of whatever's going wrong with him now."

"He dreams. They're so bad that he physically manifests the burns from the gas."

She let out a puff of breath and buried her face in her hands. "God. To have to relive that."

"He often stays awake during the day. He can't move or even speak. He's just trapped there, awake and unmoving for hours. I thought... I gave him some relief."

When she looked up, her eyes were reddened. "I'm sure you did. I'm sure the few days that you fed him were good too."

"But not enough."

"Far from it."

"But you're here now. You'll take care of him, since I can't."

She pushed back the chair and paced. "That's not the issue, Blacque. I'm a vampire. I shouldn't give a shit about another vamp. We aren't clannish like wolves."

"But you care." He watched her, his heart beating so rapidly that he thought he'd have a heart attack. "And you'll take care of him."

She turned to face him. "Blacque, his maker—our maker—is insane. He has power over us. He created me to try to lure Bleu back to him, but I got away. He's offering rewards. Yves has hunters looking for him. How likely do you think it is that Yves is having me watched? I rode into town and walked straight up to his lair. Do you understand?"

He tried to speak, but nothing came out. Blacque rose to his feet and then sat back down. "Arcada... The town will protect him. If someone attacks..."

"I know, but Bleu doesn't stay inside the city limits. He can't. He has to hunt sometime."

"I guard him during the days, but I can't take care of him at night. I can't feed him, and I can't be his lover, April. Not anymore."

She whirled away, anger and frustration radiating from her very essence. He could taste it in the air.

"Do you understand that Yves doesn't want his death? Not yet, anyway." Her voice was harsh and faint. "I don't scar. I can't show you what he's capable of. But I can tell you." She turned to face him. "Bleeding out isn't a bad way to die, but Yves didn't want me to die that way. He didn't want me to fade peacefully. He wanted me to taste pain, fear." She lifted up her T-shirt, displaying a flat, muscular belly.

"He gutted me. He ripped me open with his bare hands and gutted me. After that, he fed and then turned me. I felt my body knit back together, and it hurt. You can't imagine how it hurt."

Blacque said nothing in spite of his sympathy for her pain. He let her talk and wondered if she'd ever told anyone about this before.

"He then dragged me away and kept me locked up, teaching me to be a vampire according to his rules. Everything he did was motivated by his obsession with Bleu. One moment he wanted to kill him, to tear him apart with his bare teeth. The next, he was so in love, so desperate to find him again that he grieved. Do you understand how much danger my great-grandfather faces if Yves finally catches him?"

Blacque nodded. Every instinct he had was screaming to find Bleu—to find him and protect him. He fought the shift that threatened, and allowed his hands to lengthen into razor-tipped paws. His breathing came hard, and he fought down panic. When he could think clearly again, he spoke.

"I have few allies in my pack, but there are some who will do my bidding." Would they shadow a vampire for him? "They will alert me if there is any danger to Bleu." If he needed to use brute force to control them, so be it.

She relaxed a bit. "I'm going to follow him too, though I told him I didn't want to hunt in his territory. I don't think it'll be too odd if I hang around with him. Family and all." Her smile was forced.

"Do you have someplace to stay tomorrow? I'll be at the shop all day working. I'll be gone most of the night, though. It's the full moon. We'll have a pack run."

"I've got a place. Until I know if he's in danger or not, I'll be in town. If Yves doesn't spot him here, I'll rabbit out of the area. He'll follow me and not look where I've been."

"Are you sure he's following you?"

"Yeah. No obvious signs, but I think it's a team of hunters. It's just a feeling, you know? I'm always looking over my shoulder."

She returned to the table and sat down to sip her cooling hot chocolate. "It's getting really old. Even though I got away from him ages ago, Yves still pulls my strings."

"It sounds like Yves needs to die permanently."

She lifted her cup to his and clinked the edges together. "I'll drink to that."

Chapter Seventeen

The light of the full moon cut across the sloping lawns of the alpha's house. Pack members milled around, forming tight circles and then breaking away to reform in new clusters. Even if he hadn't got Jeremy's warning, Blacque would have known something was up.

"The natives are restless tonight." Dane stood beside Blacque, looking out the kitchen window at the activity outside.

"You have any clue what's up?" Drusilla moved to his side and stood between her father and brother.

Blacque grinned. The moon was already pulling the beast out of his soul. "Challenge, I suppose. Jeremy tipped me off."

"Challenge? I thought everyone had made peace with this." Drusilla turned to him. Her frown hid a trace of fear on her face. "Dad, can't you get this under control?"

"Looks like your brother knows more about it than I do." Dane looked at Blacque in question.

"According to Jeremy, there's a group that's going to lure me outside of Arcada tonight. They're planning to take me on as a group. I guess they want to get it over with all at once." He couldn't help the smile that settled on his face. His wolf was hungry for blood tonight. It wanted sex, but as that wasn't on the menu, it would take blood instead.

"You don't look upset." Dru eyed him speculatively. In spite of her air of casual cynicism, he knew she was worried.

He threw an arm over her shoulder. "It's been coming. I'm ready for it."

"You sure?" Dane looked concerned. As alpha, he monitored challenges but couldn't show favoritism, even toward his eldest son. "You have a second?"

"Don't know. We'll see how everything shakes down once the fighting starts." He paced to the table and sat, fingers resting gently on the file he'd brought for his father. The contents were explosive, but not nearly as volatile as what he was about to disclose. Without comment, Dru and Dane joined him at the table. Absently he noted he was in the chair his father usually occupied when they had their little family gatherings. He swallowed.

"I've got to do it on my own tonight. No help from anyone." He sent a sharp glance at his sister. "That means you."

She licked her lips nervously but didn't protest.

"Why? Why are you doing it like this?" Dane's dark eyes were steady and cool as he studied Lukas.

"There has to be no doubt in anyone's mind that I can take them and beat them. I have to establish complete and total dominance tonight." He felt surprisingly calm, but then, he was in the eye of the storm. Things would be getting very crazy very soon.

Dane leaned back and folded his arms over his brawny chest. He was dressed similar to Blacque tonight—old jeans and a T-shirt. "Talk to me, Lukas. You're leading up to something big and bad."

"You know Oliver Bleu?"

"The vamp? Yeah, you know I know Bleu." His father's face now had an expression of wary interest.

"He's got family. She's not just vampire kin, but blood related—his great-granddaughter." He watched as realization settled over Dane's face.

"The new vampire I scented a while back."

"Yeah. It seems Bleu's maker is a bit of a nutcase. He turned April in order to draw Bleu out of hiding. That didn't work, so he's been hunting him for years. April didn't know he was here, and she's afraid Yves has trackers on her."

"So she says." Dru's eyes were bright with suspicion. "Vampires aren't known for their family ties, Lukas."

He shrugged. "I believe her. And she asked for help with keeping an eye out for him. I want to have a couple of wolves that'll be willing to watch over him when he leaves the town to hunt."

Dane sighed gustily. "The pack is under no obligation to vampires, Lukas. Doesn't matter if they're neighbors or even friends. You don't want to drag us into their garbage. It's too dangerous."

Blacque glanced at Dru. She was studying the surface of the old table, avoiding his gaze. He looked back at his father.

"I told you I gave up someone in order to take my place in the pack."

Dane looked up abruptly, the shock clearly written in his face. "Bleu? You were involved with a vampire?"

"Yeah. I was involved with Bleu. And I gave him up. For you and the pack." He swallowed hard and continued. "He cares for me. I hurt him, and I owe him."

Drusilla reached out and clasped his hand. He squeezed hers and gave her a slight smile.

"It wasn't just a fling? A dominance thing?"

"Dad, I've known him for years. The...relationship part ended before it really had a chance to start. But no, it wasn't a fling. My feelings for him..." He crushed back his emotions, taking time to get himself under control. "Love." He nodded. That was it. Love. "Not just that either. You should know... I've never been interested in women. Ever. I tried for a while. It just never worked for me."

Dane had gone pale. Blacque didn't blame him—he'd just dropped a couple of major bombs on his head. He was feeling a bit overwhelmed himself.

"You're telling me you're gay."

"Yeah, guess that's what I'm saying." He cleared his throat and looked directly at his father. "I can't do this unless all the cards are on the table. You...the pack...you all deserve to know. And I deserve to live without lying about who I am."

Dane pushed back his chair, stood, and paced for a moment, finally walking to the sink to fill a glass with water. He leaned against the counter as he sipped from the glass, studying his children. When he finished, he carefully set the glass down and returned to the table. He looked from Blacque to Dru.

"You have any major revelations you want to share tonight? This would be the time to do it." His voice sounded slightly thick, but Blacque didn't sense any anger.

She smiled and shook her head.

"You knew?"

"Yeah. Mom and I talked about it before she died. She wanted me to know that it was a possibility so that if Lukas had problems, I could be there for him."

"Shit." He seemed deflated, running his hand through his hair and then pinching the bridge of his nose. "A gay werewolf. I thought your uncle was the only one."

Dru sat up a little straighter. "You know about Uncle James? You two are pretty tight, aren't you?"

"Yeah, we're close. He never tried to hide it from me. Or from anyone." He suddenly looked up and gazed from one to the other. "He's one of the main betas in his pack. I remember he had to fight hard for his position. He told me if he didn't bust everyone's ass at least once, they'd give him no peace. Once he settled in, he was rarely challenged." He nodded. "Good strategy, Lukas. You're heading them off. You beat them down before you tell them. Tonight, you don't hold back. If you need to inflict injury, you do it. We've got a pack meeting tomorrow. You do what you have to do tonight, then tomorrow, pick a small squad to put on the vampire. I'll back you on it. I don't want to, but I guess I owe you that much."

Blacque nearly wilted in relief. That had gone much, much better than expected. His father didn't hate him. The pack would follow the lead of the alpha. Most of them, anyway. He swallowed. "I'm coming out to the pack too. If we're getting involved in something dangerous, they need to have the whole story."

"It won't be easy, Lukas. You were already fighting an uphill battle. If you out yourself to the pack…"

Dane studied his face for a long moment. Obviously he saw what he needed to see. "You make me proud. Both of you. But

Lukas, you've made a difficult choice. This won't make your life any easier."

"I know."

"It won't make your life easier, but it will make your heart happier. You can't live a full life if you're hiding who you really are." He reached out and stroked a hand down Blacque's cheek in an unexpected, gentle caress. "You go and do what you have to do."

Blacque blinked rapidly, pushing back that wave of emotion again. It had been years since he'd felt the need to cry. *Years.* Now it seemed he was crying all the time. He looked at his father for a long, painful moment and then covered his eyes with his hand. Once he'd got himself under control, he gestured to the folder.

"I hate to bring this up, especially after all the stuff I've dumped on you tonight. You need to read it."

Dane opened the folder and scanned the report. He flipped through the paperwork Blacque had enclosed to support his findings. Dane's lips thinned in anger. His anger literally crackled in the air, lashing uncomfortably against the skin of Blacque's bare arms. Dane rarely unleashed his power, but when he did, it was a fearsome thing.

"You're sure of this?" He pushed the folder to Drusilla, who frowned as she read the report. In just seconds, her anger was bubbling in the air as well. Blacque studied her for a moment, surprised to discover that she had that sort of power as well. Right then Blacque knew who would eventually become his second in command.

"Yes, I'm sure. There was skimming from several of the businesses, but mostly from the main pack account. I'm sorry."

He did feel bad for his father; betrayal by someone you trust was a painful experience.

"I'll deal with this after the run. We'll bring it to the pack tomorrow."

He knew by Dane's tone he'd been dismissed. Blacque wasn't certain he'd ever seen his father this angry before. It was quiet, intense, and lethal. He was glad it wasn't directed at him.

He exchanged glances with Drusilla. Compared to his reaction to the audits, it seemed Dane was going to adjust to Blacque's sexuality with ease. He got up and started for the door, his sister close on his heels.

"You two…"

They halted and looked back at their father. He looked severe and stern and just a little bit lonely there at the big table.

"I still expect grandchildren."

"But—"

"Lots of them. I don't care how you manage it, Lukas, just get it figured out. Soon."

"Fuck!"

He stomped out onto the porch and slammed the door. Next to him, Drusilla chuckled, and he looked back at the kitchen door. Inside he heard the unmistakable sound of his father's gentle laughter. He shook his head in confusion. He'd never figure out the alpha's sense of humor.

* * *

Running felt good tonight.

He crashed through a snowbank and startled rabbits from their late-night foraging. He stretched his legs and enjoyed the rush of blood through his long, muscular body.

The pack had stayed in a tight group tonight. Following his nose rather than the tracks in the snow, he caught scents layered over other scents. He had a general idea of where they were luring him, so he turned on the speed, overtaking and passing them in the darkness. When he arrived at a large open meadow, he shifted and stood tall and naked in the snow, waiting for his challengers.

They arrived soon enough, silently surrounding him, dark shadows against the luminescent white of the snow. Blacque kept his eyes shifted to their animal nature, using the wolf's night vision to track his opponents.

The gold of his piercings glinted in the moonlight, and they grew chilled and painful in his skin, raising his awareness just a bit more. A group of four moved in and circled him like ghosts. Several other pack members lingered at the perimeter of the meadow, huddling in small groups. Their distress was palpable.

He spotted Michella to his left. She was pale gray, long, and lanky. She and Mallory policed the grounds, keeping other wolves at bay.

"Lukas Blacque. You have been challenged by these wolves. Do you accept?" Michella had shifted back to human. She stood tall and naked and full of bitter contempt for him. Mallory shifted as well. He tossed Blacque an apologetic smile.

"Four to one doesn't seem fair, Michella." He looked at the other beta, but she simply glared, waiting for Blacque's answer.

"I accept."

He didn't bother to shift. Blacque was in this for the impact tonight. He let his hands lengthen into wicked, deadly claws and bent at the knee, relaxed and easy. The four wolves circled him silently, and he went still, letting all his senses tell him their intent. They were young and fairly inexperienced. Blacque had never been one to fight, but he'd been in his share of bar brawls, where he had to hold back rather than let loose.

When one broke from the formation, he stepped to the side, claws slashing through the thick coat of the young wolf. The scent of blood broke their discipline; they all attacked at once, leaping at Blacque in wild abandon. He ducked, taking a heavy body to his gut, another on his shoulders. Before they were able to sink sharp teeth into his skin, Blacque tore through fur and flesh. He grappled with one and kicked at another, doing his best to guard his belly from the third.

One staggered, shrieking as Blacque slashed through the Achilles tendons of his hind legs. A crippling blow—a deathblow in the wild—but the pup would recover by the time he had to be back at work on Monday. Blacque let talonlike claws slip out from his feet and tore down low even as he grappled heavy jaws away from his throat. In just moments, all four young males lay at his feet, panting and bleeding.

He watched as they crawled away, leaving tracks of blood in the torn-up snow.

Expectantly he looked at the circle of wolves, and he smiled savagely as a large figure broke from the pack. Mallory stepped up, still grinning.

"Davidson challenges. Do you accept?"

"I accept." Davidson was huge as a human—a hair taller than Blacque, tough and bulky. His wolf was the same. But that bulk would slow him down. Blacque debated momentarily and then retained his human form.

When he found himself on his back with two hundred and fifty pounds of wolf on his chest, he nearly changed his mind.

He gripped the furry ruff of the wolf and rolled, then drew a knee up into the wolf's belly, never letting go, barely able to hold Davidson away from his throat. He dug in, feeling his claws sink into the thick muscles. The wolf opened its jaws wide, and frothy saliva dripped from his mouth. Blood ran down Blacque's arms. With a final burst of strength, he rolled again, brought his chest to Davidson's back, and twisted his head to bare the wolf's throat.

"Do you submit?"

The wolf thrashed futilely, growling, jaws snapping at the air. Blacque curved his claws over the shifter's jugular. "Submit or die, Davidson. I'm playing for keeps tonight!"

Abruptly the wolf went limp in his arms. Blacque let go and pushed himself up to his feet. His arms and legs trembled with stress and fatigue. His body was painted in sweat and blood. None of the blood was his.

"Next."

Three shadows broke from the darkness and approached Blacque on their bellies, stalking him with deadly intent.

Chapter Eighteen

Bleu looked down on the carnage in the meadow below and shuddered, partly in response to the cloying scent of blood, partly in reaction to what he'd just witnessed. Bodies lay scattered in the snow, some shivering and dragging themselves away, some lying still and silent. Blacque stood alone, bloody and exhausted and barely able to remain on his feet.

He dropped quietly from the tree branch he'd been standing on and started to move toward the clearing. He stopped when Drusilla stepped into his path.

"You knew I was here."

She watched him steadily, sizing him up. She was still dressed but close to feral. The blood had affected her as well.

"How did you know about the challenge?"

He shook his head and started toward the clearing. A powerful hand clasped his arm, and claws bit into his skin. Obviously he wasn't going anywhere.

"It's not over."

"He's fought everyone. Who's left?"

She nodded toward the clearing. Michella was striding toward Blacque. Mallory stood there grinning, and with a laugh, he moved in as well.

"The lieutenants? But he's all in, Drusilla." He tried to move, yet she prevented him.

"How'd you know about this? Lukas wouldn't have told you."

He turned to her and glared down into her dark eyes. "How could I not know? I heard it...smelled it miles away. I can guarantee I'm not the only predator out here tonight." He looked toward the forest. "Some of your injured might not make it home."

"That's their problem." Her voice was hard and bitter.

"Drusilla, are you all right?" A young male came into sight, a slender woman behind him. As he watched, other figures surrounded them, some in wolf form, some on two legs. They all looked at Bleu distrustfully. Some faces were familiar, others he knew by scent. He was surprised to see a few who were clearly elderly.

"I'm fine, Jeremy." She looked at the small crowd. Bleu guessed these were Blacque's supporters, or at least wolves who were neutral. "Bleu just pointed out that the blood is drawing predators. If there's anyone out there you care for, go guard them." Several of the shifters dropped away and ran within the trees. Drusilla was angry, but it seemed she cared enough to save the lives of her brother's challengers.

She turned back to him, fury sparking in her eyes. Some of the remaining wolves huddled uneasily. Clearly they felt her rage as it washed over them. However, Bleu smelled fear on her as well. She did a good job covering it.

"You shouldn't be here. This isn't for outsiders to see."

"I know." He turned away to watch the drama as it unfolded. There was nothing he could do to stop the fight, nothing he could do to help. He could only watch as Blacque faced down two of the most powerful wolves in the pack.

"Why hasn't he shifted?"

"He's proving a point to us."

He looked down at her, wanting to ask but choosing to remain silent. He felt movement in the air, and then April was next to him, staring down at the meadow. The few wolves who were still on the ground were pulling themselves away, groaning and gasping but alive.

"God, the reek of blood carried for miles." She glanced past Bleu and smiled coldly at Drusilla. "Good thing I've already fed."

Dru growled. Bleu wondered if there would be another fight for him to worry about.

"Why aren't you helping him?" Bleu couldn't help the squeamish fear that settled in his stomach.

"Bleu, you don't want to piss me off right now. I'm not real happy with you."

He looked at her in surprise. "He left me, not the other way around."

She whirled on him, fury on her face. April smoothly inserted herself between them. Her face was pale, almost serene, until she bared her fangs. He settled a hand on her shoulder and coaxed her to the side.

"You should never have started anything."

He stared at Drusilla, letting the silence stretch out between them.

"Would it have changed anything? Would it have prevented what's happening out there?"

At his side, April went stiff, and he followed her gaze back to the meadow to watch as the woman smoothly shifted into a large, powerful wolf. The man followed. He was larger than the female and slinking carefully around Blacque. Why the hell wasn't he shifting?

The pair stalked him with breathtaking precision—clearly they were a team. They worked together instinctively to move Blacque across the meadow, out of the blood, putting him on a slope. They'd have the advantage there. On two legs, Blacque's balance would be inferior to theirs. As the female struck low, the male swept to Blacque's side, going in at his hip. They pestered him, wearing him down with feints and bluffs. He appeared exhausted, and Bleu was unable to tell if the blood that smeared Blacque's body was his or that of his earlier opponents.

One of the wolves struck, and Blacque went down on one knee. A fresh wound gaped open on his side. He didn't make a sound. He moved smoothly to his feet, a fierce grin on his bloody face.

"He's good. No one's ever tested him before. I knew a few weeks back when he unleashed his power on the pack…" Dru took a deep breath, clearly torn between pride and fear for her brother.

"His power?" Bleu couldn't look away from the fight. Blacque was good, but he looked to be wearing out. How long had he been fighting? When Bleu had come upon the scene, the place was already a bloody mess.

"We all have a latent power…like…I don't know how to describe it. My father can use it to discipline others. He can force them to shift. Blacque got angry a couple months ago when Michella challenged him. He backed her down with his power and scared her pretty bad, but I guess she got over it."

Bleu winced as Lukas made a clumsy lunge forward and collapsed to his knees again.

"How far will they take this fight?"

"As far as they want. Challenges this high in the pack can end in death."

Bleu couldn't prevent the hiss that escaped. His fangs dropped, and it was only April's restraining hold on his arm that kept him from interfering.

"Have a little faith, Oliver." Her whisper was so soft, he barely heard it. All around them, the pack had gathered. Even the injured had remained behind, guarded by the wolves who were still on their feet. When Blacque went down, there was a moan of despair, a growl of anger.

"If they'd had the balls to challenge him at the start, he'd have had them."

"You know that's not how it works, Jeremy." Dru's voice was so calm, she could be watching the sunset instead of the possible death of her brother.

Blacque made his move when Mallory dived for a killing blow. He caught the big wolf by the throat and slashed with his hands. Blood sprayed over the snow, and the wolf yelped, shifting quickly to his human form. He lay on the snow, clasping his throat. He'd recover, but now Blacque had only Michella to contend with.

He crouched. All traces of fatigue had left his body. Michella was low, slinking with her belly close to the snow. As they faced off, Bleu thought of the hours Blacque spent pounding on the heavy punching bag in his basement. Suddenly his fear fled. Blacque was smart, and he was a damn sight stronger than any other wolf Bleu had met.

Michella charged him, and he struck, a brutal uppercut to her jaw, snapping her head back. Her body continued to hurtle forward and slammed into him. They rolled, and Blacque came up on top, pounding into her with powerful blows that broke bone and tore sinew. She finally went still. Bleu couldn't tell if she'd submitted to Blacque or if she was unconscious.

Blacque pulled himself upright, carefully watching his opponents. Once it was clear they were down for good, he looked toward the pack. He must have compelled them to move, because suddenly only Bleu and April remained at the edge of the forest.

A shadow moved up next to him, and a powerful male stood beside Bleu. Dane Blacque, come to witness his son's victory. He looked at the bloody meadow and sighed.

"I'm gonna need to bring in a witch." He looked up at the brilliant sky and shook his head. "No chance of rain, that's for sure. A heavy snow might help."

"You could drag in some dead animals. I scented a herd of deer a couple of miles into the forest."

Dane looked over at April as though seeing her for the first time. "You're the new one...the Honda."

She gave him a sly grin. Dane tore his gaze away from her and looked at Bleu. "This is about you." He didn't look pleased.

"No, this is about Blacque. He's not doing this for me. He's doing it because he has to." Dane wasn't listening. His gaze was once again fixed on April's lovely face. Bleu let out a low hiss. "Keep your hands off my great-granddaughter, wolf."

Dane gave him a cocky smile but turned away to look back toward the gathering. The wolves crowded tightly around

Blacque. His deep voice carried across the meadow, clear and strong.

"I didn't plan to take a place as beta, but the fact is, an opening came up. So I'm taking it." He had a foot on Mallory's arm, making sure the male didn't move. "We'll talk about this more at the meeting tomorrow. But for now, it's over. Unless anyone else wants to challenge me?" The menace was clear in his voice. No one accepted his offer.

"You all know Oliver Bleu?" He looked the pack members in the face, one at a time. "Well, he's mine. I protect him. And since he's mine, he's yours as well."

That didn't go over as well. He could literally sense the uneasiness that ran from wolf to wolf. Bleu watched Blacque's battered face, stunned by what his wolf was saying. He hadn't expected an outright declaration of ownership. He felt as if he'd been kicked in the gut and lifted into heaven in one stroke.

"Do you understand?"

"You're a faggot?" The wolf who was dumb enough to open his mouth went down to the ground with a yelp. Blacque hadn't even moved. "You want to rephrase that, Travis?" The young man writhed on the ground. "Sorry! Damn it, Lukas, let up!" After a few more seconds, Blacque relaxed, and the younger male crawled to his feet.

"Try it again, Travis." Blacque's voice was soft with menace.

"You're...gay?"

"Yeah. I'm gay." He looked the group over again. "Dane still wants grandkids from me. I'm not sure how this'll work out, but I promised him."

Bleu saw him shoot an angry look toward Dane. "Anyone else have something they want to say?" Heads shook in the negative. Michella was off to his side, squatting on her haunches. She was cradling her arm. "Michella still holds her position. Mallory...does not."

Bleu saw a woman whom he assumed was Mallory's mate kneeling on the ground next to him. She looked distressed and angry.

"What's he done, Blacque? What did he do?" She didn't question her husband's guilt.

"He needs to tell you. It isn't my place." Blacque remained upright, but Bleu sensed the weariness that radiated from him. He glanced at Dane, but the alpha remained in place. This was his son's moment.

"You all go home now. If you need care, we'll get you a ride back to the alpha's house. Go in groups. This blood is probably drawing other predators. I'll see everyone tomorrow afternoon." He dismissed them, and for a few moments, members of the pack milled about, some reaching out to touch Blacque, others throwing him confused looks. He'd managed to defuse any lingering anger and resentment.

Dane stepped out from the trees and moved to his pack members, then pointed to a large van that was parked on a nearby road. The young man Bleu recognized as Jeremy dashed off to the van, most likely to bring it closer. Bleu remained in the trees, watching as the alpha began to restore order to his pack.

With a sigh of relief, he leaned against a tree, ready to wait it out. He and Blacque had some talking to do. He wasn't leaving until they did.

"Lukas. You did good." Dane reached out and clasped Blacque's bloody arm. Blacque was tempted to scrub off the sticky stuff with snow, but he'd just hurt his skin. He'd have to wear it home. He nodded at his father, too tired to think of anything to say. "You made a real mess here."

"You told me to do damage if I needed to." He spotted Bleu up at the tree line and fought the sudden need to go to him, to let the vampire hold him and soothe his pain. He knew it wasn't time for comfort. He still had to present his best dominant face to the pack.

"I knew you'd come out on top, but I didn't think you'd break them." In spite of his words, Dane looked pleased.

Dru was suddenly at his side, stroking his arm. "Blacque, you need to get home. I swear, you had me scared to death at the end."

He snorted. He'd been scared at the end too. Mallory and Michella both were fresh and bloodthirsty. He'd only been able to take them through trickery. Once Mallory went down, Michella's focus was shot. He'd noticed in the past how closely linked they were. It was a pity to break up such an effective beta team, but it was necessary.

"So what are you going to do about Mallory?"

Dane's face grew dark with anger. "He cheated his wife. He cheated the pack. What do you think I'm going to do?"

"Shun him?" Drusilla sounded furious. No doubt if it were up to her, the punishment would be painful and long.

"Exile. He's no longer to set foot in our territory."

Which meant the wolf would have to quit his job and leave the county completely.

"I didn't have access to his personal finances, but I ran his credit. He's in debt up to his neck. His house was going to be foreclosed on. He has a second house outside of town. Mallory's been living a double life."

Dane sighed. "His wife and family don't deserve this. His idiocy will bring all kinds of grief on them."

Unlike most women in her position, Mallory's wife would land on her feet. The pack would make sure of that.

"Anyhow, I'll talk to him tomorrow before the meeting. Tell him to pack and get out." Dane started up the slope and toward where his former beta had fallen, but Mallory was gone. His trail led to the forest.

"You want me to go after him?" Blacque didn't want to hunt the wolf, but it was his battle, not Dane's. Not tonight anyway.

"No. You go home, get some rest. I'll tend to Mallory."

"I'll give you a hand with him." April was at Dane's side, smiling flirtatiously at him.

"No, you get back into Arcada. This isn't a good night to be outside the city limits." Bleu was at her shoulder, glaring at Blacque's father. Blacque looked from one to the other, and then to April's sly smile. He'd known she was going to be trouble; he simply hadn't anticipated this.

"I'll go too." Drusilla tugged at her father's arm, drawing his attention away from Bleu's great-granddaughter. Blacque suddenly had to suppress the urge to laugh. Dane and April the vampire! He shook his head, watching the three as they headed into the trees.

"He's too old for her." Bleu's anger thickened his accent.

"Bleu, she'll eat him alive. Don't worry." He started to walk, his weariness making his mind as heavy as his body. Cold began to settle into his limbs. He'd been injured many times during the challenge, and it was finally beginning to take its toll.

"So now I'm yours?" Bleu sounded peeved. Somehow Blacque knew it was an act. Bleu was pleased at being publically claimed.

"I had to put it in terms they'd understand." Blacque looked at him, peace finally settling over his soul. It felt good to have it all out in the open. No one hated him—not openly, at least. Now he could focus on the threat to Bleu. The only way he could keep the vampire safe was to keep him close. Well, it was a good excuse anyway.

"I'd say it's really the other way around. I'm yours. Tried to turn off the feelings..." He trailed off and walked faster, slipping a bit in the snow. "I can't. You fucked up my brain, I guess. Hell, maybe you fixed my brain."

"So you outed yourself for me?"

Blacque grinned and kept walking. He'd done it for himself. Bleu was just a nice side effect of the decision he'd made.

Bleu grabbed his arm. "Blacque, stop. Do you even know where you're going?"

"Don't know..." He looked around, noticing that the world was a bit hazy at the edges. "I didn't do it for you. I did it for me. I want to be part of the pack. I want my family, but I can't have either if I'm always hiding." He started walking again. "I did it for me so I can try with you. So I don't have to live the rest of my life wondering."

Bleu restrained him again, chuckling warmly. "You're heading in the wrong direction. We need to get you home. Soon." He slipped an arm around Blacque's waist, and to his amusement, Blacque felt his cock begin to lazily fill. In spite of his sore, weary body and the frigid air, the damn vampire still had that effect on him. He looked down at himself and laughed.

"Lukas, can I make a suggestion?" Bleu smiled at his amorous display. "Will you please allow your wolf to take the burden? I think he'll help you home better than I can."

"That's a good idea, Bleu." He grinned foolishly and relaxed, then dropped down to all fours. Immediately the world was clearer, and his body was warmer. He still hurt like hell, but as they entered the forest, Blacque walked as close to Bleu as he possibly could, enjoying the feel of true freedom for the first time in his memory.

Chapter Nineteen

Blacque watched the sticky blood melt away from his skin and swirl down the shower drain. He leaned heavily against the shower wall, soaking up the heat, the water, and the feel of Bleu's strong hands on his body. He was healing more slowly than usual, but given his unusual expenditure of energy and adrenaline, that didn't surprise him too much. What *did* surprise him was when Bleu had to half carry him into the bathroom and then strip and manhandle him into the steaming water, but that was a nice surprise.

He looked away from the tile floor and laid his head back against the wall, relaxing, putting himself into the vampire's capable care. He was loose, weary, and warm. When Bleu ran a soapy hand over his cock and behind his balls, he gave a drunken grin.

"I can't believe you're horny. You can barely stand on your own two feet, but there you go!"

Blacque thrust hips forward, laughing rather foolishly.

"Did you have something to drink out there?" Bleu pumped a soapy hand along Blacque's very erect shaft. "Or are you just happy to see me?"

"It's the adrenaline from fighting, I guess. And I'm happy—" He groaned as Bleu slipped a finger into his ass.

"I'd fuck you here and now, pup. But I'd feel like I'd be taking advantage of you." Bleu leaned in and kissed him slowly, letting their lips slide together. "It's been far too long."

"Do it!" Blacque's laughter had faded away, and he was suddenly stone-cold sober. He blinked rapidly, dislodging the beads of water on his eyelashes. For the first time that night, he looked up at Bleu, suddenly aware that they were together and that he'd just announced to the entire pack the vampire was his. Bleu backed away slightly and gazed into his eyes. He was so beautiful. Blacque had to swallow hard before he spoke.

"You look good." And he did. His skin was smooth; his color was warm. Blacque reached up and stroked Bleu's face, letting his gaze wander. His callous fingers strayed over silken skin, tracing the angles of Bleu's cheekbones. He closed his eyes as he shuddered in reaction to the arousal that washed through his body. He indulged in a kiss, a heated caress, and the knowledge that he'd no longer be lonely. Blacque opened his eyes and looked at his vampire's full, beautiful lips, his elegant nose. He ended up gazing into those deep blue eyes. His thick black hair was slicked back from his high forehead. Blacque's cock was hard and brushing against Bleu's erect shaft, but Blacque ignored his arousal. He was desperate to touch and to hold, knowing that this time he didn't have to hide. He knew there was a future for them.

"You gave me a gift, Lukas. I wanted to stay alive long enough to pay you back."

Blacque groaned and then leaned forward to rest his head against Bleu's shoulder. When the vampire's strong arms came around him, he melted. He reached around Bleu's waist and held him tight. "I was frightened. I was afraid you'd let yourself go."

Bleu ran his hands over Blacque's back, stroking gently. "Oddly my insomnia returned. But in the past couple of weeks, it's faded. The dreams have let up as well. I can't remember ever being so desperately unhappy, yet with the dreams gone, I've felt strangely at peace." Bleu propped his chin on Blacque's head. "Life goes on, though I'd much rather it go on with you."

"Yeah. Me too."

Bleu laughed, and Blacque looked up quizzically. "You are the master of the understatement, pup."

"And you talk too much." Heat rose in his body, and now he *wanted*. He growled and thrust his hips into Bleu's, feeling their cocks slide together. Though he'd never been with another man, Blacque suspected there was no one in the world more perfectly suited to him.

"As usual, your actions speak much louder than words." Bleu leaned in and ran the tip of his tongue along Blacque's jaw, ending with a slight nip on the throat. Suddenly Bleu was the aggressor, and Blacque shivered with anticipation.

"Do you need to feed?" Blacque's cock hardened even more at the idea.

"Strangely enough, no, I don't." He smiled. A sultry, sensual expression lit in his eyes. "But I will. I always crave you." He pressed Blacque into the tiled wall, kissed his mouth, then finally slipped his tongue between Blacque's lips. He plundered, he claimed, and he made sure Blacque was breathless with need before breaking the kiss. He leaned in closer and nipped Blacque's earlobe.

"Turn around, pup. I'm going to fuck you now."

His head spun. Bleu reached up to change the angle of the spray and turned it into a warm mist that caressed their bodies.

He ran his hands down the wolf's massive arms, grinning as his palms skated over bulging muscles. *Mine.* The knowledge raced through him like fire, heating his very blood.

"Arms up over your head, and don't let them down until I tell you."

Obediently Blacque turned and stretched his arms high up on the wall. Bleu stepped back just a bit, greedily surveying the long, powerful lines of the wolf's back, following his spine down to his muscular ass and legs. He reached out and stroked along Blacque's lower back, just above the swell of his buttocks.

"You had more work done." The vines twisted down to his hips and ass. It was still new and slightly raised.

"I was hurting."

The tattooing was a form of self-mutilation. Bleu hadn't really understood that before. Without warning, his eyes burned with tears. He hadn't really understood how hard this experience had been for Blacque. When he spoke, his voice was a hoarse whisper.

"I don't want you to get any more tattoos. No more piercings either. I don't want you to hurt anymore."

Blacque had been watching him over his shoulder, but now he turned away and pressed his forehead to the wet tile.

"I knew that I'd hurt you. I'm so sorry, Bleu."

"No blame in this, pup. You did what you thought was right. I should never have seduced you in the first place. Not for the reasons that I did." He leaned in and kissed Blacque's neck right were it curved into the shoulder. He was exquisite.

"What reasons?"

"I wanted you. I wanted your blood, and I wanted your body. I'd wanted you for years, and when the chance finally presented itself, I took it without thinking about the consequences." He reached around and tugged on the golden bars in Blacque's nipples. "I was stupid enough to underestimate your sense of responsibility. I certainly didn't expect to fall in love with you."

Blacque quaked under his hands. He shivered more as Bleu's hands drifted lower and plucked at the golden rings piercing his sac.

"Fear. I was afraid, Bleu. That's all."

He pulled at the wolf's balls while running a finger along the tender spot behind them. Blacque gasped, and he smiled. His own cock was hard and aching, but he owed this to the wolf. He owed him so much. Bleu palmed his ass, kneading the firm muscles there, then slipped the tips of his fingers between his cheeks.

"Are you afraid *now*, Lukas?" He pressed lightly on the star of his opening and then retreated. He moved his hand away and leaned into Blacque's powerful body. "Are you afraid?"

"Hell yes!" Blacque's voice was hoarse...full of need and heat. "I've never been in love before, Bleu. I'm scared as shit."

"You love me?" He wrapped his arms around Blacque's torso and held him tightly. How long had it been since he'd been loved? Felt love? For the first time in nearly a century, Bleu felt he was more than just a predator. He belonged to someone. He buried his face in Blacque's broad shoulder, letting the wolf support his weight for just a moment.

"Yeah, I do." Blacque twisted slightly and looked into at Bleu's face. "Will you just fuck me now?" He gave that tiny smile, and everything fell into place. They were both right where they belonged.

* * *

They were downstairs. Blacque looked around the dimly lit room. He'd been down here every day since Bleu had left and had grown to hate the space. Now it was a good place again. He'd finally broken down and laundered the bedding, taking away the last vestige of Bleu's presence. Now he was back. Bleu was reclining on the bed, leaning on his elbows. He was grinning at his handiwork.

Blacque looked up at his hands, which were bound to the top of the punching bag. His naked body was pressed into the heavy leather. Shit. From now on, every time he looked at that bag, he'd get a hard-on. He sighed and rested his cheek against the leather.

When Bleu's hand smacked his ass, he jumped. He hadn't heard him approach.

"You know, Bleu, we were in a perfectly good shower…nice and warm…" He looked over his shoulder, staggering a bit when the bag shifted as well. He'd have to work to keep his balance.

"I've been fantasizing about this for a while."

He could hear the smile in Bleu's silky voice, and it excited him. He smiled back. He tugged at the bonds, feeling deliciously powerless.

"All stretched out like that, you are so fucking beautiful." He was close, so close that his breath caressed Blacque's shoulder. He went tense, waiting for the bite, but it didn't come. Instead Bleu reached up and pulled the loose end of the rope. Blacque's arms dropped, and he shook them, bringing circulation back to his fingers.

"Reach around the bag…like you're hugging it."

He followed Bleu's instructions, feeling the rope loop around his wrists. He was still bound but more comfortable. He sighed when Bleu returned and began nuzzling his shoulders. He pressed his cheek against the battered leather, letting his eyes drop shut as strong hands kneaded his sore muscles. He'd nearly forgotten about the challenges until Bleu's hand gently stroked over a slowly healing bruise on his ribs.

"You're amazing. You won every challenge tonight. There's no one in your pack who can defeat you."

"Yeah, there is." He let more of his weight rest against the bag, spreading his legs a bit as Bleu's hand glided down his ass. "My old man."

"Are you sure?"

Bleu's fingers moved away and then returned, slippery and cool with lube. Blacque's belly twisted in arousal.

"Yeah. I'm sure."

"Well, I'm not. You were magnificent, Blacque. A force of nature."

Blacque flushed with both pleasure and pride. He rolled his face against the bag and pressed his forehead into the leather as Bleu slid a finger into his hole. His balls felt full and heavy, and his cock was hard and throbbing with every heartbeat. When Bleu stroked his gland, precum began to well up from his cockhead. He arched forward to grind his hips into the punching bag. The scent of sweat and leather and sex began to fill the air.

Blacque was eager, but Bleu moved slowly, carefully, coming back again and again with his fingers loaded up with lube. He fondled Blacque's sac, smearing it liberally with the slippery stuff. Blacque tightened his hold on the bag, doing his best to turn and look at the vampire.

Bleu's face was pale and taut, and his eyes burned with heat. His damp hair was pushed back from his face but dropped into messy waves at the sides of his head. When he saw Blacque looking, he reached up and pushed his face back toward the punching bag.

"Don't watch," he growled.

"Fuck me," Blacque whispered. His need had effectively bound him as tightly as the rope around his wrists. His legs were weak. Sweat began to roll down his chest. Every time Bleu's fingers brushed and pulled at a piercing, his hips rocked forward, causing the bag to swing slightly.

Bleu's finger returned to his anus, and he pumped smoothly while adding another finger, and then a third.

"Just do it!"

"I don't want to hurt you." His voice was adamant, though Blacque knew he was near his limit as well. When he felt the blunt head of Bleu's cock sliding up his ass, he nearly wept in relief.

He pressed in slowly, stretching and burning his passage while Blacque impatiently bucked back against him, needing that pain, feeling it heighten his arousal. Bleu's hand dug into his hip, holding him steady. He drew back and thrust again, and then again, until finally they were fully melded, skin to skin. Blacque heard a despairing moan and distantly realized that he'd made that forlorn sound.

It wasn't going to last long. He knew it and had no doubt the vampire knew it as well. He didn't want slow and gentle. He needed to feel Bleu take him, claim him. He needed to be joined with Bleu in every possible way. As the vampire's strokes grew stronger and deeper, he held on to the bag, not even trying to meet him. The force of Bleu's strength nearly sent him off balance. Only his hold on the leather bag and the other man's hand on his hip kept him from staggering forward.

He heard Bleu's breathing. It sounded labored and frantic in his ear. He heard his own grunts every time the vampire's hips thrust into his body. His ass ached, and the pain... It felt so damn exquisite! No human could take a fucking like this, and probably few werewolves could withstand it either. Bleu was pounding him into oblivion, slamming into him again and again, pouring his very heart and soul into Blacque's body.

The pressure built, the tension of his climax tearing from his back to his balls, and his fingers shifted, wicked claws punching deep holes into the leather. His back arched, and Bleu's hand wrapped around his cock to stroke hard and fast, in time to his thrusts.

"Come, pup. Come in my hand!"

Blacque wept with the need to release, and before he could speak—to beg for it—teeth punched their way into his shoulder. Blood dribbled down his skin, and he shouted, curses and prayers mingling as he spilled, his seed slicking up Bleu's hand, pulling the orgasm out even longer.

Bleu's body went tense behind his, and he broke away from the wound that was freely bleeding, his body shuddering and flexing as his cum filled Blacque's ass. It was cool and soothing, and after Bleu wrapped his arms around Blacque's body, he carefully lapped the blood from his skin even as he panted and groaned in bliss.

They came down slowly. Bleu reached around and pulled the rope, releasing them both from the bag. On weakened legs, they slipped to the floor, still spooned together, the vampire's arms anchoring Blacque to consciousness and reality. They lay on the rough carpet, both too overcome with exhausted emotion to communicate with words.

Chapter Twenty

Somewhere in the darkness, the phone was ringing.

Bleu jerked awake, his heart racing from the dream he'd just had. He reached up to his face, felt for blisters, but his fingers touched only smooth skin. When he closed his eyes, he recalled the sad, loving expression on the face of Yves as he leaned in for a last kiss that ripped Oliver from one life into another.

Bleu had allowed himself to drop into the shallows of sleep, content to lie next to Blacque for the entire night. He pushed his face into Blacque's powerful neck, overpowered by the realization that he'd nearly lost the werewolf not once, but twice. He had no intention of letting his pup walk away again, even if the wolves didn't want him around.

The phone in the kitchen went silent, and then he heard the sound of a cell phone. Someone wanted Blacque, and it was important enough to rouse him in the middle of the night. He slid out from under the covers and moved silently to the stairs. In just seconds, he was in the kitchen when the landline began to ring again.

"Yes?" The caller was silent, but in the background, Bleu heard voices raised in distress. "This is Bleu. Lukas is asleep."

"Get him." The voice was female, harsh with emotion. Bleu sensed movement and held out the phone for Blacque.

"Yeah? Michella? What's up?" His voice was sleepy but sounded slightly alarmed. Bleu walked to the window, still shaken by his dream. Granted, he rarely slept at night, but the dreams had always come during the day. He gazed out the window into the darkness, trying to puzzle out the change in his habits.

"Lukas, your father and Drusilla didn't come back from the meadow."

Bleu turned and listened. He could clearly hear both sides of the conversation.

"They were going after Mallory. It hasn't been that long." Blacque glanced up at the clock.

Uneasiness began to show on his face, and it echoed in Bleu's gut. Something was wrong. Badly. His mouth went dry when he recalled that April had gone with them. When Blacque looked in his direction, that realization was on his face as well.

"A call came to the house, Lukas. Alice took it. He said for Bleu to go back to the meadow." She paused, and when she spoke again, her voice was broken. "It was Mallory. They have your father and your sister."

"Who?"

"I don't know, Blacque! But he has them!"

"Yves. He must have paid Mallory for his help." Bleu spoke through the hands that covered his face. Yves was here and using Blacque's loved ones to draw him out. He must have known April wouldn't have enough influence over Bleu to lure him back to his side.

Blacque placed the phone in the cradle and then turned to face Bleu.

"I'm so sorry, pup. I had no idea he was here. I was suspicious of April, but I didn't expect this." Grief filled him; he'd been so happy to have his great-granddaughter in his life. He'd trusted so easily.

"April came to me a few days ago. She told me Yves might have had her followed. She warned me, Bleu. If she's involved, she doesn't want to be." His face was stiff and cold, but his voice gave Bleu some hope.

Still, he slid to the floor and sat on the chilly tile. Yves was here, just minutes away. He certainly had Dane and Drusilla, and possibly April as well.

"Mallory spoke for Yves. I wonder how long he's been in his pay."

"Your Mallory will probably not live through this. Though Yves freely uses informants, he despises those who are unfaithful."

"Saves me the trouble of killing him, then." Blacque stalked into his bedroom. When Bleu roused himself to follow, the wolf was dressing.

"No, Blacque. This is my problem. It's taken too many years of my life and hurt too many of my loved ones. I have to be the one to end it."

"He's got my family, Bleu." He pulled a ragged sleeveless shirt over his head. His muscles bulged, and for the first time, Bleu realized his arms were probably too bulky to fit the sleeves of most average shirts. That was why he had all those sleeveless work shirts. Numbly Bleu dressed, watching the wolf.

"Blacque, I don't know what we're walking into. I don't know how strong he is or how many people he's got with him." Bleu sat on the bed to pull on his boots. "I can move faster than you. I don't want to hang back and wait."

"We're taking my truck. You aren't going alone." He slipped his feet into tennis shoes instead of his normal steel toes. He was dressing to shift. He could slip out of the shoes on the fly.

"Blacque, I can't risk you. I'll go to him, and he'll free your family. I'll come back as soon as I can."

"*You are not going with him!*"

Blacque's rage was like a hot wind whipping through the room, prickling and biting at his skin. He paced, glaring down at Bleu. "I said you were mine. I'm a wolf, Bleu! I've chosen, and I will not... I cannot let you go with him!"

Bleu sat unmoving, not willing to risk enraging Blacque again. In this state, he'd charge in blinded by fury. He watched as the wolf paced, slowly bringing himself back under control.

"How strong is he, Bleu? Really?" He turned, his eyes burning like fire.

Bleu looked away. "I only know that he's become strong enough to be killing me from half a world away."

"The dreams?" Blacque froze, looking at him in horror.

"I doubt he even realizes what he's been doing. For years they've come to me during my day sleep. In just the past few days, I've been free of the dreams. Just before the phone rang, I had awakened from a nightmare."

The fear did not fade from Blacque's eyes. "Because he's here, in the same time zone."

Miserably Bleu nodded. The dreams had ceased just after April's arrival. It couldn't be coincidence. "The dreams were so...obsessive. They seemed fixated on my face, on turning me. When I dreamed of Yves, the images were strangely idyllic, yet they terrified me."

"You were experiencing his memories. His memories were your nightmares."

Bleu rose and faced the wolf. "You see, Blacque? If he can manipulate my mind from halfway across the world, what will he do to me when we're face-to-face? Like you, I know I don't have the strength of my...alpha."

Blacque reached out and gripped his forearm. "You have me."

Sadly he shook his head. "I will submit to him. And then I will escape, just as April did. I will return to you."

"What about Dru and my father?" He gripped Bleu's arm even tighter.

"Yves is insane, but he's got honor. He was an officer and a gentleman back when that term actually meant something. He said if I came to him, he'd release your family."

"What about April?"

Bleu closed his eyes against the grief that swamped him. "I doubt that she still lives. If she does, he will not release her. He'll want to keep us both. She's his gift to me."

He pulled his arm loose. "Go to your father's house, Blacque. Be with your pack. They need you." That was the key to maneuvering Blacque out of the way. Duty. The same damn sense of duty that had pulled them apart in the beginning. Bleu used it ruthlessly. "Until your father returns, you are the pack alpha. You cannot leave them adrift."

"Michella—"

"I heard her; she sounded terrified. She's strong, but not enough to hold them together. Now go to your people, Blacque. Let me tend to my responsibilities."

The wolf clenched his jaw, the muscles in his neck flexed. He fisted his hand, and Bleu got a peek at the lethal claws his pup could call forth at will. Finally Blacque gave a jerky nod of agreement. His control was hanging by a thread.

"If I haven't heard from you by dawn, I'll come for you."

"Your family will be back by then, Blacque. I promise."

"But not you?"

Bleu smiled and stepped close to Blacque, then clasped the back of his head. He leaned in and kissed him lightly. "I'll do my best to come back to you, Blacque. As soon as possible." He pulled away, trying to put space between them. With unearthly speed, Blacque caught his arm, slammed him against the wall, and pressed his body close. There was no arousal to interfere with clear thinking. Their passion was crystal clear, uninhibited by lust.

"You are *mine*, Bleu." Blacque kissed him fiercely, his tongue pushing past lips and teeth, thrusting with an aggression that had been foreign to his behavior until now. Bleu went submissive, letting the wolf ravage him with his fear and his grief. His hands kept Bleu caged against the wall. He branded Oliver with his lips and his hands and with his body.

"Mine."

"I'm yours, Lukas. My heart is yours." He looked into Blacque's eyes, watching as the heat and anger faded into something poignant and deep. "I love you, Blacque. With all that I am."

He was caught in a crushing embrace, and for an endless moment, Bleu let himself be loved by the most selfless creature he'd ever known in his long life. He wrapped his arms around the wolf, and they simply stood, their bodies entwined as completely as their souls.

All too soon, Blacque pulled away, setting him free.

"Be safe, Oliver." He stood to the side and watched as Bleu left the room.

Bleu couldn't resist one final look over his shoulder. He grinned. "Be back soon." He turned away and headed out into the darkness. In a heartbeat, he was in the forest, moving with the speed only a vampire could summon. The cold wind in his face froze the tears before they could fall from his eyes.

* * *

The meadow was still foul with blood. The snow had been churned up, and silence lay heavy over the clearing. Dane hadn't had a chance to call in help to get the site cleaned up. Briefly Bleu wondered if a witch could have given him an edge on Yves.

He knew the vampire was nearby. His power floated through the air as though it were something tangible. Pain slashed through his head, overlaid with a vivid image of a beautiful boy, ebony hair hanging over his pale forehead. He was looking up with such love in his eyes...

Yves was thinking of those early days, when Bleu had been flush with his infatuation. He pushed the image away, replacing it with one of Yves tearing the throat out of a young prostitute. He channeled the horror of seeing his lover dangling a youth from his hand, blood running down his face and arm.

The boy had looked just like Oliver.

The blanket of Yves' power faltered. Bleu grinned. The bastard could dish it out but wasn't too happy when retaliation came his way.

"Oliver." The voice came like a whisper inside his mind. It throbbed with such joy at his presence. The voice held such gratitude that his lover had finally come. Bleu looked around, knowing he had to be close.

"Oliver." The voice came to his ears, and without thinking, Bleu flexed his legs, jumping lightly into the lower branches of a giant fir tree. From there he saw the prone form of Dane. He was bound with a silver chain, and the wind told him the alpha was bleeding. He caught the sent of freshly spilled blood. Drusilla. If she still lived, she'd be similarly bound.

He pushed from the tree and landed in the snow, then stepped over the cooling body of the wolf Mallory. Bleu had no doubt the man's payment was folded neatly inside his wallet. As a gentleman, Yves would never break his word. Of course he probably had promised Mallory payment, but not that he'd live to walk away and spend it.

He scented the air again, searching for April, but like their maker, her scent was masked. Automatically he whipped around and looked downwind.

"Yves. I've come back to you." Yves had been forced to travel from France in order for Bleu to "return" to him, but that made no difference; Yves' throbbing power blanketed him once again, lush with joy. Oliver gasped, nearly losing his balance. For just a moment, he felt an answering joy in his heart. His eyes filled with tears, and his groin filled with blood.

More of Yves' emotions. He wondered if the vampire was using his power intentionally, or if he was simply caught in the perfect storm of his maker's wild magic.

"Yves." His voice was full of false love and feigned hope. "Please show yourself to me."

He turned slowly, looking in all directions. A glint of light caught his eye, and Bleu froze, watching as his maker moved so smoothly over the bloody snow that he very nearly levitated.

The full moon illuminated the meadow, painting it in shades of purple and lavender and gray. Except for the stench of blood, there was a macabre beauty to the scene.

Yves approached. The body of Bleu's great-granddaughter dangled from his hand. She was broken and limp, black blood dripping from the tips of her fingers. She'd fought him and had fallen to this creature that Bleu had once loved.

He carelessly tossed her to the side, and while Bleu was desperate to reach her, he remained in place, determined to play the part he'd assigned himself.

He wouldn't return to France with Yves. The idea was repugnant. But Bleu looked at his maker and knew that Yves wouldn't return either. He felt the cold intent of the killer settle over his heart. That muscle grew cold and hard in his chest as he studied the stunningly beautiful visage of Yves Artois. He'd changed so little over the years. His aristocratic face was just as finely etched. His elegant body was carried as proudly as ever. His white dress shirt was spattered with blood. A few droplets had smeared along his high cheekbone. He reached up and ran a bloody hand through his dark blond hair, as expertly cut as it had been nearly one hundred years ago.

"Oliver."

He reached out an elegant, long-fingered hand, and memories of that hand stroking his naked skin flooded Bleu's mind. His breath caught painfully in his chest as long-ago sights and sounds came back in a rush. Endless nights spent in Yves' elegant flat. Hours making love with the windows thrown open. He recalled soaking in a gigantic tub, one man at either side of the bath, their long legs tangled and stroking. Yves threw back his head and laughed in sensual delight.

The back of a hand to his face when he questioned the blood on Yves' uniform...

Laughter as they danced to the little band in the sleazy nightclub that catered to men of particular tastes...smuggled champagne and forbidden delights under the cover of darkness and a tablecloth...

Yves' face, eyes dancing with cruel hunger as he bent to drain the life from Oliver...

Bleu's memories were sharp and astringent, allowing him to free his mind.

"Yves. What have you done to my friends? My great-granddaughter?" He took a deep breath, fighting for composure, fighting to crush the horror washing through his gut. Yves looked about, appearing confused.

"I smell only wolves, Oliver. April...she lives. She will accompany us home to France, my love." Again, a push of sweet nostalgia, of joy and love. Bleu countered it with images from his memory, forcing a confused frown to Yves' face.

"Why are you angry, Oliver?"

"You turned me, Yves. I did not want this life." He stood still and quiet, letting the other vampire absorb his words.

"April said something similar."

"She did not wish to be a vampire either. Neither of us is well suited to this life." He glanced in her direction, but she was still and silent, her body too loose to be feigning unconsciousness.

"She said I did wrong by turning you."

Finally Bleu let out a breath, taking advantage of Yves' momentary lucidity. What had happened to bring his maker to this point of insanity? Was he simply too old? Too battered by the decades—perhaps centuries—of turmoil he'd survived?

"My end was horrible, Yves. I saw my friends blown to pieces right next to me. I saw them choking and dying horrific deaths in the mud of the trenches. I watched my own flesh eaten away while I lived." He looked calmly at Yves. "I earned my death, Yves. Not as punishment, but reward. I didn't deserve these endless years of memory."

To his surprise, the other vampire's eyes filled with tears. Yves reached up and touched his cheeks as though unable to comprehend his own emotion. He blinked, and as Bleu watched, sanity fled from those expressive gray eyes.

"We are reunited in death, Oliver. I have a place in the mountains, right at the border of France and Spain. It is so lovely. We will be so happy."

"Will you let my friends loose? I will go with you only if you free them." He moved a bit closer, hoping to keep Yves talking. He had no false hopes. He was reeling under the elder vampire's power. Every time he cleared his mind, Yves pushed his way back in.

"You have no friends. Only wolves."

"Yves, you told them that if I came to you, you would free the alpha and his daughter."

Sudden cunning flared in Yves' face. Anger made him pale and feral-looking.

"You stink of wolf. He claimed you as his own."

Bleu had to fight to hide the dismay that swept through him. Yves had been hiding, watching the challenge. He knew about Blacque.

"Those were his words, Yves, but they are not my words."

The vampire drew closer; the nostrils of his aquiline nose flared. "You stink of his seed. You have taken another with your body. You came to me from his bed!"

Just like that, Yves struck, throwing Bleu backward with what felt like the force of a train. Over the years he'd fought many other vampires, but he'd had his strength then, and none were a match for the insane fury of his maker. Bleu shut his mind as best he could and leaped into the air, barely dodging the next charge. He clasped his ribs, feeling broken bones knitting themselves back together, and he was suddenly, profoundly grateful that he'd taken blood from Blacque.

Yves rushed him. Ironlike fingers sank into his flesh; razor-sharp fangs struck at kill zones. Bleu ducked and rolled, bringing Yves to the ground for a moment. He didn't bother with nerve grips; the other man's insanity deadened him to pain. He heard the vampire gasp as the air was forced from his lungs. Bleu rolled away and once again regained his footing. He panted, doubled over with pain.

He had to use his brain. He couldn't defeat Yves with his body. He spared a glance around, looking for weapons, desperately racking his mind for any trick that might work. From the corner of his eye, he saw movement. Was it April? His heart began to pound.

Yves launched himself, covering yards with a single leap, and Bleu took a blow to the shoulder as he caught the slashing hand and twisted it hard enough to snap it. Yves landed with a howl of pain and anger.

Bleu crouched, opening his senses, feeling stealthy movement all around him.

Wolves. Dozens of them.

He needed to keep Yves distracted, off balance. Bleu began to walk backward, moving back out into the blood-soaked snow at the center of the clearing. That would mask the scent of the wolves. His foot caught a branch, and he went down, unable to avoid the coming attack. Yves straddled him and clasped his forearms, bearing down hard enough to make Bleu certain the bones in his arms would shatter. It was a nightmarish replay of the last few moments of his human life. This time there was no love in Yves' expression, only rage and the fury of a man betrayed.

Before those wicked fangs found their mark, a gray blur whipped through Bleu's line of vision, struck Yves, and threw him from his body. Another streak and then another, never engaging, worrying the vampire as a boxer baits a bull. The vampire's attention was torn from Bleu, though he scrambled to stay in possession of his prize.

He screamed, lunging at one wolf and then another, some blows going wild, others striking home. Through the noise and confusion, a tall figure emerged in the meadow. Blacque was there, striding steadily, a half dozen wolves following at his heels. He watched as the vampire struggled with the fury of the pack. Bleu staggered to his feet, taking a moment to glare at his lover through the chaos of the battle. It was then that Yves broke away and came at Bleu with death in his eyes. He caught Yves' weight in the chest, not resisting but rolling with the blow. They plowed through the foul snow, half blinded by ice and blood and dirt. They rolled and grappled. Bleu slashed with his fangs, opening great tears in Yves' chest and throat, then finally in his beautiful face. Blood poured over him, making his grip slippery and unsure.

Yves shrieked. The sound was so feral, so deafening that Bleu was certain any remaining wildlife would flee the area forever. He braced the other vampire's body above his, using arms and legs to hold him away from his vulnerable throat. He groaned with the effort, feeling the muscles of his arms and legs begin to tremble. He had seconds, just seconds to win this fight...

A flash of silver came from nowhere and wrapped around Yves' naked throat, snapping him backward like a dog on a choke chain. His hands flew up, and once again he screamed. The cry broke off, and a fist burst through his chest. In horror, Bleu watched as a pair of powerful hands grabbed and twisted Yves' head until his neck broke with a sickening crack.

He didn't die right away. He continued to gaze at Oliver with desperate love in his eyes. Bleu looked up to see Blacque many yards away, standing still as a statue. As Yves began to crumble to the ground, he looked up to see Drusilla. The silver chain still smoldered against the skin of her hands. April struggled to free her fist from his chest—his heart was clasped firmly in her palm. Dane held him by the skull and lowered the dying vampire slowly to the ground.

Bleu choked back a cry, crawling over to his maker, feeling the wrenching separation of Yves' soul from his own. April bent over double, staggering until Dane steadied her.

"What's happening?" Blacque was finally there next to Bleu, his strong hands holding him back from the other vampire. Yves reached out a hand, desperately searching for his offspring.

"Keep him back, Lukas. He's trying to pull energy from them." Dane pulled April away from Yves and held her tightly in spite of her struggles. Bleu lunged against Blacque's hold, frantic to obey the unspoken command to return to his maker's side.

With a sigh, Yves dropped his gaze and then looked at Bleu once again.

"Oliver."

He shuddered, and then it was over. Bleu went limp, looking out at the world as he lay on his side in the snow. He looked at Dane and Drusilla and saw burns where the silver chain had bound the two werewolves. Drusilla looked down at her hands as though she finally realized her skin was being charred by the silver. She cried out, throwing the metal to the ground. Another wolf came to her side and licked the lesions on her skin. April was limp in Dane's arms. He held her like a child, but his eyes were fixed on Blacque and Bleu.

"He thought the silver would weaken us. It burns, but as soon as we woke up, it was easy enough to break loose." He took a wide path around the body of the vampire and settled April on the ground next to Bleu. "Will she be all right?"

"I don't know. Makers usually take their offspring when they die. I don't know why we were able to survive his death."

Blacque growled in his ear. "You knew his death would mean your own?" His arms went dangerously tight around Bleu's torso, causing him to gasp in pain. The broken ribs hadn't mended yet.

"I told you to stay at the house. I told you to stay with the pack!"

"The pack was already on its way out here." He continued to glare at Bleu.

"We felt Mallory die." It was Michella, newly shifted to her human form. She was blood streaked and naked and really quite impressive. "Then the alpha called us. Lukas arrived when we did."

Bleu looked around and saw wolves shifting into ghostly human shapes. An old woman limped over. She'd taken a fierce blow to the leg. It began to heal as he watched. Another woman was bent over Mallory's body, rocking and quietly crying. His wife. The bastard had put her through hell this day. Hopefully Yves had paid him well. She'd need it.

"Why? You had your alpha safe. You could all have got away from him. Did you have any clue how lethal Yves is...was?"

The enormity of what had just happened settled in. This pack of wolves had destroyed one of the most powerful and unpredictable vampires he'd ever known in all his years. He began to shake, grateful for Blacque's strong arms around him.

"He claimed you." A young man was squatting on his haunches a few feet away, balancing on his fingertips. "He stood up in front of us all, and he claimed you. That makes you ours as well." The kid didn't look too pleased about it.

"Well fuck." Bleu literally didn't know what else to say. He struggled from Blacque's arms and staggered a bit as he regained his footing. He looked down at himself—his clothing was torn and bloodstained, and he had too many injuries to count. He'd need blood and a safe place to lie for the coming day. As though catching his thoughts, Blacque looked up toward the mountains.

"Morning's coming. We need to get you two to cover."

April moaned a bit incoherently, and Bleu reached for her, feeling better even as he clasped her hand. He bit his lip, not caring that his fangs showed.

"It was her...us...I think." He looked up at Blacque. "We're blood kin as well as sharers of the same maker. We survived because of our blood ties. When his power left us, we supported each other." He knelt and gathered April into his arms.

"You don't have to, Bleu." Blacque was looking at him worriedly. He carried her a few steps and then paused. "Where am I going?"

"My house." Blacque moved up on one side, Dane on the other. He didn't protest as the alpha relieved him of his burden. He was sadly grateful for Blacque's support at his side. He began walking, his feet dragging in the snow, wondering how he was going to make it to cover before dawn.

"Hey, Bleu. This way." Blacque tugged his arm. "I've got the truck. We'll drive." Bleu looked at Blacque in confusion, but he followed, relieved he wouldn't have to dig a hole out in the forest. The driver's side door was ajar. Bleu crawled in, then reached out to take April from Dane's hands. Blacque climbed in, and then the passenger door opened. Drusilla slid in next to him. He eased his great-granddaughter onto his lap, and he tucked her head under his chin. The truck rocked, and Bleu looked back to see a number of injured shifters being loaded into the bed of the truck. There was a slap on the door, and Blacque started the engine. As they began to ease out onto a narrow, rutted road, Bleu could see the shadowy figures of wolves running beside the vehicle.

The slider window opened, and he looked back at Dane. "We can get to the big house faster than your place, Lukas. There're a couple of rooms in the basement." The window snapped shut, and Bleu felt himself begin to list to the side. April struggled a bit and then went still again.

"Welcome to the pack." Drusilla smiled, reaching over to pull the unconscious vampire into her arms. "We'll take *real* good care of you two." She gave him a slight push. Bleu was glad to find his head resting on Lukas Blacque's wide shoulder.

As the truck jolted from dirt road to smooth highway, he fell asleep with a smile.

Epilogue

The muscles in Blacque's arms and back strained as he eased the engine from the hoist to the compartment of the Studebaker. He gently guided it into place, grinning as he unbuckled the straps that held it to the metal balance bar. Not much longer now, and she'd be running. New paint glistened, and the freshly upholstered seats had gone in the night before. By tomorrow, he'd have the engine completely finished. He hoped.

"I know you aren't worried, Blacque, but I am. He's much too old for her."

Blacque straightened and stared at Bleu. "You're still talking about April?"

"And Dane. Can't forget Dane."

He grinned and turned away. "You're saying that my father is too old for April?" He lifted a brow in question. "She's old enough to be my mother, Bleu."

"But...she was just a child when she was changed."

"She was older than you. Besides, if Dane's robbing the cradle, what exactly have you been up to?"

If vampires could blush... Wait—there was definitely a pink cast to Bleu's smooth cheeks.

"Dane is a player. I mean seriously, how many offspring does he have?"

"You worried that he'll get her pregnant?"

Bleu let out a sound of exasperation.

"Frankly, Bleu, if Dane manages to get her pregnant, I'll be really interested in seeing what their baby will turn out like. It'll be the first vampire-shifter cross I've ever heard of."

Bleu groaned and reached out to pull him close. "You know, I think I have an idea about that engine hoist."

Blacque glanced over at the sturdy piece of equipment. It could be raised high, and the balance bar that dangled from it had loops at either end. He grinned, feeling his cock begin to fill. "I'll like seeing you all stretched out on that hoist, Oliver." The vampire reached around and pinched his ass.

"Think again, pup."

"Are we interrupting?"

They both jumped and moved apart like a pair of errant schoolboys. Michella sauntered into the engine bay, followed by a smaller, very pretty human woman. The human looked normal enough, but power radiated from her. He shivered in reaction. "I know it's the weekend, but I was hoping to catch you. Alone." Michella smiled sweetly at Bleu, who smiled back with equally false sweetness.

"I've got some work to do in my end of the shop."

They'd installed a large rolling door between the two businesses, making it easier to move their work back and forth. Blacque gestured toward his office and followed the two women inside. He grabbed a folding chair and set it next to the chair across from his desk. The two women sat side by side.

"Lukas, I'd like you to meet Angie. My wife."

He looked at her in surprise and then back to the human. She had wavy blonde hair and bright blue eyes, and it took only a second for him to place where he'd seen her before.

"You're the witch who came in last fall..."

She nodded. "Quite a mess you made out there. But a little concentrated rain and a new layer of snow, and it was good as new."

He nodded, still gazing from one to the other. Finally Michella spoke.

"We've been together a few years now. Last year, we went out of state on vacation. We got married."

"Congratulations."

Like him, she'd kept her personal life very, very private.

He waited for her to continue. Michella fidgeted and then looked up at him. "We want to have a baby. Your baby."

He felt his cheeks go warm. He'd known this day would eventually arrive, and now he was tongue-tied and at a loss. He glanced out the window and saw Bleu back at the Studebaker, leaning into the engine compartment.

"The thing is, Blacque, I really, really don't want to have sex with you to get pregnant." He looked back at her in surprise. "I thought we could just go into a clinic. There's one about an hour from here." She swallowed hard. "No one would need to know; they'd just know that you're the father we chose. No fuss, no muss."

Angie hid a smile behind her hand, and then she spoke. "We aren't the only ones like this, Blacque. That woman from Nevada? The one staying at your father's house? She came here hoping to do this without the sex part. She's got a human husband. They made the decision together, but I know she'd feel much better if you'd consent to doing it artificially."

"And since you came out"—Michella looked steadily at him—"it's given us courage. Angie and I aren't the only ones going public to the pack." She reached out and took her wife's hand. "You made life better for us, Lukas."

He sat back in his chair, looking up at the ceiling. That damn cobweb was still up there. With a sigh, he got up, excused himself, and grabbed the broom from the corner. He knocked it down and then returned to his chair. He propped his booted foot up on his desk.

"Sure. Why not? It's a new century. Well, it was a few years ago." He looked up and saw Bleu leaning in the doorway, a lopsided smile on his face.

"Guess it can't hurt to try something new."

THE END

Belinda McBride

While Belinda's upbringing seemed pretty normal to her, she was surrounded by a fascinating array of friends and family, including a polyamorous grandmother, a grandfather who is a Native American icon, and various cowboys, hippies, scoundrels, and saints.

She has a degree in history and cultural anthropology, but in 2006 made the life-changing decision to quit her job as a public health paraprofessional and stay at home fulltime to care for her severely disabled, autistic niece. This difficult decision gave Belinda the gift of time, which allowed her to return to writing fiction, which she'd abandoned years before.

She has two daughters, six Siberian Huskies, and an array of wild birds that visit the feeders in the front yard. She supports no-kill animal shelters, and donates platelets twice monthly at her local blood center.

As an author, Belinda loves crossing genres, kicking taboos to the curb, and pulling from world mythology and folklore for inspiration. She is committed to taking her readers on an emotional journey and never forgets that at the end of the day, she's writing about love.

Loose Id Titles by Belinda McBride

Belle Starr
Blacque/Bleu

"Educating Evangeline"
Part of the anthology Doms of Dark Haven
With Cherise Sinclair and Sierra Cartwright

"Hunting Holly"
Part of the anthology *Doms of Dark Haven 2: Western Night*
With Cherise Sinclair and Sierra Cartwright

Available in ebook at Loose Id and other ebook sellers.
Belle Star *and* Blacque/Blue *are also available in print.*

CPSIA information can be obtained at www.ICGtesting.com
Printed in the USA
LVOW081940070113

314713LV00001B/53/P